SONS OF PERDITION

TOBY NEIGHBORS

MYTHIC
adventure
PUBLISHING

Sons of Perdition

Copyright © 2025 by Toby Neighbors

ISBN: 978-1-952260-96-4 ebook

978-1-952260-97-1 print

Mythic Adventure Publishing, LLC

Idaho, USA

1

Jude Olson had planned everything. The hardest part was waiting. He sat in his car until exactly 5:45 pm. Up and down the street, people were returning home. That was what Jude wanted. He wasn't attempting to hide anything.

From the trunk, he retrieved a propane torch and a sledgehammer. The weight of the tools felt good in his hands as he walked. It was the first time he had really felt anything since Alison left him. There had been rage, of course. Frustration and sadness, but mostly rage, yet it was dulled by a numbness that overshadowed everything else in his life until that moment. Walking up the front entrance to the house with the heavy tools gave him a sense of clarity that he had rarely felt in his thirty-seven years.

There had been a time when Jude's hands were soft and unaccustomed to labor. But he had grown. He had come to understand and even admire what he could accomplish using his hands in honest labor. Tools were empowering in his hands. It made him wonder if the way he felt was the same as a medieval king might have felt taking up his sword for battle.

Jude wasn't going to battle, but he wasn't making a polite visit, either. The house had a wide front porch that sat empty. Furniture may have once graced the wide boards to give the porch a warm, inviting appeal. Yet today, the bare space was cold and unwelcoming.

The house belonged to Alex Metford. He was a manager in a corporation that had offices in one of the high-rise buildings downtown. Jude didn't know what the corporation did and didn't care. Nor was the fact that Alex's lawn was in need of trimming or that his landscape bushes next to the house were dying. What was important was that the front door was made of oak and had a stout bolt lock. Fortunately, despite the ruggedness of the door, the homebuilder had used mostly subpar materials. The door jamb, for instance, was made of soft pine, which meant it only took one swing to break the bolt lock through the soft wood it was extended into.

The sound of the sledgehammer crashing into the door was heard up and down the street. Jude felt the neighbors looking at him, which was the reason he lingered on the porch for a moment. He wanted to be seen, to be remembered. There was no reason to hurry. Jude knew what he would find inside.

Stepping past the splintered door, Jude entered the home. It was the very definition of breaking and entering. The floor inside was dirty. There was dust and the accumulation of dirt that was a result of poor housekeeping. Jude kept his own home, which was much smaller than Alex's, clean. He had learned that the discipline of cleaning was almost therapeutic. But he wasn't surprised that Alex kept his home in a disheveled state. The man was rarely here. He worked a lot, and on the rare occasion that he actually left the office at five o'clock, it was to come straight home and drink himself into oblivion, which he did almost every Friday evening. The drinking couldn't wait until he arrived home either. He would start in his car, drinking good whiskey straight from the bottle. By the time he got home, he was drunk, which was when the real damage was done.

Jude could smell the booze. It was a potent odor in the home, but was soon to be replaced by an even more offensive stench.

"What the hell!" Alex shouted, dropping the bottle of cheap gin he had been holding as Jude came around the corner and into the living room.

It was a bachelor's home. There was a single piece of furniture. It was a leather recliner with electric controls, which was why Alex hadn't sprung up when the door was knocked open. His shaking hand had pressed the button to bring his feet back down to earth, but it took nearly twenty seconds before the motor shut off. And the booze made quick reactions, such as leaping to his feet, impossible. Instead, he dropped the bottle he had been holding and sagged forward. He lurched up and forward on unsteady legs just in time for Jude to lash out with the same hand he had held the sledgehammer with. That hand was empty, and he thrust it forward, palm first, straight into Alex's nose.

The inebriated man crashed backward, his arms and legs flailing. He bounced off the chair and hit the small side table next to it, where the television remote was resting beside a bucket of ice, where a second bottle of cheap gin was sweating. Both went flying across the dirty carpet that showed impressions where other furniture had once been neatly arranged.

Jude turned around. The only other item in the living room was a large screen television poorly mounted onto the wall. Jude could have pulled it down easily, but he wasn't there to harm the home. He had come to kill Alex Metford, so he settled for jerking the electrical plug from the outlet.

Silence descended inside the sad, unkempt home. Alex was gasping, but his nose was bleeding, so he was left to gulp raspy breaths through his mouth. Jude walked into the kitchen. It was filthy. Dirty dishes, pots and pans, mostly take-out containers, lined every inch of the countertops and clogged the sink. There was a stiff, wooden chair next to a tiny breakfast table. Jude took it and returned to the living room, where Alex had managed to turn over. He was sitting on the floor with both hands cradling his nose. It was bleeding a lot, the red flow staining his wrinkled business shirt and the carpet in front of him.

Jude grabbed Alex by one arm and hoisted him up. He was not gentle. Alex was pushed onto the wooden chair and nearly toppled over, but Jude held onto him long enough to steady the drunken man, who was sobering up quickly. Although not fast enough to defend himself or realize how much danger he was in.

Taking the extra-long belt that Jude had bought just for the occasion from around his waist, he slung it over Alex's chest. With quick movements, he fed the thick band of leather under his arms and around the wooden backrest. He fastened it tight enough to hold Alex upright in the chair but not so snugly that he couldn't breathe.

"Who are you?" Alex asked.

"My name is Jude Olson. That ring any bells, Alex?"

"No... should it?"

"Oh, yes, it absolutely should," Jude said, moving around in front of his prisoner.

There was no guarantee that the neighbors had called the police yet, but they would soon. When they heard the screaming, they would call 9-1-1 as fast as their trembling fingers could manage. Jude lit the propane torch with a cheap cigarette lighter, the plastic kind that would easily hold a fingerprint. He dropped the lighter onto the floor and turned the valve on the torch so that the flame went from yellow to bright blue.

"Look, if you want money, my wallet is in my coat pocket," Alex said.

"I'm not here for money."

"You can have it. Take whatever you want," Alex stammered, more from fear than the alcohol. "My car's in the garage."

"I don't want your car," Jude said. "Do you remember September twenty-third, Alex? I know you do."

"What?"

"September twenty-third. I know the day is burned into your memory, just as it is in mine."

"I don't understand."

"Yes, you do."

"I had an accident that day."

"No," Jude said calmly.

"I did. I... I hit... a deer on the way home."

"It wasn't a deer," Jude said. "It was a woman. And she lived for exactly eight minutes."

Alex started to argue, but instead, he screamed as Jude held the torch under his still-dripping nose.

2

Evan St. Cloud was the first police officer to arrive on the scene. He stopped his squad car in front of the house. The front door stood open, an ominous sign, and there were neighbors on their front lawns watching despite the cold evening temperatures.

Evan picked up the radio transmitter and pressed the activation switch on the side. "Dispatch, this is Victor thirteen; show me responding at two-one-seven Hummingbird Lane."

"Copy, Victor thirteen," the scratchy voice of the police dispatcher said.

Evan checked his rearview mirror, saw people walking toward his cruiser on the street, then got out of the car.

"Officer, he's gone," an older woman from across the street said. She was standing on the edge of her lawn, wrapped tightly in a flannel bathrobe. "I seen him. He was parked right here for nearly half an hour."

She pointed at the curb she was standing over.

"Who's that, ma'am?" Evan asked.

"I don't know," she said. "But I seen him take a sledgehammer to Alex Metford's front door. To be honest, I'm not really surprised. He's been a mess since Cindy took the kids and left him. But he had it coming. The man's a lush."

"Alright, thank you, ma'am. Please stay where you are. I'm sure I'll have more questions for you in a minute."

Evan walked around his police cruiser. It was getting dark outside, and the home was completely dark. Evan kept one hand near the grip of his service pistol, and with the other, he pulled out a small flashlight.

"I think someone's hurt in there," a next-door neighbor said. "We called nine-one-one when we heard the screaming."

"Someone was screaming in this house?" Evan asked, clicking on his flashlight and shining it toward the open front door.

"Sure was," the neighbor said. He was a middle-aged man with a protruding stomach and thinning hair combed straight back. Behind him stood his wife and a preteen boy. "Something awful — never heard anything like it."

Evan could see that the door frame was broken. He mounted the steps and shouted into the house. "Police department. Is there anyone inside?"

No response wasn't really a positive thing, although it made Evan feel a little less nervous. The report from dispatch had initially been signs of a break-in at the residence, but had been updated with information of the alleged perpetrator fleeing the scene. Evan wasn't worried about walking into a dangerous situation. That did sometimes happen, but in most cases, the police arrived too late to catch criminals in the act.

"Police department, call out if you can hear my voice!" Evan shouted as he stepped into the dark house.

Again, there was no response. Evan was hit with a horrid stench that he couldn't place. He reached out, found a light switch, and flipped it on. Porch lights came on, as did the overhead light in the entryway. There was nothing to see directly ahead, so he moved forward and turned the corner.

The body was strapped to a wooden chair, and Evan placed his free hand over his mouth and nose. The smell of burned human flesh was powerful. The victim was clearly dead, yet protocol required that Evan be sure. He found the light switch on the wall, turned it on, and noticed the burn marks across the victim's body. It registered in his mind that the poor wretch on the chair had been tortured and probably killed. Evan reached out with two fingers, touching the neck. It was surprisingly cool to the touch. There was no pulse.

Evan reached up and took hold of his radio's shoulder-mounted transmitter. He pushed the switch on the side and said, "Dispatch, Victor thirteen, roll a supervisor to my location and a bus. I have a non-responsive adult male with obvious burn wounds."

"Copy that, Victor thirteen, sending help to your location."

Evan turned and left the body. There was nothing he could do for the man, and his job was to clear the residence for any threat or other occupants who might need help. It took five minutes. By the time he got outside again, he could hear sirens approaching. The officer felt dirty, and the stench of burned human flesh was still in his nose. Taking a deep breath, he felt grateful for the cold night air, but it didn't help with the odor. It would stay with him for a while.

Evan walked back across the street to the woman in the robe. She hadn't moved. His breath was coming in little puffs that showed condensation in the night air. An unmarked car with police lights in the grill arrived from up the street just as an ambulance arrived from the opposite direction.

"Is he... dead?" the woman asked.

"I need you to tell me everything you saw," Evan said, taking out his phone and starting the dictation app. "Don't leave anything out."

3

Ron Flanagan had seen burn victims before. He had seen them overseas as a squad leader in the army. And he had seen them in vehicle accidents as a first responder as well as a detective working cases. They were rare but not unheard of. There were much faster and cleaner ways of killing someone. Burning them alive was rarely an act of passion or a response to danger. The only time people were burned alive was to send a message or in an act of revenge.

By the time Ron arrived on the scene, there was a full tech squad poring over the house. A pair of Emergency Medical Technicians were lingering by their rig, watching videos on Instagram while they waited for permission to collect the body. The Medical Examiner was already there, too. He was a small man with thick glasses and an abundance of energy. Ron wished he could tap into the small man's energy and give himself a boost. It was going to be a long night, and he needed all the help he could get.

Getting out of his car, Ron was immediately met by the supervisor in charge. It was an old friend, Marshall Owens.

"What do we have?" Ron asked.

"Crispy critter," Marshall said. "Neighbors called it in. We've got eyewitnesses to the perpetrator and some doorbell camera footage, which should be available soon. Seems like the perp wasn't worried about getting caught."

"Well, that's a welcome change," Ron thought.

The only thing worse than a random crime with no clues was a high-profile case that would require weeks of intensive detective work. If they had eyewitnesses and video evidence, they could move forward pretty quickly.

"Patrolman St. Cloud was first on the scene," Marshall added.

On television, the detectives rushed into the crime scene to poke around, but in real casework, it was better to talk to the witnesses first. Ron wanted a frame of reference before the crime scene was burned into his memory.

"You responded to the call?" Ron asked the patrolman, who was waiting patiently to give his report.

"Yes, sir. Nine-one-one call came in of a suspected burglary in progress. I headed this way. More calls updated with the suspect fleeing the scene in a silver Ford Explorer."

"Did you catch sight of the vehicle?"

"No, sir. But the neighbors all did. According to Miss Julian Evergreen," he said as he pointed to the house directly across the street from the crime scene, "a white male, mid-thirties, wearing blue jeans and a black tee-shirt, parked in the aforementioned Ford Explorer across the street from the residence owned by an Alex Metford. He stayed in his vehicle for over twenty minutes, then retrieved a sledgehammer and what appeared to be a blue canister."

"Propane torch," Marshall said. "Buy 'em in any hardware store."

"The perp went up the front walk, busted open the door with the sledge, dropped it, and went inside."

"Are we getting prints?" Ron asked.

"Oh, yeah, lots of 'em," Marshall said. "This one's gonna be a walk in the park."

Ron hoped the older man was right. In his experience, no case was foolproof. A good lawyer could cast doubt on just about any crime. Ron's job was to gather evidence. It was a bit like putting together a puzzle. The goal was to find enough pieces of the puzzle so that a jury could make out the picture. You never had the entire puzzle, and sometimes the pieces didn't fit right. But it sounded like they had gotten lucky, and maybe the perpetrator was careless.

"Guy goes inside, tortures the victim with the blow torch, then hits the road right before I arrived."

"Was the vic alive when you entered the scene?" Ron asked, hoping maybe the unlucky bastard had lived long enough to name who killed him and perhaps why, too.

"No, sir, DOA. I believe the perp made sure of that before splitting."

"We've got footage of this animal coming and going," Marshall said. "The neighbors all saw him. No mask. We'll nail him."

"Tell me someone got the license plate," Ron said.

It was rarely as helpful as it might sound. License plates could be altered with a little electrical tape. They could be swapped with another car. Most people didn't know their license plate number and wouldn't notice if their plates were swapped. If the car was stolen, then the plates were worthless, but if the perp was as sloppy as it seemed, they might get lucky.

"They did," Marshall said. "Evan already ran 'em."

"License plate is registered to a Jude Kindle Olson of twenty-two-seventeen east Warnock Road."

"A local?" Ron asked.

"Seems that way," Marshall said. "No record, but we did a little internet sleuthing while we were waitin' on you, and this Jude

Olson fits the description. We'll put him in a lineup once he's in custody."

"Have you sent officers to his place of residence?"

Marshall nodded. "Practically doing your job for you, Flanagan. You owe us both a beer."

"If this pans out, I'll buy you more than a beer," Ron said. "I don't need this headache."

He was feeling the tension building inside him as a news truck approached from the opposite end of the street.

"Keep those goons out," he said, pointing at the truck. "I'm going inside. Can you spare Patrolman St. Cloud?"

"He's all yours, Ronny boy. Place nice."

"I always do," Ron said as he headed toward the house with Officer Evan St. Cloud on his heels.

4

Twenty-two-seventeen East Warnock was a pleasant little cottage. Jude had bought it shortly after getting engaged. He was fixing it up with the plan that they could move in after the wedding. The police officers sent to check it found the house empty, but there was a sign in the yard that read *Olson Construction and Refurbishing*. It didn't take a genius to realize that the same Jude Olson currently wanted in connection to the homicide of Alex Metford was the same man who owned the construction company.

Meanwhile, Ron worked the scene through the night. By morning, he had affidavits from eight different neighbors who saw the perpetrator bust into the house and flee the scene afterward. They also had video footage from doorbell cameras. The cameras showed a man who looked exactly like one Jude Olson on social media going into the home with the sledgehammer and propane torch.

On top of that, they had fingerprints from the sledgehammer, the propane torch, the lighter, and the belt used to hold the victim in place while he was tortured to death. Nothing in the sad little home appeared to be missing, but they couldn't be sure it wasn't a robbery. Ron had a solid start on the murder book, which was a three-ring binder with copies of all the affidavits and evidence receipts, along with a timeline of the crime. Nothing had been difficult, but it was still wearisome. By dawn, Ron was ready to find his suspect. He and Evan St. John, now out of his uniform and in his civilian clothes, had breakfast at the Cracker Barrel and then made their way to the Olson construction offices. It was a small, rented space in an industrial row. It was large enough for a work truck, some materials, and a little office. A plaque, just like the yard sign, hung over the man-door leading into the office space.

Ron tried the door handle. It was locked, but a silver Ford Explorer was in the parking space adjacent to the building.

"It's locked," Ron said to St. Cloud, who was checking out the Explorer. "Anything?"

"Nothing," Evan replied. "But the plates match. This is our suspect's vehicle."

Ron turned back to the door and knocked. It was a long shot, but it was possible the murderer might be in the building. Ron drove an unmarked Chevrolet Malibu with over a hundred thousand miles on it. It was a plain vehicle and didn't scream police if a person didn't look too closely. It was possible that they might be mistaken for potential customers, even though it was early on a Saturday morning.

"What now?" Evan said.

Ron felt a lump forming in his gut. He needed sleep, but time was of the essence if he hoped to find his man. All the evidence in the world was useless without a suspect in custody. Plus, the Explorer being at the construction office was a bad sign. If Olson had a second vehicle, one not yet registered, perhaps, he could be in another state already.

Before he could answer, Ron heard the lock click in the steel door of the construction office. His breath caught in his throat as he turned, and Jude Olson opened the door.

"Let me finish my breakfast, officer. Then I'm all yours," he said.

5

Jude Olson was in an interrogation room. He was amused at how much it looked exactly like the rooms criminals were questioned in on television programs. He admired the craftsmanship of the room. It was a small space. The walls were covered in foam padding that would soak up any sounds made inside. There was a metal table that had been bolted to the floor, which was unpolished concrete. The door was mounted with big, industrial hinges that swung the door out instead of into the room. One wall had a small window in it. He could see his reflection as he sat patiently at the metal table.

When the detective came in, he had a three-ring binder in one hand and a digital dictation device in the other. He was wearing a rumpled suit, and there were dark circles under his eyes, but he seemed upbeat for a man who had obviously been working all night long.

He turned on the recorder and set it on the table.

"This is Detective Ron Flanagan, badge number two-one-eight-seven-three, interviewing Jude Olson on December eighteenth, 2025. It is nine-thirty-seven in the A.M."

He went on to read Jude his Miranda Rights, which had already been done when the detective arrested him at his construction office. Jude had been living in what was supposed to be a break room for nearly six months. He had a cot with a sleeping bag in the small room, along with a refrigerator, microwave, and hot plate. Jude had learned to cook a good variety of one-skillet meals since moving into the tiny space while he spent his free time renovating the house he had bought. Of course, all that had stopped a couple of months back. He was nearly finished with the little house, but couldn't bring himself to work on it any longer. So, it sat unfinished while Jude lived in his office.

"Do you understand your rights, Mr. Olson?" Ron asked.

Jude nodded.

"Please respond verbally for the audio recording," the detective insisted.

Jude knew he was being video recorded, but he didn't mind going along with the detective's wishes. It wasn't his intention to make trouble for them. This was all part of his plan, after all.

"Yes, I understand my rights, Detective Flanagan."

"Can you tell me where you were yesterday at five-forty-five pm?"

"I'd like to speak to a lawyer," Jude said.

That made Detective Flanagan sigh. He was obviously tired, and Jude didn't want to torture him.

"Do you have a lawyer?"

"No," Jude said. "But I'm willing to confess everything to Lance Brown. He's a lawyer with the prosecutor's office. You get him down here, and I'll answer all your questions."

The look in Ron Flanagan's eyes was pure hunger. A confession was a home run. A confession meant no more work on the case. He could file it as solved and move on.

"You want ADA Brown?"

"Lance Brown, yes," Jude said. "I'll confess once I have certain considerations in place."

That dimmed the hunger in Flanagan's eyes a little, but he still got to his feet, turned off the recording device, and opened the door.

"I'll be back," he said.

It took over two hours to get Lance Brown to the station. Jude sat alone in the small room the entire time. It was a change. He was used to staying busy, but all that was behind him. He was no longer fully in charge of himself. Others would have a say in all that he did, and there would be a lot of solitude, but that was just fine with Jude. He didn't mind being alone. And for the first time since losing Alison, he was able to savor something again. He relaxed in the uncomfortable chair inside the claustrophobic interrogation room and waited.

Lance Brown looked hungover and grouchy. He was the type of man who obviously cherished his weekends. Jude understood the feeling. One could work tirelessly through the week; it only made time off on the weekends sweeter. But there were always exceptions in life, and Jude knew he was nothing if not exceptional.

"What is this, Mr. Olson?" Lance Brown said as he came into the interrogation room. "Please tell me you didn't do something rash."

"I will tell you everything I've done," Jude said. "But first, I need assurance from you that the death penalty is off the table. Write that up. I'll sign it and then I'll answer all your questions."

"Are you saying you killed Alex Metford last night?" Lance Brown asked.

"Sign first, talk second," Jude said.

Lance looked shocked. He bent down over the table, and Jude caught a whiff of bourbon on his breath. Jude knew some people needed a little nip in the morning to steady themselves after a night of hard drinking. It was a shame to think that a young man like Lance Brown was already so far gone down the road to perdition.

"Mr. Olson, you're in a lot of trouble here. I highly recommend you get yourself a lawyer. I can recommend someone."

Detective Flanagan pulled the prosecutor out of the room. "What the hell are you doing?"

"He's obviously disturbed," Brown said. "You don't know the situation."

"I know you recommending lawyers isn't going to help anyone."

"That's not true, detective. I understand you want a confession, and I'll do what Mr. Olson has asked, but you need to know something. Two months ago, his fiancée was killed, probably by Alex Metford. She was jogging and got run down."

"I remember that case," Flanagan said.

"Then maybe you know the particulars and why we couldn't prosecute."

"That has nothing to do with this crime," Flanagan said. "Will you support what he's asking for?"

"He wants the death penalty off the table. I can do that for the Metford case."

"Then do it!" Flanagan ordered.

Thirty minutes later, Jude was reading the legal document. It was full of hitherto and aforementioned type language, but basically said what he wanted it to say. It was restricted to the case of the Alex Metford homicide, although that was fine with Jude. He had committed no other crimes in the recent past.

Jude signed. Detective Flanagan sighed with relief ... and then the confession began in earnest.

6

M r. Olson, can you tell me where you were yesterday at five-forty-five p.m.?" Flanagan asked.

"I had just gotten to the house on September twenty-third when Alison was killed," Jude said. "We were three weeks from the wedding and had already moved in. She insisted that we wait for marriage before becoming intimate, and I thought I had a lifetime to be with her, so I agreed. But I was trying to finish the kitchen in our new home, and she wanted to lose five pounds before the wedding. I don't know why. She was perfect just the way she was. I told her so, many times, but I guess she wanted everything to be perfect."

"I didn't ask about the night your fiancé was killed, Mr. Olson," Detective Flanagan said. "Please tell us where you were last night."

"I will, but first, you need to know what happened to Alison. It's still listed as an accident, but it wasn't. She was run down by a drunk driver less than a mile from her home."

"Jude, please, we've been through this," Lance Brown said.

"We've been through the case many times," Jude replied. "We both know who was responsible for Alison's death."

"There are no witnesses to the crime and no evidence," Lance said.

"Because the police didn't act fast enough. Tell me, Detective Flanagan, why didn't the police look into Alex Metford immediately after Alison's murder? He was pulled over for a busted headlight and a cracked windshield two miles from the scene. He had an open bottle of alcohol in his vehicle. Yet, he was sent home with just a warning. It took the police an entire week to follow up. I've never understood that."

Ron Flanagan sighed and looked at Lance Brown.

"Officer Dave Murphy pulled him over," Brown said. "In the report he made days later, he said he let Metford off with a warning because the driver claimed to have hit a deer. He was rattled but not drunk. It was too dark for the officer to see if there was blood on the vehicle, and as he was unaware of the hit-and-run at that moment, he didn't use his flashlight to inspect the vehicle. When he did finally report the stop, five days later, Metford had used a power washer on his car and sent it in for repairs. There was no evidence to connect him with Alison Whitney's death."

"You called it all circumstantial," Jude said.

"Yes, that's all we had," Lance Brown said. "Your fellow detectives brought him in and questioned him about the incident. They found him to be unreliable, but he stuck to his story, and without a confession, there was no evidence to tie him to the accident."

"It wasn't an accident," Jude insisted. "Alex Metford is a high-functioning alcoholic."

"Was," Flanagan interjected.

"His drinking was on the verge of out of control," Jude continued. "Did you know he had two reprimands in his work file for drinking on the job? Did you know that's why his wife left him and why he didn't fight for custody? Did you know that every Friday during his lunch break, he would leave the office, drive to a liquor store, and buy enough hard liquor for a frat party, or that he would begin drinking it on his drive home? Did you know that he takes the same route to and from work every single day, and that it passes by Alison's home? Yet, it's all circumstantial. The cop who pulled him over didn't run a breathalyzer test. He didn't inspect the vehicle, which had obviously been in an impact with something. And he didn't file a report."

"We've been over this," Lance Brown said. "I'm sorry for your loss, Mr. Olson, but the justice system isn't perfect."

"No, it isn't," Jude said. "But it should be. I'm going to see what I can do about that."

"Can you answer a question then, Mr. Olson?" Detective Flanagan asked.

"I was at the home of Alex Metford yesterday at five-forty-five pm," Jude said calmly. His eyes never left Ron Flanagan's. "I busted down his door with a sledgehammer. Then I broke his nose with a palm strike. He was already drunk. I don't think he even felt the punch. I put him on a wooden chair and secured his body there with a belt I brought with me."

"And you killed him?" Detective Flanagan pressed.

"I spoke to the Medical Examiner who took care of my Alison," Jude said. "I had to press him pretty hard, but he confessed to me there was evidence that she lived for about eight minutes after being run down by Alex Metford."

"Oh, God help us," Brown said as he leaned against the metal table.

"There was a traumatic injury to the brain," Jude went on. "So, there's no way to know if she was awake and aware of her injuries during the eight minutes before the cerebral swelling caused her vital functions to cease. But what if she was awake? What if she felt it all? Can you imagine that? Laying in a ditch, your bones shattered, knowing you're going to die and you can't do anything to stop it? Alex Metford can imagine it. At least, he could have. Yes,

I killed him, Detective Flanagan. I took my time. Eight minutes, to be exact. And I made sure that he knew why he was dying."

"You are confessing to the premeditated murder of Alex Metford?"

"I killed him after he confessed to the drunk driving murder of Alison Whitney."

Jude fell silent.

"Is that enough?" Lance Brown asked.

He was pale, and there was a thin sheen of sweat on his upper lip. Jude wondered how a man could be a criminal attorney and be so squeamish.

"We're going to have to work through the details," Flanagan said. "But you don't have to be here, counselor."

"Thank God in heaven," Lance Brown said. He practically jumped from his chair.

"Thanks for finally getting something right," Jude said, holding onto the legal document they had both signed.

"May God forgive you, Mr. Olson."

"I'm just the instrument in his hand, Mr. Brown," Jude said.

7

At the arraignment, Jude pled guilty. Two weeks later, he was sentenced for the crime.

"Having heard your confession, Mr. Olson," the judge said. "And taking into account the bargain made with the prosecution's office, I hereby sentence you to life in prison. You will be transported to the Supermax Correctional facility in Duncan County, there to serve your sentence. Do you have anything to say to the court about this matter?"

"Justice is served, your honor," Jude said. "Thank you."

The judge frowned as he banged his gavel on the desk and waved to the bailiffs to take Jude away. He already had handcuffs on. The last two weeks were spent in a small cell with a bed and toilet. The county jail where he was detained had a small library and a simple system for dealing with inmates who were considered to be dangerous. Jude Olson was, without a doubt, the most dangerous man who had ever stepped foot into the jail, but he did nothing to cause problems.

The food was bad, the conditions less than optimal, but he had expected as much. Jude knew what it was like to live in the lap of luxury. He had spent the night in suites that cost ten thousand dollars a night and in mansions with the rich and famous. But that was in his younger days when he was exploiting his talents for personal gain. It hadn't taken long to realize that having everything a person could ever want left one without much to live for. So, he had given up his posh lifestyle and taken on a simpler life, but one with much more in the way of intangible rewards.

Since Alison's death, he had decided to simplify again, which is exactly how he would have described his two-week vacation at the county jail. It wasn't exactly luxury, yet he slept well, took naps, had others who prepared his meals, and did his laundry. He was kept isolated, which was fine for Jude. He hadn't expected anything different. The Christmas holiday had passed, which Jude had known would be hard emotionally. It was one more reason why the solitude in the county jail with no trappings of the season was probably for the best.

After his sentencing, he was loaded onto a bus with twenty-seven other felons. His seat was in a cage near the front. The bus made three stops. The first was to the minimum security prison, where three white-collar criminals were turned over to the guards. The second stop was for a combined facility. The medium-security prison was the oldest building and looked frightening with its towering stone walls. Jude saw inmates in orange jumpsuits in a wide recreation yard there. All but two of the remaining felons on the bus were turned over to guards at the second stop, who quickly separated those bound for the medium security facility from those unfortunates going to the maximum security prison. It had even higher walls and several tall chain-link fences with razor wire looping the top. Jude saw his first guard tower there, and the correctional officer with a rifle that was held ready in case trouble broke out. It didn't, at this time, and the bus set off for the new Supermax prison in Duncan County.

It was January, and there was snow on the ground. Jude

wondered how much he would miss the outside world. It was impossible to say. He would rather have been on a tropical beach sipping a frozen beverage and watching the surf roll in and out. He had some trepidation about his plan by that point. Perhaps it was crazy putting himself in prison. Perhaps he would go crazy there. He felt reasonably confident he could get out if he really wanted to, but getting out held very little appeal to him. There was a wound he could not assuage with luxury, hedonistic pleasure, or mind-numbing medications. It never left him. The ache of it was raw and terrible. He would never see Alison again. He would never hold her hand, kiss her lips, or hear her laugh again. That realization was worse than any torture could ever be.

He had heard it said that if a person hadn't loved, they hadn't really lived. He had certainly loved Alison. She was the first person who had ever really seen him. His father was gone before he was born, and his mother was an addict. Jude had lived in various boys' homes and foster care facilities throughout most of his child-hood. When his mother cleaned up and managed to get custody, it was always short-lived and often more dangerous than being in the system.

Jude had learned to blend in and go along to get along. But he had also learned what made him unique and, eventually, the system worked in his favor. When he got out, the world was his oyster, but he was still hiding his true self behind a mask and keeping everyone at a distance. Alison had been different. She knew nothing about him when he asked her out. She had said yes because she saw something in him that she liked, not because he had money, influence, or the rarest of all traits a man can possess. He had given all that up when he met Alison, and it had been the best choice of his life until the day she died. Then came pain like he had never known. The lack of justice for her death only compounded that hurt.

The bus entered Duncan County. Jude saw the sign and the

overgrown fields beyond. They were laden with half-melted snow. In the distance, he saw mountains, but nothing close by that seemed appealing. And then the supermax prison came into view. It looked like a fort. Cinder block walls rose around the facility. They were painted black. The gate was big and heavy, with a guard facility built on top that had wide windows. They were tinted so that a person on the outside couldn't see in. But the bus whined as it slowed, and the gate crept open as if it was being pulled by teams of languishing inmates instead of hydraulic pistons.

The bus stopped, and the guards inside unlocked Jude's cage.

"This your new home, boy," the guard said. "On your feet, inmate."

Jude felt the derogatory names as though he had lost his personhood. But he knew boys in the foster care system who had treated him the same way. He shook off the insults and the trepidation the guard was foisting onto him. The leg irons only allowed for short steps. He had to shuffle off the bus, and the other inmate wasn't let out of his cage until Jude had been turned over to the guards. Four of them walked Jude down a long path inside a series of tall chain-link fences.

When they reached the facility, his leg irons were removed, and he was searched. This included the removal of his jumpsuit from the county jail. He was required to open his mouth while a guard with rubber gloves and a tongue depressor searched for contraband hidden inside his cheeks and under his tongue. They forced him to raise his arms, turn around, squat, and even lift his scrotum. Jude had no contraband or weapons.

He was sprayed with some type of hard chemical intended to kill vermin that often infested inmates at the county level. His head was shaved, and he was given two minutes to shower in a small stall. The water was cold, and the soap was rough, but he scrubbed himself clean and washed off.

Naked and shivering, he was given clothes that he put on while being watched by no less than four guards at all times. Two had clubs, two others had firearms at the ready. Jude gave them no reason to mistreat him.

"This is the Duncan County Supermax," one of the guards told him. "You'll be in a cell with another inmate unless you can't play nice. Otherwise, you'll have two hours of rec time in the yard every day and showers twice a week. When the buzzer sounds, you put your feet on the ready line. Is that understood?"

"Yes," Jude said.

"You got two choices here, inmate. You can do what you're told when you're told, and eventually, you can earn some privileges. Or, you can resist, and life will be harder and harder for you. I don't recommend it, but the choice is yours. What you should put out of your mind at this moment is escape. It isn't possible, and any attempt will result in bodily harm or death. Is that clear?"

"Yes," Jude said.

They didn't know him. They didn't know what he was capable of. But they would learn soon enough. And he wasn't looking to escape. He had a mission, and he had sacrificed a lot to set the wheels of the justice system in motion. All that remained was to see justice served.

He was given a pillow, a set of sheets, a blanket, a plastic cup, and a short-handled toothbrush. Inside the cup was a small tube of toothpaste and an individually wrapped bar of soap. With his new possessions in hand, he was marched into a building with three floors. There were cells on each of three floors, or tiers, as he was soon to learn. Each one was open in the center, with a railing and what looked like chain link fencing that kept the opening on the second and third tier from being accessed. It was still an imposing sight from the bottom. There were stairs enclosed in the same chain-link on either end of the room.

"This is cell block alpha, your new home," the talkative guard said. "You're on tier three, cell three-five-three. Your cellmate is Hitchcock."

"Tell me what he's in for," I said.

"We don't talk about convictions," another of the guards said.

"Killed his old lady and the guy she was cheating on him with," the talkative guard said.

"Munson! What the hell, man?"

The look of surprise on CO Munson's face was almost comical, but I had seen it a thousand times. Looking over my shoulder, I saw that the guards all had name tags on their uniforms. The angry guard's name was Pax.

"Don't be angry at him," I told the guards.

For a second, they looked confused, then the one named Pax reached out a hand and slapped Munson on the shoulder. "Just busting your chops, man."

They all chuckled nervously, and we stopped in front of the stairs. There was a door on rollers, but with no handle or locking mechanism that I could see. Munson and the other guards had radios pinned to their uniforms. Munson took his and asked someone in another part of the prison to open the stairwell door. A buzzer sounded, and the door slid open.

"Everything is operated by computer in a different building," Pax said as he gave Jude a gentle push forward.

They walked up the stairs. Jude wore thin-soled slip-on canvas shoes. The guards wore heavy, steel-toed boots that clanked on the metal stairs. At the top of the third-tier landing, they radioed in for the door to be opened again. When it did, they walked through.

"Home sweet home," a man named Baxter said.

"Cell three-five-three," Munson said into his radio. Another buzzer sounded, and the door, which was one piece of heavy steel with an opening in the center, slid to the side.

"Step in and hold your hands through the opening," Munson ordered.

I went inside the small room. It smelled of body odor and sweat. A big man with dark skin was on the bottom bunk. He was so tall his feet hung off the end. He sat up, looking at Jude the way a hunter looks at a stag that suddenly appears in the forest.

"Hitchcock, meet Olson," Pax said. "Show him the ropes around here."

"I look like a tour guide?" Hitchcock sneered.

As the cell door closed with a resounding thud, Jude set his personal effects on the upper bunk and turned around. He could feel the big inmate moving behind him. Sticking his hands through the opening in the door, Munson began to remove the cuffs.

"Hitchcock," Jude said calmly, "you aren't going to threaten or hurt me."

"Good luck, Olson," Pax called out as the guards left. "You're going to need it."

8

When Jude turned around, he found the big man standing near the foot of his bunk. He could have easily reached out and touched Jude, who was thin and a few inches short of six feet tall. There was no getting around Hitchcock unless the big man turned sideways, and then it would be uncomfortably close. The big man was breathing hard but not moving. There was a strange trembling on his cheeks as if he were trying to move an unmovable object.

"We have a lot to learn about each other," Jude said calmly. "Go sit in the corner."

Hitchcock grunted angrily but obeyed. He folded his big body up and sat on the dirty floor of their cell.

Jude didn't know when the power to influence people came to him. He thought maybe it had to do with his bodily changes during puberty. At first, it seemed fantastic to him, but over time, he began to see that many people were born with incredible abilities. Some could throw a ball so much better than regular people. Jude certainly understood that. He couldn't throw a ball, or run very fast, or jump very high. He wasn't handsome by conventional standards. He wasn't smart enough to understand the stock market or build rockets. Even in his chosen profession, he wasn't as good a builder as many carpenters and contractors he knew personally.

What he could do was dominate the will of other people. He didn't know the mechanics, but he knew how to use it. He could will other people to do what he wanted by speaking a command to them. That was why Munson had told him what Hitchcock was in prison for. And it was why Alex Metford had confessed to killing Alison. Jude could have caused the murderer to go to the police and confess, but he quickly saw that the law was actually impotent to mete out justice. They postured and proclaimed their supposed powers. Yet, in the end, the best they could offer was fractional recompense to society, which was to say to people at large, not to the victims who deserved justice. Murderers like Alex walked free every day. Those who were convicted often only served a few years in prison for the crime of stealing another person's life. How was that justice?

"Don't worry, we won't be sharing this tiny space long," Jude said. "But for now, I need you."

"Who the hell are you?" Hitchcock stammered.

"It's hard to deal with, I know," Jude said. "I've been powerless many times in my life. Most people in my position would feel the way you are feeling now. Big felons like yourself are intimidating, wouldn't you agree?"

"Who... are... you?" Hitchcock said.

"We can start with names. That's fine. Mine's Jude. Tell me your name."

"Marcus Hitchcock, but everyone calls me Money."

"Money, I like that," Jude said.

"How you make me do what I don't want to do?" Money asked.

"It's a talent I picked up," Jude said. "Are you a murderer, Money?"

He frowned. "Yeah."'

"How many people besides your wife and her lover have you killed?"

"Six."

"Six people?"

"Gang life, dog. It ain't for the weak."

"No, and neither is prison life, I suppose."

Jude turned to the small shelf above the sink. There were books on it—the Bible, the Book of Mormon, the Quran, along with The Fountainhead by Ayn Rand, Rebel Yell by S.C. Gwynne, and a Calvin and Hobbs cartoon book.

"Interesting reading list," Jude said. "Are these yours?"

Money didn't respond. Jude looked over at him. "I can make you answer."

"The Bible's mine. The rest are from the prison library."

"Good to know," Jude said. "I like to read. Tell me what your typical day is like here?"

Another sour look crossed the big man's face, but he answered. "I'm on kitchen detail. So, I do my exercise after my morning nap. Then they come get me for lunch. I work in the kitchen through dinner time. I get an hour in the yard in the afternoon, too. Then I'm back in here for the night."

"You cook?"

"I do the heavy lifting," Money said.

"And get plenty of calories working down there, too, I imagine. From the looks of you, I'd say you eat a lot. What's my schedule going to be?"

"Man, I ain't going to help your skinny—"

"Tell me!" Jude said, raising his voice a little.

"You'll be on rookie rotation for the first couple of weeks," Money grumbled. "Breakfast comes early, probably six in the morning. I don't keep up with it. Tier three gets group exercise in the yard every afternoon. Showers after breakfast two days a week."

"Which days?"

"Beats the hell outta me. I don't keep no calendar."

"It's the same every single day?"

"That's right. And these jokers in here gonna twist you up like a pretzel, white boy."

"That won't happen," Jude said. "The rest of my time will be in here?"

"That's right. Or in the infirmary, I'd bet."

It was Jude's turn to chuckle. The big inmate didn't know him and couldn't conceive of what Jude was capable of. Jude could do more than influence what a person thought or how they acted. He could actually take control of a person's internal organs. He could order a person's heart to stop beating if he so desired.

"How do I get books from the prison library?" Jude asked.

"Old man Kelly brings the library cart around a couple of times a week."

"Can we make requests?"

"Man! I don't know!"

He was angry, sweating, and trying to break free from Jude's invisible hold over him.

"Maybe this isn't going to work," Jude said. "You stink, Money. This entire cell smells like a shoe box with old sneakers inside. Go to sleep."

The big man's head flopped back, and he snored slightly. Jude pulled the rumpled sheets off the lower bunk. He didn't want to sleep down below the hulking felon, but he had a pretty good idea that Money had some hidden contraband. Most of it wasn't hard to find. There were two granola bars tucked between the mattress and the wall. The bed was made of a slab of steel with a thin, rubber-coated mattress. Jude checked the edges and found two razor blades and a spoon with the handle ground down to a point.

Satisfied that he had everything the mattress was hiding, Jude flopped it up onto the upper bunk. He would let Money sleep on the hard steel and see how that suited the big man. He sat on the lower bunk and looked around the cell. Nothing jumped out at him initially. When he laid back on the steel bunk he discovered a small pocket made from butcher tape on the bottom of the upper bunk. Inside was a baggy of unmarked pills and a color photo of a naked woman that had been folded into a tiny square.

Jude wasn't interested in weapons or drugs. He moved to the books and thought about what Money had said. They were all from the prison library except for the Bible, that was his, which meant he didn't have to give it up. Jude plucked the Bible from the shelf and thumbed through it. The beginning and end were whole, but in the center, a section had been cut from the pages, and a burner phone was hidden inside.

"This might actually be handy," Jude said.

He was going to make the prison his home, and it would take some time, but soon, he would have whatever he wanted, including a private cell. He could have killed Money, but he needed information, and he wanted the big man to spread the word about him. Fear was a powerful motivator, and prison was a dangerous place. Jude had to make sure he understood the place, and that included the prisoners as well as the guards.

An hour later, guards came to escort Money to the kitchens. By that point, Jude had made his bed and was relaxing with Money's copy of *Rebel Yell*. The guards ordered the big man to put his hands through the opening in the door. Jude woke him, and he got to his feet, his joints popping from being stuck in an uncomfortable position. The guards locked Money's hands behind his back with handcuffs, then opened the door. Jude watched the procedure, propped on one elbow. The guards noticed that he had the bigger man's mattress, and Money was limping. They probably thought that Jude had bested the larger man in a physical altercation. Jude wasn't bothered letting them think it.

Lunch arrived an hour later. It was a cold sandwich, bologna with cheese, and a piece of limp lettuce. There were raw carrots and celery in the next compartment, not fresh and crisp but old and chewy. The fourth compartment had a generic pudding cup. There was a paper cup of iced tea and, beside that, a small carton of two percent milk. The meal was unappetizing, but Jude forced himself to eat some of it. The pudding wasn't good, but it was better than the rest of the meager meal. He saved the carrots and celery in case he got hungry later and ate the sandwich as fast as he could. Jude hadn't had milk with a meal since getting out of the foster care system, but he drank the contents of the small carton, knowing it was decent calories. The tea was more water than tea, what Alison had called weak tea. It wasn't sweetened, although it wasn't water either. He saved it, sipping on the beverage while he read until the paper was nearly saturated and he had to pour the rest down the sink.

That afternoon, Jude was taken out to the yard for exercise. The yard was not like he expected. There were no ball courts, no bleachers to sit on, no weights to exercise with. It was a bare patch of muddy ground. The inmates all walked. It wasn't coordinated, but the prisoners quickly segregated based on race, and it was better to stay within the bounds of one group than to let the others catch up and surround you.

Jude found himself in a group of white men who were neither large nor tattooed like the prisoners involved in the Aryan gang. Most of them looked ragged, worn down from prison life, and absolutely terrified. Jude recognized the man who had been on the prison bus with him and moved closer.

"I'm Jude," he said. "Tell me your name."

"Miller," he said softly. "First name's Oscar, but everyone calls me Miller."

"Nice to meet you," Jude said. "We came over here together."

Miller nodded. "You settling in okay?"

"It's an adjustment."

"Who they have you in a cell with?"

Miller nodded his head toward a slim man with tattoos on his face and neck. He had brown skin and jet-black hair, which was slicked back. The man walked with swagger among a gang of Latinos.

"T-bone," Miller said softly. "I thought he was going to kill me for that lousy bologna sandwich."

"He took your food?"

"Everything but the celery," Miller said.

"Things will get better," Jude said. "Trust me on that."

Jude was the first person to break from the pack. There was an immediate sense of tension from the prisoners and the guards. Things in the prison functioned on routine. When someone broke that routine, bad things tended to happen. The Latin gang saw Jude approaching. The larger members moved to meet him. It wasn't hard to tell that even though the Latino gang was the smaller of the prison groups, it was one of the toughest and held the white and black gangs at bay.

"You aren't going to hurt me," Jude said loud enough for the group to hear him. "You will step aside. I'm going to talk to T-bone."

The big men grunted as they tried to resist but couldn't. They let Jude through, and he approached Miller's cellmate.

"Man, you must be loco. I ain't gonna lie, I thought you was dead come walking over here like this. Pedro, show him how it is."

"Stay where you are," Jude said to Pedro.

T-bone's eyes opened large. It was part shock and part fear as he realized his soldiers weren't obeying him.

"I said somebody end this pendejo!"

"No one is going to hurt me, T-bone. Tell me, are you a murderer?"

He tried to turn suddenly and nearly fell down. The prisoners were still walking, and someone helped him stay on his feet. When he spoke, it was like a growl.

"Yes," he snarled.

"I thought so," Jude said. "You will have a brain aneurysm when I walk away."

"Screw you!" The felon snapped.

Jude walked back across toward the group where Miller was watching him. The moment Jude left the group and stepped out into the open, T-Bone screamed. He grabbed his head and fell to the ground.

"Help! We need help!" One of the Latin gang members shouted.

"Medic! Something's wrong with him!" Another bellowed.

An alarm sounded and everyone got down on the ground. Jude hurried over and dropped down beside Miller.

"He won't be eating your food anymore," Jude said.

"Man, what the hell did you do?"

"I carried out justice, Miller."

The man looked at him as if Jude was crazy. They were lying on the ground, and the guards were out with shotguns, watching the prisoners. A pair of inmates in medical smocks hurried out and picked up T-Bone. The man was limp. They put him on a gurney and rushed him back inside. Once they were gone, a guard blew a whistle and everyone got back up on their feet.

"Tell me, Miller, are you a murderer?"

The other new prisoner didn't hesitate. "No way, man. I'm innocent. They got the wrong guy."

"Tell me the truth," Jude said.

"I am. I didn't do it. I'm not supposed to be here."

It was Jude's turn to be shocked. He knew Miller couldn't lie to him. If he had committed a crime, he would have to confess it. And yet he maintained his innocence. To Jude, it was another example of the broken criminal justice system.

"I think maybe we're going to be friends," Jude said.

"Yeah, man, sure thing," Miller said quietly. "Thanks for helping me out."

"My pleasure," Jude said. He knew he was in the right place. It might not be easy, but he was on a mission. He could make the sacrifice if it meant making a difference in the world.

9

"Tell me what happened," Rick Jennings said.

He was the warden of the Duncan Supermax, with over five hundred high-security inmates to keep tabs on.

"Doc says it was some kind of brain issue," Captain Derek Foster explained. "They'll have to do an autopsy to be sure."

"No trauma?" The warden asked.

"No, sir, no incidents at all," Foster assured him.

The proclamation was factually correct, but it still made Sergeant Tyler Munson cough. He tried to hold it in, but he couldn't.

"You have something to add, Munson?" Jennings asked.

"Well, sir, I agree with Captain Foster. Only, there was something odd that happened."

"You were on duty?"

"Overwatch, sir, north tower."

"And?"

"And sir, one of the new inmates crossed over and spoke to Perez just before he collapsed."

"Spoke to him?"

"We didn't see anything," Foster insisted. "Munson was watching via the binoculars. I didn't mention it because there's nothing to tell."

"Is there any way to know what this new inmate said?" Asked the Warden.

"We could ask him," Munson said.

"Like he would tell the truth," Foster scoffed. "Sir, it was just a freak accident. Perez was probably walking around with that brain disorder half his life."

"Get a full report," Jennings said. "And I want the name of the new inmate who spoke to him."

"We only had two come in today," Munson said. "Jude Olson is his name. Small guy. Gave us no trouble when we brought him in."

"Not even a cross word," Sergeant Howie Pax chimed in. "He's in three-five-three with Hitchcock."

"Alright, thank you. Let's get back to our posts. Derek, a moment, please."

The other corrections officers filed out of the office. Jennings wasn't happy. The truth was, he had taken the job at the newest, most high-profile prison in the state because it was a step toward getting on the board of the Bureau of Prisons. Duncan Supermax was a joint experiment between the state and federal governments. It housed the most dangerous prisoners in the state, including those on death row, as well as high-risk inmates in the federal system. Normally, the state and federal government had their own facilities. But Duncan was a way to test new methods in corrections management, while isolating the risk from the exceptionally violent offenders.

Jennings took off his glasses and rubbed his eyes. He could feel a headache coming on. Foster went over to the K-Cup coffee maker the Warden kept in his office. He put a pod in the machine and slipped a mug under the spout before holding down the button that got the machine to brew a single cup of coffee.

Jennings put his glasses back on and opened the file on the new inmates that had arrived that morning.

"Do you know anything about this Olson character?" Jennings asked.

"I read the file," Foster said from across the room. "The guy cooked the drunk who ran over his fiancée. Can't say I blame him for that."

"He made a plea bargain. Confession in exchange for removing the death penalty. Wonderful. We get to deal with him for the next fifty years."

"I don't know why he didn't fight the charges," Foster said.

"Does it really matter? I'm more concerned with how much trouble he's going to cause us."

"None that I can see," Foster said. "The guy did nothing but talk. Since when is that a crime?"

"When you're the last person to speak to someone before they die, it's a problem."

"I don't know what he said. But to be honest, I'm more surprised he was able to say anything at all. T-Bone was a shot caller for the cartel guys in here. My intel says he has connections on the outside, too. Maybe Olson is from down south. Anything like that in his file?"

"No," Warden Jennings said. "He was a model citizen. Not even a parking ticket before he committed premeditated murder."

"You think he's crazy?" Foster asked.

"Might be. He burned his victim to death with a propane blow torch. That is one nasty way to die."

"And then he walks right through the Latin crowd like he's the king of the world. They don't lay a hand on him," Foster said, picking up his coffee and blowing on the scalding liquid.

"He could be a problem," Jennings said. "Let's keep our eyes open. Any more funny business and I want to know about it."

"Yes, sir," Foster said.

"Anything else going on? What's the scuttlebutt with the guards?"

"You mean the Corrections Officers, sir?" Foster acted as if he was offended.

"Sorry, Derek."

"I'm just yanking your chain, sir," Foster said. "Nothing's changed. Lots of talk about New York State. That liberal governor up there is a real piece of work."

"Our guys are happy with the current state of affairs?"

"We're always one step away from an insurrection around here, sir. But the bottom line is that our COs make as much or more than any officers in the country. Plus, we've got great benefits. The boys have all seen you fighting for them, and it counts in their book. I think we're okay across the board here, Warden—nothing to worry about. One accident is not going to ruffle anyone's feathers. Besides, no one was involved. Unless the ME comes back with poisoning or something, we're in the clear on this one. Just bad genetics, that's all."

"Good," Jennings said. "Now get out of here. But make sure you bring that mug back clean."

10

The walk in the afternoon wasn't bad. Yard time in the county lockup had been twice as long, but the fresh air was nice. Back in his cell, Jude climbed into his bed and took a nap. He could only doze. There was still a sense of danger that kept his nerves on edge, even with his cellmate gone to the kitchens.

The food schedule at the prison seemed odd. Lunch was late, dinner was early, and if Money had been straight with him, breakfast would be very early in the morning. His dinner was spaghetti, overcooked with bland marinara sauce, a piece of cold toast, and steamed broccoli. If there was any meat in the spaghetti sauce, Jude couldn't find it. Dessert was applesauce that was just poured onto the tray. More milk and tea. It wasn't tasty, but it felt good to have something warm in his stomach.

An hour after he finished his meal, Money returned to their cell. He smelled of garlic, although even that was an improvement over his usual body odor.

"What the hell, man?" Money snarled as soon as the door to the cell closed. "You can't take my mattress."

"I can, and I have," Jude said as he lay propped on one elbow. "Lay down on your bunk and don't speak unless I ask you a question."

For a moment, he didn't move. The tremble of effort was back in his face. The big man was trying to resist, but couldn't. He sat down on the bunk, then turned and lay down flat on the cold steel. The cells on tier three weren't as cold as those on the ground floor. What little heat was pumped into the prison rose to the upper floors.

The noises of the prison were getting louder. Some inmates opened the flap in their metal door and shouted to their neighbors. Some just cursed and screamed for no reason at all. Jude heard it, but the sounds mingled into a cacophony of white noise in his mind. He lay on his bed reading. The only sound that registered in his mind was Money's noisy breathing.

Having a cellmate was not ideal. But it was somewhat necessary. Jude wanted information, and Money had it. When the lights eventually went out, they began to talk.

"Tell me, are you in a gang, Money?"

"Everybody in a gang up in here. The inmates, guards, everybody. We all got our allegiances, and we all got to pay our way."

"What do you mean, 'pay your way'?"

At first, Money didn't answer, then he said quietly, "You'll see."

"Money, you're going to answer all my questions truthfully. What does it mean that everyone pays their way?"

"Means if you want protection, it's gonna cost you something."

"What gang are you in, Money?"

"Can't you tell by the color of my skin, dog? I'm in the Brotherhood."

"What other gangs are there?"

"Mexicans, Aryans, fags and the guards. And within each one, there's levels. Just like the prison. We up here on tier three. Ain't so bad, really. Gets hot in the summertime though, I ain't gonna lie.

But we got more privileges than them down on the bottom. That's where they send them mad dogs. You feel me?"

"The shot callers for the gangs?"

"Some of 'em," Money explained. "Others is just straight-up killers. They only let 'em out one at a time, and they keep 'em caged in they separate yard. They got screws workin' for 'em, yo. They carry messages and move people around for 'em. They the real wardens in this joint, fo sho. They tell you do something, you do it. Don't matter what it is. You want to live long in this hell house; you do what the devil requires."

Jude thought about that for a while.

"What do they make you do, Money?"

"I'm in the kitchen, see? I'm part of the pipeline."

"Pipeline for what?"

"For whatever they want. It come in through the kitchens. I get it, pass it along, make sure everything is smooth and easy."

"Drugs?"

"Hell yeah, all types of dope in this place."

"Do the guards know?"

"Lookie, on the outside, the cops want to stop all the drugs, but on the inside, they use 'em."

"The guards are on drugs?"

"Nah, man, they ain't using 'em using 'em, they use the dope to keep the peace, dog. It's a whole lot easier to manage the monsters in these cages if they sailing high, you know. It ain't official but it's for real."

Jude was beginning to understand. The guards were complicit in breaking the rules. Of course, they were. Some did it because their family was threatened or because they were in some sort of moral predicament, like having gambling debts. But others understood they were outnumbered, out-muscled, and outmatched when it came down to pure savagery. So, why work to make the inmates miserable? Certain drugs mellowed people out. Sure, they were bad for the inmates' health, but the guards wouldn't care about that, especially when their own lives were on the line. All it took was looking the other way and letting a few contraband items in. The prisoners were smart enough not to flaunt the things they really wanted.

"Some of them brothers down on tier one got a whole different kind of prison experience, man. They got rugs in they cells, iPads, wi-fi, game systems, anything they want. It pays to be king; you know what I'm saying?"

"It's the same all over, I guess," Jude said. "There are those who have more than they will ever need and those who will never have what they need."

"It's a brutal planet, homie. No doubt."

Jude thought about the pills in Money's hidden stash. They were probably some kind of opiate—his little treasures and maybe a way to stick it to the system that controlled his entire life.

"Did you tell people about me?" Jude asked. "About what I did to you?"

"I told Pax that you was a person of interest."

"Pax, the guard?"

"He's in King's back pocket, dog. Do whatever the Brotherhood tell him to."

"But he's a white man," Jude pointed out. "Isn't that some sort of conflict of interest or something?"

"Man, you be tripping. Pax is our slave now. Does exactly what he's told."

That made sense to Jude, and he wondered what the Brotherhood had over Pax. It wasn't important. Jude wasn't planning to overthrow the prison's ecosystem but rather utilize it to his own advantage.

"What are the guards doing now?" Jude asked.

"I don't know. Some of them walk the tiers. They make they

rounds or whatever. I try to sleep. Breakfast comes early round here, dog. Too early."

"There are inmates in the kitchens at this hour?"

"Some, I reckon. More in a few hours to start cooking breakfast."

"What other jobs are there in the prison?"

"Everybody starts in laundry. Hot, hard work, lots of bad things happen in the laundry. Guards don't patrol it, see. Too dangerous. Cons run the laundry. They'll keep new fish like you locked up till you're ready to do anything for a change of scenery. Then they send you to the laundry, less you got some skill they need elsewhere. It's hard, dirty work. Put a cocky little scrub like you on draw duty."

"What's that?" Jude asked.

"You know, cleaning them dirty draws, dog."

Money laughed. Jude could see how such an assignment would be difficult. Working in the laundry certainly wasn't why he had come to the prison.

"Tell me about the good jobs," he said.

"They ain't many," the big man said. "Library, I suppose, food service for the admin building."

"The administrators have a separate building?"

"Yup. I never been. They say they some pretty young fillies over there working as secretaries, but I ain't never seen 'em. Food's better, though. Some fish would rather eat the warden's leftovers than what we get."

Jude didn't think that sounded appealing at all.

"They's some groundskeepers. It's hard work, but gets you outside if that's your thang. Kitchen supervisors got the most juice, though. They sit around and tell everyone else what to do. They get a piece of the action, too. You want a nip of something wasn't brewed up in a toilet bowl, you gotta pay a toll. You want something sweet, candy or otherwise, you have to pay a premium. Sups get their cut; the shot callers always get a cut and we get what's left. Crumbs from the master's table, dog. That's what we get."

Jude wasn't interested in crumbs from anyone's table. Nor was he looking for a job that would keep him busy. Everyone in the prison was doing time, but Jude had the power to leave if that's what he really wanted to do. He could force a guard to smuggle him out. Anyone within earshot was his to command. They might not like it, but they had no choice in the matter. At some point, he would leave, but he had a mission to accomplish first. Justice cried out to him. He was locked inside a facility that was full of murderers, who were jockeying for power in a corrupt prison system that they had bent to their will.

That night, he slept for a few hours and was shocked when the lights came on. Being on the top bunk there was no way to shield his eyes from the light, which was followed by an extremely obnoxious buzzing sound.

"Breakfast," Money grumbled.

"What time is it?"

"Don't matter," Money said. "You on prison time now, son. Get used to it."

A few minutes later, the flap on the door opened. Another inmate was pushing a cart full of breakfast trays. He set one on the ledge. Money was up on his feet and took the first tray.

"Give that to me," Jude ordered.

There was murder in Money's eyes. "That's my tray."

"They're all the same. Get the next one," Jude told him.

Money obeyed, but Jude realized that he had been wrong. The trays of food weren't the same. Money's had twice the amount of food the other tray had. It was supposed to be scrambled eggs, but they were reconstituted from powder and didn't have much flavor. Fortunately, on Money's tray, there was a salt and pepper packet. With the eggs, there were sausage links. It was the only real food on the tray. Fruit filled one segment, and a triangle of toast took up another. With the breakfast was a paper cup of coffee and the anchor of every meal served in the prison, a carton of two percent milk.

Money's tray had twice the amount of eggs and sausage as the other tray. There was salt, pepper, and even a sugar packet for the coffee on the big man's tray. Money stood holding the regular tray and staring balefully at Jude.

"Sorry," the new inmate said. "I didn't realize there was a difference."

"I earned that grub, you little—"

"Stop!" Jude said. "I'll give yours back, but I'm taking the sugar and the seasoning packets."

Money wasn't happy, but he didn't complain. Jude took what he wanted from the big man's tray, leaving him the majority of the food. He used a tiny bit of the salt and pepper to season his eggs.

"From now on, I get the same tray as you."

"Ain't up to me," Money grumbled.

"I think you've got the pull to make it happen," Jude said. "Otherwise, I can just eat yours."

The big man dropped down onto the metal bunk with no mattress. He had spread his blankets on the slab to try and soften it, but Jude knew it couldn't be comfortable. Still, he didn't complain about it.

The breakfast was the best meal that Jude had eaten in the prison. The seasoning packets helped, but the eggs weren't hot. The fruit was from a can and had almost no flavor. The bread was burned on one side and dry. Still, it was hard to ruin toast. There was no butter on it, but it was useful in scooping up the runny eggs. The sausage was actually good. Not top quality and made with as much gristle as meat, yet they tasted pretty good. Best of all was the sugar in Jude's coffee. It was lukewarm and weak. Coffee was one of the things that Jude enjoyed. He spent extra to get good coffee beans before he became a murderer. He would grind them himself and brew a large cup every day. Normally, he drank his coffee black, but the sugar in the prison coffee felt like a luxury that was exceedingly rare.

"Today, you are going to smuggle more condiments back to the cell," Jude said. "Sugar and salt, not a lot, just a few extra packets. Don't put them in your underwear."

Money grunted. It was his acknowledgment of the order, and enough for Jude to know the big man would do exactly what Jude told him.

11
_____

After another inmate picked up their empty trays, Money went back to sleep. It was tempting for Jude to follow the big man's example, but he realized the upper bunk had been a mistake. The lower bunk had advantages. He would have to move down there once Money had been moved out of the cell, and it was Jude's private domain.

Instead of sleeping, he stayed at the door. The flap opened on hinges from above, which made it necessary for Jude to hold the flap open with his hand. But he could see through the opening to the far side of the tier and even down to the second tier. There were guards patrolling each one, and some inmates had jobs that required them to be out of their cells. Most were cleaning. Some inmates pushed brooms; others wiped the railing around the open center section with rags. Mops with cotton yarn heads were swiped over the floors. Jude wasn't sure how clean anything was actually getting, but he was more interested in the interactions between the guards and the inmates. Most didn't speak to the guards; they kept their heads down and made a show of doing their work. Yet a few spoke, mostly in low tones, while they pretended to clean near where a guard stood.

Jude didn't see any commerce between the guards and the inmates. Jude was certain it must happen. Eventually, an old black man with white hair came up the stairs. Two other inmates, both black and muscled, carried a book cart up the stairs. When they got to the third tier, the old man pushed the cart around, while the carriers waited. The librarian interacted with inmates in each cell, while the younger, muscled pair spoke to the guards. Jude wasn't certain, but it seemed like one handed something to a guard.

The man looked in Jude's direction, but he was certain that he wasn't the only inmate watching through the opening in his cell door. Some were talking. They either made bad jokes or called out to the old librarian, who ignored them and took his time pushing the book cart along. Jude noticed that most inmates didn't take a book. Reading wasn't a habit for most of the prisoners. Jude had learned the joys of reading as a youngster. Books weren't cool like watching television in the foster care system. Although nothing was more important than video games to children with little or no access to them. But Jude discovered that when he sought out books, the authorities in the group homes seemed to think he was doing something good. The other kids often left him alone when he was reading. Furthermore, he could lose himself in a good book. He might have been in a dorm room with a dozen hyperactive children, yet in his mind, Jude could be on alien worlds or in fantastic kingdoms.

He could read just about anything, but what Jude was drawn to the most were books where the hero overcame injustice. From comics to novels, his favorite reads were those with a happy ending. They gave him hope in a world where regular people rarely overcame the obstacles in their lives. So many people settled for whatever was easy. Jude had learned that hard work led to opportunities and was a reward in its own right. He often took time to reflect on a job well done. Construction had afforded him the privilege of being able to see what he had built with his own two hands. He could rip out a rotting roof and replace it. He could take raw wood and build just about anything his mind could conjure up. That had been rewarding to him on a level he had never experienced as a child growing up or as a young adult who could impose his will on others. Money, privileges, and affection that were coerced could not compare with the satisfaction of money earned and affection freely given.

But Jude had also learned that no matter how hard a person worked, and how diligently one adhered to society's laws, bad things still happened. Injustice was everywhere. His work ethic and moral code hadn't kept it at bay. Alison had been killed in the prime of her life, just days before she was to be married. All Alison had wanted in life was to be a wife and mother. She said it was her calling to raise a family. Jude wasn't so sure he was meant to be a husband and father, but Alison's devotion to him made him want to rise up and meet the challenge.

Then suddenly, through no fault of his own and nothing that Alison had done wrong, she had been snatched away from him. Even worse, the heinous act wasn't punished. Alex Metford went on with his pathetic life. He lied his way out of trouble, and the people who were supposed to punish him did nothing. They knew he was guilty, but their system of justice had rules that tied their hands. Jude had cast off those bonds. It hadn't come without a price. He was in prison, after all. The highlight of the day had been a packet of sugar in weak coffee, but still, he wouldn't let society's shortcomings keep him from seeing justice preserved.

Nor was he in a hurry to act. The opportunities would come soon. He was certain of that. The first was the librarian. Old man Kelly was what Money had called him. He stopped in front of Jude's cell and spoke.

"You must be the new fella," Kelly said. "You want a book?"

"I do," Jude said. "What have you got?"

"What do you like?"

"Fiction mostly, or history, biographies."

Kelly picked up a clipboard. It had a short pencil tied to it with a piece of yarn. He looked at the page. "Money's got his limit of books allowed in your cell."

Jude stood up. He grabbed the Book of Mormon, the Quran, and *The Fountainhead*. He pushed them through the opening in his cell door.

"We're returning these," Jude said.

"He might not like you doing that with his books," Kelly said.

"We've got an understanding," Jude said.

"If you say so," Kelly replied.

"How long have you been here?"

"Since they opened four years ago. Been all over really, all the big joints. This one ain't too bad, I suppose."

"You getting out?"

"Nah, wouldn't know what to do if I did," he said with a chuckle. "Prison life is all I ever known. You want a book?"

Jude had already said that he did. He had even returned some of Money's books. Old man Kelly had marked them off his list. But he had also forgotten what Jude told him he wanted.

"Yes, please," Jude said. "Fiction, history, or biography."

"Got that," Kelly said. "Yes, sir, we got lots of that. I like a man who enjoys reading."

He pulled two books from his cart and pushed them through the slot.

"Thank you," Jude said.

"My pleasure. Be back in a few days."

The books were worn with soft covers that had been reinforced with transparent packing tape. Jude set them on the floor and continued looking out the window. It was only a matter of time before the guard came. Old man Kelly made his rounds and returned to the stairwell. His younger assistants took up the heavy cart and preceded him down the stairs. The guard who had spoken to them started toward Jude's cell.

"Looks like I'm being summoned," Jude said out loud, but Money was asleep. He lay on his back, snoring softly, his big chest rising and falling in a steady rhythm.

Jude brushed his teeth quickly and checked his hair. It was still buzzed off. He didn't like the look, but had to admit it was easy to take care of. He would need a shave before long, although he didn't have a razor. That would have to change soon, but it made sense not to give new arrivals anything they might use to kill themselves with. There was a heavy sense of doom that could overwhelm a person upon arrival at the supermax prison.

A buzzer sounded, Money stirred on the metal bunk, but didn't get up. Outside, the guard named Pax was standing by.

"Looks like you're the man of the hour," Pax said. "How'd you convince Hitchcock to give up his mattress?"

"I can be very persuasive," I replied.

"Well, you're coming with me, Olson. The King wants to meet you. Can't say why, but if he wanted you dead, he would have had Hitchcock do the deed, so I guess you shouldn't be too worried. Hands out!"

Jude extended his hands. Pax snapped on a pair of cuffs and then took Jude by the elbow before radioing in to have the cell door closed. The buzzer sounded, and the door slid closed. Jude was becoming accustomed to the ominous thud of the door sliding home and the lock engaging.

"Tell me who this King is," Jude said.

"Head of the Brotherhood, and I mean the very tip top. He's a nasty one, that's for damn sure. Calls all the shots on the inside and outside."

"What does the Brotherhood do on the outside?"

"What don't they do?" Pax said, before keying his radio. "Open north stairwell, tier three."

The buzzer sounded, and the lock on the door to the stairs released. Pax pulled it open and led Jude through, then closed it behind them. The chain linkage rattled as the door slammed and the lock engaged. They started down the metal steps.

"Drugs, guns, prostitution, influence peddling, money laundering, human trafficking, they do it all. Got their fingers in lots of otherwise legit enterprises too, sports betting, music production, land speculation. They have contacts all over the world. Lots of money. That's why Delvin Amon goes by King. It's his kingdom."

"It doesn't matter that he's locked up in here for the rest of his life?"

Pax chuckled. "Being in prison is like a rite of passage for them. On the gang level, you have to fight, steal, and even murder to become a full-fledged member. Sort of like a made man with the mob, only not so clear cut. You want to rise up through the ranks of the Brotherhood, you have to prove yourself on the inside as well as the outside."

Jude found the notion to be absurd. There was no glory in going to jail. It was a dangerous, brutal place. But that was another failing of the justice system. The prisons didn't reform criminals; they trained them to be stone-cold killers.

When they reached the first floor, Pax called in again, and the door was unlocked. He led Jude past several cells with inmates grunting, cursing, and even screaming through the slots in their doors.

"We call this place the madhouse," Pax said. "All these baddies have a little something in them."

"What do you mean?" Jude asked.

"I mean, they aren't just crazy; these animals are possessed. Watch yourself at all times, or you might end up in a world of hurt, and if one of them lays into you, we won't stop them until they're done. No guards are risking their safety for you, Olson."

"You will protect me at all times," Jude told him.

A strange look came into the guard's eyes. He didn't say anything, but he stopped looking at Jude and started looking around, alert for any signs of danger.

"This is you," Pax said. He triggered his radio, "Open one-zero-niner, please."

There was a buzz, and the door slid open. Inside the cell was exactly the same dimensions as his own. Only there was no lower bunk. Instead, there was a leather zero-gravity chair with an ottoman. The floor had an exotic African rug covering the bare concrete. On a table next to the chair was an iPad, a mobile phone, and a package of cheap cigars with plastic filters. There was no ashtray that Jude could see. On the bookshelf were several books held upright by bottles of whiskey.

Standing in the center of the room was the king. He was barefoot and bare-chested. He stood on one foot, with the other against his knee, and his hands were pressed together in front of his chest. Jude guessed it was some type of yoga pose. The man's skin was light brown, and he had a thick afro hairstyle. Jude could see the end of a rolled joint sticking through the dark curls and smelled the skunky odor of marijuana mixed with the stale stench of cigar smoke.

"This him?" the king asked in a gravelly voice.

"Jude Olson," Pax said. "Murderer sentenced to life. He just arrived yesterday."

"Your cellmate is Money Hitchcock," the king said.

Jude nodded. "He is. You are never going to hurt me ... or order anyone to hurt me."

The king chuckled. It was a strange, grinding noise, but there was unmistakable menace in the sound.

"Heard about you. Money says you got some magical powers or something."

"Or something," Jude said.

"I can use a cat like you."

"I'm not for sale."

"I can make your life miserable."

"Same," Jude said. "I can also make it end."

The king laughed again. Pax was standing beside Jude, but with his back to the open cell. The screaming and grunting from the other inmates had stopped.

"I don't get threatened very often," the king said. "Not in my own kingdom."

"This isn't a kingdom. It's a prison. What do you want with me?"

"I want to know if you've got the juice to back up what you claim you can do."

"Good," Jude told him. "The moment you can't see me anymore, you will slam your head against the wall until you're dead."

A new look came over the hardened criminal. It was fear.

"Don't do that. I can do a lot for you in here. I can do a lot for you out there. Maybe even get you out."

"I don't want out," Jude said. "I don't want anything from you."

"Everyone has their price. You can be my second in command. There's lots of bad people in this joint. It's a dangerous place, especially for a cat like you."

"There are no cats like me," Jude said. "But there is a new king. Officer Pax, close this cell door."

"Don't!" the king shouted. "Ain't nobody threaten me and live!"

"If you want to do something about it, I'm waiting."

Delvon Amon tried to lash out at Jude. He managed one step, then froze. He filled his lungs, most likely to shout orders to the members of his gang who were listening for them. But no words came from his open mouth. Pax called in the order to close the door to the cell, and it slid shut. Jude waited for a moment. Then they both heard Delvon Amon, AKA the king, scream as he ran toward the door and slammed his head into it. The resulting boom was louder and more ominous than the clang when it shut.

"Holy sh—" Pax started to say.

"Let's move," Jude ordered. "Don't call it in. Let someone else find him."

"I... I should take you... back to your cell, I suppose."

"No," Jude told him. "What else is down here?"

"Kitchen, laundry, maintenance, and the library."

"Where is the guard station?"

"Wouldn't you like to know," Pax said, eyeing Jude warily.

"Yes, that's why I asked. Now let me tell you something, Officer Pax. I'm not going to cause trouble for you or any of the guards. But I'm here for a purpose. You've seen what I can do."

They both looked back toward the king's cell. Blood was beginning to emerge from under the heavy, metal door.

"You know that there is no way to resist my will."

"That's impossible."

"And yet, here we are," Jude said. "You believe in the supernatural. You said it about those other inmates."

"They're possessed," Pax said. "Strange, I've never heard 'em stay so quiet."

"They'll be quiet around me," Jude said.

Pax called for another door to be opened. They passed a room with reinforced glass windows. Inside, there were guards sitting at folding tables in plastic chairs. Jude saw two vending machines, one of which was refrigerated and dispensed sodas.

"Break room?" Jude asked.

"Now you know," Pax replied.

Opposite the guard's break room was the library. It wasn't very big and had nothing but books inside. There were no magazines or newspapers, no computers, movies, or music, just books. Jude stopped in the doorway. Across from him was a desk, a small card catalog of all the books in the prison library, and more of the rolling carts stacked with books. At the desk was an ancient-looking computer and a nice leather chair on casters. High up on the far wall were narrow windows that let sunlight into the room. To his left, large metal shelves held several thousand books.

Jude turned to Pax. "Old man Kelly is about to go on an extended vacation. What's he in for?"

"He stole a car with a baby in it back in the seventies," Pax said. "He claims he didn't know the kid was in there. But he killed it and threw it into a ditch. They caught him a few days later, and he's been locked up ever since."

"Why didn't he get the death penalty?"

"He confessed in exchange for leniency. Sound familiar?"

"Yes, and it's time for justice to be served. When he's gone, you are going to give me his job."

"I can't do that. You haven't been here long enough to be eligible for work detail, and all new inmates go to the laundry."

"You will make an exception for me," Jude said. "I want Oscar Miller to be my assistant."

"I want a million dollars and a first-class ticket to Tahiti, but it's never going to happen."

Jude turned to face Pax. "All you have to do is let me speak to the warden," Jude said. "You will assign me to be the new prison librarian when Kelly dies. You will assign Oscar Miller to be my assistant."

Pax forced himself to swallow. There was sweat at his temple, and his eyes were shifting around. He was clearly uncomfortable.

"Who are you?"

"Nobody special," Jude said. "Just another son of Perdition."

12

There were seventy-two Correction Officers serving at the Duncan Supermax prison. Fifty-eight were basic officers with no rank. Nine were Sergeants, and three were Captains, with two special floaters who worked filling whatever roles were needed. The Sergeants were in charge of day-to-day operations and had the most interactions with prisoners. They weren't assigned to areas, stations, or specific roles such as escorting inmates to their jobs in the various prison areas. They were reserved for special assignments and had more freedom to move around the prison. Howie Pax was a Sergeant. His best friend was Sergeant Tyler Munson. They often worked the same shifts, but Munson was what was known as a "clean CO", meaning he had no affiliations with the gangs that were the unofficial shot callers. Munson would one day be a lieutenant, one of the administrators over the correctional officers. When he retired after thirty years on the inside, he would most likely take a role in the union and spend his twilight years very well off.

So it was that when Sergeant Munson saw the blood coming

from under the door of Devon Amon's cell on tier one, he immediately sprang into action.

"Open one-zero-niner," he radioed in. "We have a medical emergency. Roll a medic."

The guards in the control room didn't usually need to respond verbally, but one did to Munson's call. As the door buzzed and started to open, a husky voice said, "Medic is on the way."

Duncan Supermax had a full-time physician on staff. As one might guess, it was not a highly sought-after position. The guards and inmates generally agreed that the doctors who worked in prison were those who graduated from medical school at the very bottom of their classes. Most were barely competent, and none of them had people skills. Some were extremely intelligent yet had trouble dealing with sick people who wanted more from a doctor than the ability to dispense the correct medication. Others, like Doctor Bill Smith, who served at the Duncan Supermax, were simply not good at their chosen profession in any way. How Bill Smith had passed medical school, no one could say. He was odd, hard to get along with, clumsy, slow, and forgetful. But he was on duty, and there was no help to be given to Devon Amon. The man had run headfirst into the steel door of his cell. The blow to the head had been so severe that it crushed his skull. Capillaries in his sinuses burst. The bone fragments cut into his brain, which swelled. He died a few minutes later as blood ran from his nose onto the floor. Some of it stained his expensive, hand-woven rug, although most of it ran under the door and into the walkway outside the cell.

Officer Tyler Munson cared about the inmates. He couldn't really help them, but he could be fair, which was not the normal. Nearly ninety-five percent of all the COs working were compromised in some fashion. So, treating the inmates fairly was a kindness. Sergeant Munson, upon seeing Devon Amon lying in a pool of his own blood with the top of his head dented in like the fender of a used car, sprang into action. He rolled the inmate who called himself king onto his back and checked for a pulse. There was none. He checked for breathing. There was none. So, Munson immediately started CPR. It was a wasted effort, but he slept better knowing that he had tried to save the inmate's life.

Doctor Bill Smith, looking as generic as his name when he arrived, immediately pronounced Devon Amon dead. He oversaw the removal of the body. Munson stayed until more guards with members of the maintenance workers arrived to clean up the blood. He wondered what would happen to the furniture in the dead inmate's cell. It was worth more used than he had paid for any furniture in his own home when he bought it new. That was just one of the many paradoxes of the prison system. Munson didn't approve, but he also understood the incredible strain on the inmates, who lived in hard conditions under the constant threat of mortal danger. His own safety and well-being depended on the ability to placate those prisoners so that they didn't snap under the pressure and turn violent.

Once the clean-up began, Munson began the complicated process of moving through the prison's many gates and reinforced doorways to reach the administration office. The warden rarely ate food inside the main facilities. Duncan Supermax had three structures that were built for the inmates. The central structure was where Jude and four hundred other prisoners were housed in Cellblock A. East of that structure was a one-story building with its own bathhouse and exercise yard. Known as Cellblock B among other names, it housed the inmates sentenced to die for their crimes. Death row, terminus, and Hell's Waiting Room were just a few of the names the smaller facility was called. To the west of the main building was Cellblock C, otherwise known as the Nut House. It housed the criminally insane inmates with special facilities that allowed them to be studied by doctors and researchers who didn't consider them guilty of the crimes they were imprisoned for. But they were most definitely a danger to others, both the guards and the medical staff who looked after them. Their facility was larger with its own kitchen, bath spaces, and an isolated exercise yard.

In front of all the inmate buildings was a separate, isolated, and fully secured administration building. It was the warden's domain, a series of offices that included the computer controls for the prison and the parole board's conference chamber. It was the only building with direct access to the outer gate.

Munson made his way to the admin building, where he was put into a temp office to begin writing a report of the incident he had uncovered. There wasn't much to tell. He had spotted the blood, radioed for help, administered CPR, and, finally, failed to revive the inmate. Eventually, Munson's direct supervisor, Lieutenant Derek Foster, came and took him to meet with the warden. Rick Jennings was clearly upset by the death.

"You know what this means," Jennings said. "I want the entire facility on high alert."

"Already there," Foster said. "But it was only a matter of time. The king was bound to fall. The gangs always eat their own, eventually."

"It appears to have been a suicide," Munson said.

"No... no, that never happens. These are high-level shot callers; they don't get depressed and kill themselves. I've worked prisons for nearly thirty years, gentlemen. I've never heard of a person killing themselves in this fashion."

"Come on, warden, inmates pull all kinds of stupid stunts. Amon probably didn't intend to hit the door that hard. "

"Either way, we have a power vacuum. Half of the Brotherhood will be fighting to claim the King's spot in their hierarchy, the other half will blame the Aryans and start killing them."

"We should have a battle Royal in the yard. Let them kill each other. No one would miss a single one of them," Foster said.

"I don't like that sort of talk, Lieutenant," Jennings said.

He was no fool. His job was managing the resources of the prison, from food to guards; it was all about the data. Jennings knew all his top people and kept track of them. He knew Foster was old school and that he managed his COs with a soft touch. As long as they weren't hurt, Foster didn't care about the conditions of the inmates.

Most people didn't, but the few bleeding heart liberals who did were very vocal and had a lot of pull. And not just with the board of prisons, but with state and federal government officials. Corrections was a branch of Law Enforcement, which had become a very dangerous field to work in. Resources were being whittled down by foolish people who actually believed that most criminals were simply in need of social services, not law enforcement. That made it harder for people like Jennings to operate safe prisons, while at the same time having to put his own neck on the line for any incidents that occurred in those prisons. It didn't matter that the reason for most inmate uprisings was the lack of guards.

His job was a careful balancing act where one wrong step could prove fatal to himself, his career, and the people he oversaw. The stress of it was beginning to take a toll on the warden. He understood that prisons were run mainly by the inmates themselves. The guards and administrators laid down the boundaries, but everything on the inside was carried out by the inmates themselves. Understanding that meant giving them enough leeway to ensure that life continued in an orderly fashion for the inmates. The death of Devon "the King" Amon would send shockwaves through the entire prison population.

He sat down by his computer and brought up the log that showed when each cell was opened and for how long.

"Who opened one-zero-niner this morning?" Jennings asked.

Foster and Munson looked at each other and shrugged. They had no idea.

"He wasn't scheduled for yard time or showers," the warden said. "But someone had that cell open for several minutes."

He immediately brought up the security footage. Rewinding the video feed that showed the cells on the ground floor, he saw Howie Pax escorting a prisoner.

"Who is this?"

Foster and Munson leaned over each of the warden's shoulders to get a closer look at his computer monitor.

"That's Olson," Tyler said. "New inmate, Jude Olson. Cell three-five-three."

"What's he doing on tier one?" the warden demanded.

"We'll have to ask Sergeant Pax. There's bound to be an explanation."

There would be, and Munson could guess what it was. Pax was his closest friend, but the man had inherited debts from his father, who died from a heart attack that was probably brought on from the stress of his mounting debt to illegal sports bookies. Howie's father had been the poster boy for why sports betting should have stayed illegal. Those debts didn't go away just because the old man died. Howie had a wife and a son of his own. When the Brotherhood found out, they bought up all the debt. Howie was forced to work for them in the prison to pay it off. He would never rise above the rank of Sergeant, but as long as he did his job, he wouldn't be penalized for helping the Brotherhood on the side. Of course, those kinds of deals, which were a practical reality of the prison system, got very murky when a guard was attacked and killed by the inmates. Munson hoped nothing like that ever happened on his friend's watch.

"It's his second day and the second death in the prison," Warden Jennings declared. "Something's up."

"What could it possibly be?" Foster said. "They don't touch. I don't see Olson doing anything to the king. They just talked."

"He can't be an inside man in the cartel and the Brotherhood,"

Jennings said. "My short hairs are standing on end. I didn't reach the age I'm at by ignoring my intuition."

"What do you want to do?" Foster said.

"Get them both in here," Jennings said. "I want Sergeant Pax in this office and inmate Olson in the parole room ASAP."

"Copy that," he said as he adjusted his pants and smoothed the front of his uniform shirt. "I'll radio Pax. You go get Olson."

"Full irons," Jennings said. "There's something about that inmate I do not trust."

"Yes, sir, warden," Munson said before he set off through the maze of gates, walled corridors, and locked doors to retrieve the prisoner.

13

News of the king's death traveled through the prison like wildfire. In cell one-three-three, Forrest Sunday, AKA the General, sat at his desk. Unlike the king, the general used his cell like an office. Memos went out on scraps of toilet paper written in code with felt-tip markers. He had a phone, of course, a burner with several prepaid cards that allowed him to reach his people outside the prison. Unlike the king, Sunday wasn't the top dog in the Aryan Nation. There were secret members in high society. Men who ran Fortune 500 companies secretly helped operate the Aryan Nation behind the scenes. Sunday was one of their loyal soldiers, a "General", who helped command the men in the field. Of course, the prison systems were a big part of their illegal drug empire.

Sunday took a square of toilet paper. He wrote in neat block letters. The message was simple: move forward against any weakness in the Brotherhood. The African-Americans in state and federal prisons were the Aryan Nation's biggest rivals in the drug game. The loss of their top guy would weaken them. Weakness was an opportunity in prison, just as it was in business, in sports, and maybe most importantly, in politics. The Nation had a few members in the Halls of Congress, too. Their reach was wide and deep. White power was poised to make a comeback.

The General took the square of toilet paper, pulled it carefully from the roll, and handed it through the flap in his door where a member of the Nation who pushed a broom for the prison maintenance crew was waiting. He took the note and moved off down the corridor.

"Screw?" Sunday asked.

"Don't call me that," CO Bert Slater growled.

Sunday knew he could call the man whatever he wanted. Slater was in the Nation. He had pledged his allegiance and even taken the job as a Corrections Officer in order to help the Aryan Nation. But Sunday didn't want to exacerbate Slater. He respected a good soldier no matter what uniform he wore.

"Sorry," Sunday said without meaning it. "What are they saying?"

"The king is dead," Slater whispered.

Sunday already knew that, so he waited for the guard to say more.

"No one knows why. He rammed his head into his cell door so hard it crushed his skull."

Sunday whistled. That was a bad way to go.

"Who's responsible?"

"That's just it. No one is taking responsibility."

"Has to be someone," Sunday said. "Find out. I need to know."

"Copy that."

The guard moved off. Sunday looked around. There was no one out of their cells except for the inmates from tier three doing cleaning. Across the room, Sunday could see the king's open cell. A pair of inmates was busy moving the furniture out of it.

He returned to his chair. Forrest Sunday was tall, nearly six and a half feet. His once-blond hair was kept shaved to stubble on his pale scalp. He had no tattoos that would show if he wore a long-sleeved shirt, or even if he bared his forearms. But his upper arms, chest, and back were covered with tattoos declaring his allegiance to the Aryan Nation. He settled back in his chair and opened one of the drawers in his desk. After removing some files, he popped open the false bottom. Inside was an iPad with 5G connectivity, a burner phone, some marijuana, and a shiv that was made from an old cooking spoon. It was shaped like a dagger with serrated edges. Sunday knew that one day he would probably die with that weapon in his hand. But what more could a man ask for in death, he thought.

He dialed a number from memory. The phone kept no records of calls made or received, and Sunday didn't have any numbers saved on the burner phone. There was no way for the feds to bug it even if they did know of its existence. Sunday was careful not to text his orders or questions to his superiors. Text messages had a way of showing up even after they were read and deleted on both ends. Somewhere, there would be a server with the messages saved, and they would no doubt show up at the most inopportune time. Instead, he called the people he needed to talk to.

"Go!" A voice on the other end of the wireless line said almost as soon as the phone rang.

"It's the General. The king has fallen."

"Copy that," the voice said.

There was a click, and the line went dead. Sunday snapped the burner phone closed. He had done his part. Others would decide how and when to take advantage of the vacancy at the top of the Brotherhood's food chain. All Forrest needed to worry about was his own little kingdom in the Duncan Supermax.

A knock on his door summoned him back to the flap. He opened it, saw the black slacks of a guard, and the tiny tattoo on Slater's thumb just above the nail bed. It was actually the Aryan

Nation motto written so small that it required a magnifying glass to read it. But Sunday knew what it said.

"What?"

"New info. That fish, the one that broke through the Cartel's lines during yard time yesterday," the guard said, pausing for the General to remember what he was talking about.

"Oloff?"

"Olson... Jude Olson," Slater corrected. "He paid a visit to the king just before he killed himself."

"You don't say? Is he one of us?"

"Not that I know of," Slater said. "I didn't do the intake, but I read the file. No record, no ink, no affiliations."

"What's he doing here?"

"Killed a guy with a blowtorch. The file doesn't say why."

Burning someone was brutal. Burning them to death takes real nerve. Most people don't have the stomach for that kind of torture killing. Sunday was fascinated.

"I want to meet him. But not directly. Have Pearson make contact."

"On our behalf?"

"Not initially. I want more info. If he's a believer, then we'll meet. If he's not, we need to make him one."

"Copy that. I'll get word to Pearson."

Sunday dropped the flap. It snapped closed and ended the conversation.

14

J ude was reading on his bunk when the door to his cell opened. He looked up, not bothering to hide his annoyance.

"On your feet, Olson," Munson said.

"Is something wrong?" Jude asked as he slid down from his bunk.

"No, but we need to move. The warden wants to see you."

Jude had known it was coming. He was a little surprised that they were on to him so quickly. There was no doubt the inmates were talking, but Jude didn't think Officer Pax would give him up. Howie was still struggling with what he had seen and what Jude had ordered him to do.

As soon as Jude's feet hit the floor, Munson pulled out the shackles.

"What's with all that?" Jude asked. "Tell me the truth."

"The truth is that the warden doesn't like the inmates and doesn't trust them," Sergeant Tyler Munson said. "That means leg irons and shackles. Turn around."

Jude didn't resist. He didn't like being chained up as though he were a wild animal. Even worse, he didn't like being seen in shackles by the other inmates. It sent the wrong message, namely that he was vulnerable. But there was nothing he could do about it. He would just have to stay vigilant in case they were attacked along the way.

One chain went around his waist, and another linked to the first hung down to the chain between his ankles. Both of his hands were cuffed to the chain around his waist. Jude thought it was extremely unnecessary, but no one had asked him. He could have ordered Munson not to use the chains, but that might result in trouble for him. Jude wanted the guards on his side. He was willing to use his ability to control people in order to get justice. Although it was a slippery slope back to using the power to get whatever he wanted. He had vowed to himself not to do that, and so he let the guard chain him up.

They left his cell and went across to the nearest stairwell. Most of the cells were empty. Unlike conventional prisons, the cells were not left open. Any time the inmates weren't in an authorized activity, such as exercise in the yard, showering, or working in their respective jobs, they were kept in their cells. Jude was supposed to spend twenty-three hours a day in his cell unless he had earned the right to join a work detail.

Fortunately, with most of the tier busy working, there was little exposure and risk. Stairs in leg irons were a challenge, especially with his hands bound to his hips, which kept him from using the handrail with any sort of leverage. Munson took hold of Jude's arm at the elbow and helped him. He was a no-nonsense type of guard, but Jude got the impression he cared enough that he didn't want to see Jude fall.

When they finally reached the ground floor, Munson escorted Jude outside through a door he hadn't used before. They came out in a long walkway between tall chain-link fences with razor wire across the top. There was a locked gate at the end. They passed through several outdoor walkways and gates before finally reaching the admin building.

"What's this?" Jude asked.

"Admin center," Munson said.

Jude was glad that he didn't need to compel the guard to answer his questions. Officer Munson wasn't friendly, but he wasn't rude either. He spoke when spoken to and answered questions directly. In many ways, Jude sensed that Munson was different from the other guards, although he wasn't sure why he felt that way about him.

Munson took Jude into a wide room with an elevated desk along one wall. There was a single chair facing the elevated desk. The guard put him there and then radioed in.

"I have inmate Olson for the warden," Munson said into his radio transmitter.

"Copy that," a voice responded.

The wait was nearly half an hour. Jude wondered if he was being watched. There was a camera in the corner of the room, but he could see no lights on the device to indicate that it was turned on. Munson spent the half hour leaning against the elevated desk with his eyes on a door that led into the admin building. When it finally opened, a man in a suit was escorted inside by another Corrections Officer in uniform.

"Inmate Olson," the suited man said, "I'm Warden Jennings. Welcome to Duncan Supermax."

Jude stood up, his chains rattling. "It's nice to make your acquaintance."

The warden smiled, but it was thin and felt insincere. Jude felt himself in the presence of a dangerous man.

"You spoke to inmate Amon this morning," Jennings said. "I want to know how and why."

It occurred to Jude that he could be in a lot of trouble. "You will never hurt me or allow others to hurt me."

"No one is trying to hurt you," the other guard, an older gentleman with gray in his short-cropped hair, said.

"But we must insist that you answer the questions," Warden Jennings said. "Why did you see Amon?"

"He sent for me," Jude replied.

The warden frowned and glanced at his companion, but didn't hold the disapproving look, "Why? What did he want?"

"Just to meet me," Jude said. "I think he wanted to recruit me."

"The leader of the Black Brotherhood wanted to recruit a white man? I don't think you're being honest with me."

"I am, but I can see why it's odd. Perhaps the king was losing his mind. He did harm himself; I'm told."

"He tried to recruit you, and you turned him down?" The older guard asked. "That's a dangerous move on your part."

"I didn't come here to serve him. I came to serve justice," Jude said.

"Did Amon seem erratic or unstable to you?" The warden asked.

"No," Jude replied.

"And why did he want to recruit you of all people?"

"You would need to ask him that. I just got here."

"Maybe it has something to do with what happened to inmate Perez during yard time the day before," Jennings pressed. "What did you speak with him about?"

"Do you know that Oscar Miller is an innocent man wrongly convicted?" Jude asked, ignoring the warden's question completely.

"He was judged by a jury of his peers."

"Wrongly," Jude insisted. "The legal system is far from perfect, and I'm certain he's not alone in his innocence among the inmates here."

"Why are we talking about inmate Miller?" The warden complained.

"I think he was cellmates with Miller," Munson said, speaking up for the first time since telling Jude to sit and wait for the warden.

"Is that right?" Jennings said. "And I get the impression that maybe Perez didn't treat his new cellmate well."

"That would be the case," Jude replied.

"And you decided to help?"

"I thought maybe I could convince T-Bone to show Miller a little more respect."

"And what did you do to inmate Perez?" Jennings asked.

"I talked with him."

"You talked with him, and he died. Just like you talked with Devon Amon in his cell this morning ... and he died."

"I believe that the king killed himself. Am I being accused of some wrongdoing relating to his death?"

"You're not being honest with us," Jennings said. He was getting angry.

"Calm down, warden. I'm telling you the truth."

Jennings took a deep breath, and then he smiled. It was much more genuine than the first time.

"I don't believe in coincidences," Jennings said as he reached out a hand and leaned against the elevated parole desk. "In my job, when things don't add up, they have to be investigated. Somehow, it seems that you are involved in the deaths of two inmates."

"One died of natural causes. It was tragic, but not an act that anyone could have initiated. And the other killed himself while alone in his cell. I don't think anyone was involved in either of those deaths."

"Don't toy with us, Mr. Olson. We've been doing this job a long time."

"I'm not toying with you, sir," Jude replied.

"We will get to the bottom of this," Jennings insisted.

"No doubt. Let me ask you a question, Warden. What is your mission here at this prison?"

"I don't take questions from inmates, Mr. Olson."

"It's not rehabilitation," Jude said. "Both of the men who died here were murderers. They killed, either by their own hands or through proxies, unknown numbers of innocent people. Yet they were allowed to live. That doesn't seem fair."

"Life's not fair," the older guard said.

"Agreed," Jude continued. "But if our aim is justice, I think we can do better."

"Then write a letter to your congressman," Jennings huffed. "But if you are involved in any more incidents here in this facility, I can guarantee life will become much more difficult for you."

"I stand duly warned, sir," Jude said.

Jennings gave him a dirty look. The smile was gone. He turned on his heel and stormed out of the room. The older guard lingered for a moment.

"You're an interesting fish, aren't you, Olson?" The guard said.

"I like to think I'm interesting," Jude said.

"You murdered a man in cold blood. Planned the entire thing out and cooked him in his own home."

Jude nodded.

"So, what makes you any different from the killers in here?"

"Nothing," Jude said.

"You're saying you deserve to be here," the guard said.

"I deserve to be punished, yes."

"Fascinating," the guard said. "Get him back to his cell, Sergeant."

"Yes, sir," Munson said.

"Be seeing you, Olson," the older guard said on his way out of the room.

Jude turned to Munson. "Should I be worried about the guard?"

"That's Lieutenant Foster. He's a man worthy of respect, but I suppose that's up to you."

"Respect is not an issue. Although there's a difference between fear and respect."

"Okay then," Munson said as he led Jude back out of the door that led into the maze of gates and pathways. "I'd say it pays to know when you're being watched by one of the more powerful men inside the prison."

"Copy that," Jude said, drawing the phrase out. He wasn't actually frightened of the guard, but he did agree that it paid to know when someone had their eye on him.

Jude made it back to the cellblock in time for his hour of exercise, only to have it cut short when a group of Aryans attacked a group of black inmates. Jude made sure he was far from the conflict. No one could blame him for the attack, even though it could have been said that he technically weakened the Brotherhood, which in turn gave the Aryan Nation the opportunity to attack. He wasn't bothered by any of it, including the fact that three men were sent to the infirmary and four more were ordered into solitary confinement. Murderers would do what murderers were in prison for doing, he thought.

What was more important to him was the looks he was getting from the other inmates. They were taking notice of him. It was dangerous but also necessary. If he was going to uphold real justice, they would all soon come to fear him.

15

It was another day before Jude got the chance to take a shower. He and nineteen other prisoners were taken into an open shower room. There were five shower heads with four spouts on each. It was awkward. Some of the inmates made inappropriate jokes, but there were guards at the entrance to the room, and the water was tepid at best. For the most part, the men washed up quickly and got dressed again.

Jude was given deodorant after his shower and an extraordinarily cheap disposable razor. It was enough to get through a quick shave. There was no shaving cream, just soap, but Jude made do and managed not to get cut. The razors were all rounded up and properly disposed of. Then it was back up to his cell.

The entire prison was on edge. The death of Devon "the king" Amon left the Brotherhood facing both an internal and external struggle. Jude avoided it whenever possible. Once, he even stopped a fight that was about to break out in the yard by ordering a pair of Hispanic prisoners from jumping one of the black inmates on their way out into the yard.

"Man, what gives?" Miller asked Jude. "Why are those guys listening to you?"

"I can be persuasive on occasion," Jude replied.

From behind them, another inmate spoke up. "Hey, I heard about you," a small man said. He had dark brown eyes, and his teeth seemed too big for his mouth. He was shorter than Jude and very skinny. In fact, he looked like he didn't get much to eat.

"You won't hurt me," Jude said to the man.

"Hurt you? Me? I couldn't hurt a fly. Look at me, I'm wasting away in this joint. I'm just trying to survive, fella. But I heard about you."

"What've you heard?" Miller said.

"Some say you got juice. Some say," he stepped closer, "that you're a boss nobody knows about."

"I'm nobody," Jude said. "Forget what you've heard."

"Cool, cool, that's good, man. I prefer to stay under the radar, ya know. I ain't making any waves in this place. Too many sharks looking for an easy meal."

"What's your name?" Jude asked.

"Valentine Pearson. I know, it's a terrible name. Everyone calls me Val."

"I'm Jude, this is Miller."

Oscar Miller nodded, but didn't speak.

"Tell us what you're in for," Jude said, nudging the small man with his persuasive powers.

"Tax evasion, actually," Val said.

"You're kidding."

"No, I'm not. Don't get me wrong, I'm not a nut job or anything. I worked, paid my taxes every year on time, no funny business. Then I went to one of those riverboat casinos. Nice enough joint, the food was decent, everything was cheap. And I had exactly two hundred bucks in cash. That was my limit, you know. Just so I didn't do something stupid. So, I'm paying for everything with cash. Drinks, food, and poker chips, you know the drill. I was just having a good time. Everywhere I went, I was getting silver dollars back in change. So, I end up busted. I'm heading out the door with five silver dollars in my pocket. I walk past the big jackpot slot machine. Wouldn't you know it, the thing takes silver dollars. The casino people know how to squeeze every last cent out of you, that's a fact. So, I say, what the hell, and drop all five in for one last shot at glory. I pull the handle, the digital images start spinning, and I tap the button to stop them. I'm thinking it's going to be a bust, just like everything else I tried. But then it hit, sevens all the way across. A siren stars blaring, I'm hit with a spotlight, and confetti starts raining down. It's a casino miracle."

"How much?" Miller asked.

"Twenty-five Gs," Val bragged. "Enough to pay off my Subaru and buy myself a lobster dinner with a bottle of real champagne. Of course, the casino wanted me to stay and play. They even comped me a room, but I took the money and ran. The only problem is, I didn't report to the IRS. But guess what, the Casino did. The next thing I know, I'm guilty of trying to rob the federal government."

"Why not just pay them what you owed?" Jude asked.

"They wanted twenty grand!" Val exclaimed. "And I didn't have it."

"You couldn't get a mortgage on your house?" Miller asked. He sounded suspicious.

"Sure, could have, if my wife hadn't left me and forced me to sell the house. After the attorney fees and paying alimony, I had nothing left. No assets I could even sell to raise the money, and the IRS was piling on fees and penalties every dang day."

"They put you in Supermax for tax evasion," Jude said.

"True," Val confessed. "I was put in minimum security. It was a pretty decent place, but not all that great at keeping us contained."

"You escaped," Jude said with a chuckle.

"No one seemed to care. I would have come back, but the police picked me up. The next thing I know I'm in court again and they're adding five freaking years to my sentence! Can you believe it?"

"Thems the breaks," Miller said.

"But you didn't go back to minimum security, did you?" Jude asked.

"Medium security. I broke out of there, too. It was not a nice place. Black mold everywhere."

"Five more years?" Jude asked.

"And the judge made an example of my case, assigning me here," Val said. "Ain't no getting out of this one."

"Ten years," Miller said, shaking his head. "What's your wife going to do?"

"Ex-wife," Val said with disgust. "She already remarried. I doubt she can even remember my name."

The conversation was cut short when the walk in the yard ended. As Jude lay in his bunk that night, he contemplated the irony that murderers like Alex Metford walked free, while a guy like Valentine Pearson was in Supermax for the best part of his life. How was that justice? Jude went to sleep thinking he had a lot of work to do.

16

Jude didn't think of himself as a murderer. He wasn't an avenging angel either. Although he did believe that the United States was built on the idea that there were times when regular people had to take matters into their own hands. The Declaration of Independence stated in the very first sentence that when, in the course of human events, it becomes self-evident that the bonds that tie one group to another must be dissolved ... or something along those lines. Jude had studied it as a teenager, but he had forgotten most of what the Declaration said. Yet, that first line had stuck with him. In the course of his life, events had occurred that made it evident to him that he had to do something to shake people out of their apathy toward justice.

It began with old man Kelly. The librarian was making his rounds. He was ancient to begin with. The poor fellow had been in prison longer than Jude had been alive. And Kelly had only one hope of escape, that was through death. Besides, he had murdered an innocent child. There were parents who had been crushed by the death of their innocent little baby. Who knew how many other lives had been harmed by Kelly? He seemed like a kind old grandfatherly figure, but no one survives in prison for over fifty years without shedding some blood. They didn't put old men into supermax just to be mean. He had earned what was coming.

When he stopped at Jude's cell, he spoke softly to the old man. "When the sun goes down, your heart will stop beating."

"Never heard of that book," the old man said. "But I'll give it a look-see."

Jude knew he wouldn't. In fact, he would have forgotten what Jude said by the time he got two cells away. The old felon probably had Alzheimer's Disease, but being in prison, no one cared. He would serve his time until he couldn't take care of himself anymore, or he died. Jude was just speeding that up a little. Perhaps, it was merciful. Jude didn't know and didn't care. In his mind, justice was being served.

"What'd you tell that old man?" Money grumbled from his bare bunk.

"I told him he was going to die this evening," Jude said. "But you don't have that long."

"Screw you!" Money snarled.

He had gotten used to his new cellmate, and he was still half asleep. It was a mistake, not that he could do anything to stop Jude. Although he might have wanted to do something with his last moment of life.

"You're going to have sleep apnea and your heart will stop," Jude said, as if he was describing the weather.

Money had already gone back to sleep, and then he made a snorting sound and stopped breathing. Jude knew he could be revived, but instead, Jude climbed up to the top bunk and opened his book. He was getting a lot of reading done in prison.

Midmorning, the guards arrived to take Money to the kitchens for his daily work shift.

"Up and at 'em, Hitchcock," a guard named Neil Ray shouted.

"What's it? He sick or something?" the other guard whose name badge said Crow asked.

"Hasn't made a peep all morning," Jude said without looking up from his book.

"Damn it, Hitchcock," Ray snapped. "Get your butt out of that bunk!"

"He ain't moving," Crow said.

"Alright, you want to play stupid games, get ready for stupid prizes," Ray added. "Olson, get down here."

"What did I do?" Jude asked.

"Standard Procedure," Crow said. "We gotta take you out of there before we go in."

Jude huffed, put his book down, and slipped off the top bunk.

"Turn around," Ray ordered. "Hands behind your back."

"You won't hurt me," Jude said, just before he turned his back on the pair of guards.

"Just get over here," Ray said. "Why do you guys always have to make everything twice as hard as it needs to be?"

Jude backed up until he felt the cuffs snap onto his wrists. Ray pulled him back and pushed him roughly toward Crow, who grabbed onto Jude by the arms.

"Hey, that's not necessary," Jude complained. "I was going."

CO Ray ignored Jude. He drew his baton and went into the cell. Reaching out with his stick, he nudged Money's leg, but the inmate didn't move.

"Come on, Hitchcock, up and at 'em, fat boy," Ray said. He stepped closer and hit Money with a hard swat on his thigh. The big man on the narrow bunk didn't move. Ray reached out and pulled back the blanket covering him. Then he threw his arm across his face and made a gagging sound.

"Oh, man, he's soiled himself," Ray declared.

"Dude, I don't think he's breathing," Crow said.

"What, that's crazy?" Ray argued. He stepped close to Money

and hit him rapidly on the cheek with the flat of his fingers, a quick slapping movement meant to rouse the big man. Money didn't move.

Ray gave Money a hard shake, then checked for a pulse. Crow didn't wait for the result. He used his radio to call it in.

"Emergency medical services needed on tier three," he said into the mic attached to the shoulder of his uniform. "We have an unresponsive inmate in cell three-five-three."

"No pulse," Ray called out. "I think he's dead."

"What?" Jude asked, feigning surprise.

"He's already cold, man," Ray said. "Oh, hell, this is going to be a disaster."

"I called it in," Crow said.

Ray whirled around and shouted at Jude, "What the hell did you do?"

"Me?" Jude asked.

"You kill him?"

He was angry and still had his baton out. He raised the weapon as if he were going to hit Jude across the face with it, but Crow stepped in between them and tried to calm his partner down.

"Yo, man, cool it," Crow said.

"He killed a man!"

"We don't know that, bro. Don't do something you're going to regret."

"I didn't touch him," Jude said.

"That's a lie. What did you do?" Ray shouted.

Jude stepped back. There were inmates watching from around the tier. He could see them peering through the slots in their cell doors.

"I didn't touch him," Jude said. "He had sleep apnea. He snored all night long. It probably killed him."

"You're full of—"

The rattling of the cage door around the stairwell cut Ray off.

Doctor Bill Smith, a potbellied, balding man with bad skin and a dirty lab coat on hurried forward.

"In here," Crow said.

"He's already gone," Ray said.

The doctor went inside, checked for a pulse, but found none. With one hand, he pulled back Money's eyelids, then checked his nose. Finally, he pulled back the dead man's chin and bent down to look at the neck. With his free hand, he felt the throat before standing up and stepping back out of the cell.

"Alert the warden. He's dead."

"How?" Ray demanded.

"We won't know that until we do a full workup, but from what I saw, he suffocated in his sleep."

"And this little rat did the deed," Ray said, turning on Jude again.

When Doctor Smith spoke, he had no emotion in his voice. Jude wondered if the man could relate to regular social cues.

"There are no signs of foul play," Bill Smith said.

"I don't believe it. People that age don't just die in their sleep."

"This inmate had no signs of being choked or smothered. He does, however, have the morbidities often associated with sleep apnea asphyxiation."

"That's what I said," Jude spoke up.

"How come you're always around when somebody dies?" Ray said. "That ain't right."

"Hold it together, bro," Crow told him.

Moving the body took nearly an hour. The warden didn't show up, but Munson did. He sent Ray and Crow down to the admin center to work on their reports. Lieutenant Derek Foster came to see Money before they carried him away to where the dead bodies were kept in the prison. He did a thorough inspection of the cell, including Jude's bed and books. Expecting as much from his cellmate's death, Jude had hidden the burner phone and razor blades inside the top of his sock band. The baggy prison pants covered them, but a close inspection would land him in hot water, so he was prepared to ditch the contraband if necessary.

"There's drugs hidden under the top bunk," Foster said. "We'll have to do a toxicology report."

"Doctor says there are no signs of foul play," Munson said.

"Not surprising. Hitchcock is twice the size of poor Olson," Foster said with a grin. "But it is strange that your cellmate died. You're going to land yourself a bad rep in these parts, Olson."

"I had never touched him," Jude said.

"No one is saying you did," Munson said.

"The warden might," Foster said. "Some could say this was murder."

"Or justice," Jude replied.

Foster laughed. It was a morbid thing to do, but he wasn't put off by death the way some were. He had seen it in many forms and fashions over his nearly three decades as a Corrections Officer. He had also seen inmates commit atrocities against one another ... even murder guards. He had no illusions about the hardened felons he was paid to watch over, or the realities of life behind bars.

"Are you saying Hitchcock had it coming?" Foster asked.

"We all do," Jude replied.

17

The tension was high in the prison after Money's death was revealed. If there was one constant in the Duncan Supermax, it was gossip. Everyone talked, and Jude was at the center of those conversations. The issue came to a head that afternoon while tier three was getting their allotted hour of exercise outside.

Normally, the inmates circled the yard. But after a few minutes, the biggest men from all three gangs left their groups and started toward Jude. Miller and Val fell back, and the entire yard stopped moving except for the men stalking down Jude.

"You will not hurt me," he said in a loud voice.

"The hell we won't," a hulking man from the Brotherhood responded.

To everyone's surprise, Jude started toward the men who were threatening him. No one else in the yard made a sound. The air was sharp and cold that day, the clouds low and menacing overhead.

"Your aorta will explode right now," Jude said, pointing to the man who threatened him. They were still twenty paces apart, but the man dropped to his knees, clutching his chest and gasping.

Jude pointed to a big white man with Nazi tattoos on his neck, "A blood clot will cut off the oxygen supply to your brain."

Then, to a Hispanic man, he added, "You will have a lethal Grand Mal seizure."

The man jerked and stiffened, toppling over like a tree cut down in the forest. When he hit the ground, he began to jerk spasmodically and foam at the mouth. But Jude wasn't done. He pointed to another member of the Brotherhood, "You can no longer breathe."

One after another, he pronounced fatal conditions that dropped the men in their tracks. They died on the grassy lawn before the guards could reach the area. Just as the last of the nine men died, a siren went off. Seconds later, as Jude stood over the carnage he had caused, guards rushed in.

"On the ground! Get on the ground!" They screamed.

Everyone obeyed. No one was talking. Everyone was looking at Jude.

He got down just like the rest of the inmates. Medical staff was called out and once again Doctor Bill Smith appeared in his dirty lab coat. This time, he had a stethoscope around his neck. He was followed by two members of the medical volunteer team, whose work assignment kept them in the infirmary most of the time.

The doctor checked the fallen and declared them all to be deceased. More guards were arriving. The rest of the prison was on lockdown with everyone, even those on work duty in the laundry and kitchens, sent to their cells. Eventually, even the warden showed up.

"Him," he said, pointing to Olson. "Put him in the hole."

"Sir," Munson spoke up. "He didn't touch a single one of them."

"But he killed them," Jennings said. "I don't know how, but he did it. Get him out of here."

Jude didn't resist. The guards were almost hesitant. And who could blame them? They had seen nine of the strongest men from three separate gangs die because they were going to hurt or kill Jude Olson. How he stopped them was a complete mystery, but the guards weren't anxious to repeat what they had seen the inmates do.

Munson was the first to reach Jude.

"Don't hurt anyone," he said softly.

"I won't," Jude said as Munson put handcuffs on him, binding both his hands behind his back.

The guards picked him up gently and led him from the yard. Jude didn't resist. They led Jude to a set of stairs near the kitchens. They led to an underground chamber with a row of cells. Munson opened one. It was dark inside. Jude could make out a metal platform to one side of the room and a stainless steel toilet in the far corner.

"I'm not crazy about this," Jude said.

"It's temporary," Munson said. "Warden's orders. We'll bring you a blanket before lights out."

"Great," Jude said sarcastically.

The heavy door closed. It sounded like he imagined the closing of a crypt would sound. And there was no light in the cell. It was like being in a cave. He settled on the metal bench. It was somewhat better than the concrete floor in the tiny cell.

Jude still had the burner phone and razor blades in his sock. He took them out and put them in the corner of the cell, where they wouldn't easily be seen from the corridor if the door was opened. As he set the contraband down, he heard a metal bolt slide and a flap in the big metal door opened. Jude could see a face, but the light wasn't good enough to make out who it was.

"I talked to Howie yesterday," Munson said. "He told me that you have some kind of magical power over people."

"Sounds far-fetched," Jude said.

"That's what he said. He was still struggling to believe it. That's why he didn't report what happened with Devon Amon. He didn't think anyone would believe him."

"Do you?"

"I'm starting to," Munson said. "I think I've been pretty fair with you, Olson. I try to be fair with everyone and treat the inmates with dignity. So, I'm going to ask you to be honest with me. What's going on?"

Jude didn't answer right away. He moved over to the door and sat down where he could see through the opening. He didn't need to see Tyler Munson's face, but he wanted to see the light before he was shut up in the dark for who knew how long.

"If I tell you it's going to be hard to believe," Jude said. "And no one will believe you."

"Try me," Munson said.

"I have the power to impose my will on people," Jude began. "It started when I was fourteen years old. I can't explain how ... or why ... but when I tell people to do something, or not do something, they can't resist me."

"How can I know you're telling me the truth?"

"I'll have you do something you would never willingly do," Jude said.

"Such as?"

"How about you give me the handcuff key?" Jude said. "Or better yet, the key to this cell."

"I can't do that, Olson."

"Munson, give me all your keys right now!" Jude said. He didn't shout, and he wasn't rude, just determined. A moment later, Munson was handing over a massive key ring that jingled as the metal landed on the pass-through.

"I can't believe I just did that," he declared.

"You didn't have a choice," Jude told him. He hadn't touched the keys. They lay on the pass through. "You can take them back."

Munson snapped them up quickly as if he were in danger for having left them exposed.

"And you can do that to anyone?" the guard asked, his voice a little mystified.

The truth was Jude could only do it to those who were in the sound of his voice. If a person couldn't hear him, they wouldn't be affected. But Jude didn't tell the guard everything.

"Sure," Jude lied. "And not just that sort of thing. I can order things to happen to a person's body, too."

"What do you mean?"

"Like T-Bone having a brain aneurysm," Jude said. "I told his body to do that."

"You can tell a person's body to kill itself?"

"Essentially."

"This can't be real."

"It is. The entire prison is figuring it out. Even Jennings. He's slow, but he'll catch on eventually. There's no other explanation."

"People won't believe this," Munson said. "You're the perfect assassin."

"I could be, but until I got justice for my Alison, I had never killed anyone before."

"The man you burned alive?"

"He ran over my fiancé," Jude explained. "The cops bungled the case, and he walked away scot free."

"So, you killed him."

"I did. It wasn't an easy decision, though. I really wrestled with it, and you know what I came up with? It's pretty simple, really. I have the power to dispense justice, so I'm going to. Our prisons are full of inmates who are multiple murderers. Those men in the yard, they have killed in the past, and they would have killed me today."

"But why should you have the power to pass judgment on anyone?" Munson asked. "Because, just as I made you hand over your precious keys, I can make anyone confess their crimes. All I have to do is tell them to be honest with me, then ask."

"That's not possible."

"Isn't it? Would you like me to ask you to be honest about your secrets?"

"No," Munson immediately replied.

"Exactly," Jude said. "That's how I know. Most of the guys in here have killed many times and only been caught once. They deserve the death penalty, but our society has gotten soft. Go back and look at the file on me. Do you have access to my police report from the murder?"

"I can get it," Munson said with a note of suspicion in his voice.

"Read it. They had me dead to rights. I was seen by the neighbors breaking in. There were plenty of eyewitnesses. They saw me go into that drunkard's house. They heard his screams as he died. They saw me leave. I left the tools I used. The sledgehammer I broke in with. The propane torch. They had my fingerprints on them. I drove my car to the scene of the crime. They had my license plate number. They even had video of me going in and coming out from the doorbell cameras across the street."

"Why were you so sloppy? Why not kill him with your secret power, and no one would be the wiser?"

"Because there's really only one place where my abilities can be utilized as they should."

"Prison?"

"You got it. And do you know how I got here?"

"You were convicted."

"I confessed. I willingly confessed to first-degree, premeditated murder with special circumstances. It is the very definition of a crime that results in the death penalty. But the law enforcement and prosecution side of the equation are lazy. Even with all the evidence against me, they willingly waived the death penalty if I would confess to the crime."

Munson didn't respond. Jude could see him thinking hard. And he was in no hurry to push Munson into agreeing. He could have forced that on the guard using his persuasive powers, but what he wanted wasn't a slave, but someone who understood what he was doing and why. Even if Munson didn't agree with him, he could still recognize the merit of Jude's argument.

"I need time to process this," he finally replied.

"Sure," Jude said.

"I'd like to ask you a favor, though," Munson pressed. "Will you refrain from using your abilities on me? I promise I will not hurt you, or allow you to be hurt, if it is in my power."

It was a big ask. Jude was in prison. He wasn't dealing with a peer on even ground.

"I need more," Jude said. "Promise me that you won't hinder me from doing what I need to make it in this place."

"I can't countermand the warden ... and I can't stand by while you hurt other people."

"I don't need you to," Jude said. "But I'm going to get some special treatment. Don't stand in the way of that, and I promise not to use my ability to force you to act against your will."

To Jude's surprise, the officer's hand came through the opening. It was a simple gesture, a handshake between two men. But it was also a sign of trust. With his hand through the opening, Jude had leverage over Officer Munson. He could have hurt, permanently injured the guard, perhaps even broken out of the cell he was locked in. But Jude didn't hurt Munson. He shook his hand politely in the limited space the slot in the door allowed, then released him.

"Just one more thing," Jude asked. "How long will I be in here?"

"Hard to say. Overnight for certain. Maybe longer while Jennings looks into you, he almost never enters the cell blocks, so that's a sign you've got him shook."

"My goal isn't to hurt or hinder anything the officials are doing here," Jude maintained. "But this place is going to hurt me."

"I'll get you some blankets. You'll have food."

"But no light."

"I can't fix that. But I suppose you could break out easily enough if you really wanted to."

"Breaking out doesn't move me toward my goals," Jude confessed.

"Then I'll leave the slot open. It's not much, but you'll get some light."

"I appreciate your help, Officer Munson."

"Thanks for confiding in me, Olson. I can't say I understand what you're trying to do, so I can't condone it. But I will consider it with an open mind."

"That's all I ask," Jude said.

He watched the guard walk away for as long as he could. Even hearing the man's boots scuff the floor was reassuring. But when he was gone, there was nothing but silence. It was a surprisingly unsettling change. In the hole, Jude's thoughts were loud, his discomfort more pronounced, and worst of all, his fears seemed almost tangible.

18

Warden Rick Jennings had every prisoner who had been in the yard questioned. It was a long, taxing process, but so was dealing with the dead bodies. There were nine of them, three from each of the major gangs in the prison. They were all big, powerfully built men. It wasn't hard to see that they were the muscle for their respective groups. One man shouldn't have been able to stop them from doing what they intended, yet Jude Olson had. Worse still, there were no signs of violence on the bodies. The men hadn't been fighting; they had just been killed.

"What do you want to do?" Lieutenant Foster asked Jennings after the warden sent Olson to the hole with Officer Munson.

"We've never had anything like this before," Jennings said. "I would know about it if there had been."

"Unless the powers that be covered it up," Foster said.

"They couldn't," Jennings replied. It was a knee-jerk reaction, and he instantly knew that it wasn't true. He wanted it to be true, but it wasn't.

"Come on, warden. They killed two Kennedys; they can do just about anything they want."

"Well, there's nothing I can do about it other than call it in. We are a joint operation, so I'll make contact with the FBI. We'll get their crime lab people out here. Don't touch the bodies. Get Doc Smith away from them, that's for sure."

"And the inmates?"

"I want them questioned, on camera. There's going to be hell to pay for this mess, and it won't be me footing the bill."

And so, the circus began at Duncan Supermax. The FBI was in no hurry. A field agent was sent to the prison. He looked at the carnage, took some pictures with his cell phone, and called it in. Lights had to be directed to the yard, but that was something every prison had in spades. The grounds were lit up like a sports stadium every night anyway, and so when the crime technicians finally arrived, they were able to go immediately to work.

Meanwhile, the prison had to continue to function. A handful of kitchen workers managed to churn out a meal for the inmates. It was tomato soup, peanut butter sandwiches, crackers, pudding, and the usual beverages. At the same time, the inmates from the yard were held in three separate areas, all outdoors and all surrounded by more fencing with razor wire.

Warden Jennings didn't consider himself to be racist, despite what many university professors said to the contrary. He saw all men as equal, but not the inmates. Working in prisons for all his adult life had proven beyond all doubt that in the correctional system, segregation was the best policy. Not that felons of the same ethnicity wouldn't fight and kill each other over petty grievances or the smallest personal possessions. And while he felt that he was colorblind to skin color outside the prison, it helped to manage the inmates on the inside. So, he had divided the groups by race and left them waiting and watching. His guards were armed on the prison walls. The chain-link fencing wouldn't stop the buckshot in their tactical shotguns. If trouble were to break out, his people were ready.

The FBI did the interrogations. They were quick and thorough. It helped that every inmate's story was roughly the same. Some said Jude Olson used magical powers, others said he called down judgment from God Almighty, but to a man, they all agreed that he never touched the slain inmates.

There was video of the incident as well. With Olson in the hole and the inmates locked in the side yards, Jennings hurried back to his office. The truth of the matter was that the prison frightened him. He didn't like it, didn't like the sounds or smells of the place, and didn't like being close to the inmates. After years of correctional work, he could admit to himself that he had grown claustrophobic. He didn't like knowing there were several gates and walls between himself and the outside world.

Being the warden certainly had its privileges, not the least of which was that he was required to spend most of his time in his office, which was located inside the admin building. He could be safely outside the prison walls in a matter of seconds. And his office had windows, comfortable chairs, telephones, computers, all the trappings of normal, free life. He needed those reminders to reassure himself that he wasn't a prisoner like the inmates he was in charge of. He could leave and often did, at any time.

Safely back at his desk, Jennings reviewed the security footage of the incident. The main yard for Cellblock A was the size and rough shape of a football field. There were wide-angle cameras at all four corners. They did not record sound, so Jennings didn't hear what was said, but he watched as the big men left their respective groups almost at the same time. That spoke to some sort of coordination. Had one group started out and the others scrambled to follow, it would have taken longer. They moved from the edges of the yard where the inmates walked in bunched-up groups, the better to hide whatever illicit actions they were involved in, and made their way across the more grassy middle of the yard.

Surprisingly enough, as the inmates around Jude Olson, the unaffiliated lot cringed back in fear. Olson went to meet the men seeking him. That was a shock to Jennings. There were moments in prison life when an inmate had done something that he knew would result in his death. Jennings had seen snitches getting shivved, and inmates who had insulted a rival faction face their deaths with courage. But Jennings had never seen a lone man face down nine assailants. Three men were from the Aryan Nation. They were "muscle", the type called on to fight with bare fists. They weren't exactly assassins, as much as intimidators. All three were over six feet tall, with broad shoulders and tattoos on their necks and faces.

Three of the dead men were from the Black Brotherhood. Like their white counterparts, they were all big men. While the Aryans were thick, the Brotherhood enforcers were packed with well-defined muscles. They had long arms and big hands, thick facial bones, and scars. They had tattoos, but the ink didn't stand out as clearly on their ebony skin, so they added branding to their body art. Jennings couldn't imagine allowing someone to burn an image into his skin, but the Brotherhood enforcers were covered with brands.

The last three were Latino and completely different in both physicality and demeanor. In Jennings' mind, they were even more frightening. The Cartels didn't bother roughing people up. Even the most minor infraction was often cause for assassination. Most of the cartel members in the prison system had begun their life of crime in the Latin American countries they came from, often murdering dozens of people, from rivals to innocent family members of the people their bosses wanted dead, before ever stepping foot inside the United States. They had dead eyes, like great white sharks', and Jennings thought of them as such. They were less obvious as muscle at a glance. They fit into a crowd more easily, although they were serious men with deadly intentions. Yet, Jude Olson had faced them all down.

One by one, his attackers had fallen. Some collapsed as they grabbed their head or chest. One had what looked like a seizure. But nothing had passed between them. They were still several yards away from Jude Olson when the last of them died. He didn't get any closer to their bodies. When the sirens sounded, he immediately complied. It might have been better had he struggled or resisted in some way. Nothing about the new inmate was making sense to the warden. Not for the first time, he considered if he should just retire and find something else to do. He would be lucky to be given that chance, with nine inmates dying in a single incident under his watch. The Bureau of Prisons might fire him. Losing his job and benefits was nerve-wracking, but the idea that he could lose his pension was terrifying.

He called his wife and told her that he wouldn't be coming home that evening. She was worried, but he assured her he wasn't in danger. Their future was, but he kept that tidbit of information to himself. His wife had worked various part-time jobs as their children got older. She volunteered and was active in church, although she was completely dependent on him and his pension for financial security in their golden years. All she would receive in Social Security would be the bare minimum, and, without his pension, they would have to sell their home. He could forget about joining the board at the Bureau of Prisons after the incident that had just occurred under his watch. That dream had been shattered and was one of the reasons he was so angry at Jude Olson. It would have been better for the warden if Jude had been killed. One violent death was almost expected in maximum security correctional facilities.

Around three in the morning, after five cups of coffee from the pod machine, the head of the FBI team knocked on his office door.

"Come in," Jennings said.

"Long night, eh, warden?"

"One of the longest of my career," Jennings said.

Lieutenant Foster came in and closed the door. He didn't speak, just listened. Jennings didn't mind him being present. In fact, he was grateful to have a familiar face as he listened to the Special Agent's report.

"Can I get you some coffee, Special Agent Sinclair?"

"I would love some," the federal agent said as he sat down in a chair across from Jennings' desk.

The warden walked around and placed one of his favorite coffee pods in the machine. It began to hum. Jennings picked up a bowl with individual coffee creamers and a chrome-topped sugar dispenser and carried them back to his desk. He set them in front of Agent Sinclair and then sat down in the vacant visitor's seat so that there was nothing between the two men.

"It'll be ready in just a moment," Jennings said.

"Appreciate that," Sinclair said. "I've seen some strange things. Cattle mutilations, crop circles, ritual killings, even a few serial killers, but I gotta say: this is at the top of my list."

"Have you seen the security video?"

"I have, it didn't really help much."

"What are the inmates saying?"

"I normally wouldn't give convicted felons much credence, but in this case, they're all singing the same tune. It fits with what the video shows. No matter what we may want to believe, this was not a physical altercation."

The coffee machine finished. Lieutenant Foster took the cup and set it on the desk in front of the FBI agent, then started his own cup of coffee brewing. Sinclair added sugar but no cream to his beverage. Late at night, one's stomach often churned. The sugar could give a burst of energy, but the creamer would just make the liquid harder to digest.

Sinclair leaned back in his seat. It was tufted leather, which creaked as he moved. He took the coffee mug and held it in both hands. Outside, the temperature was just above freezing. The agent let the warmth seep into him slowly.

"What about the bodies?" Jennings asked. "Is there any sign of drugs or some other agent that might cause their deaths?"

"We can't say for certain until the full autopsy and toxicology," he replied with a sigh. "But my medical guy is good. He teaches this stuff to medical examiners all across the country."

"What's he saying?"

"That every one of the nine men appear to have died from natural causes."

"But there are assassins who do that sort of thing, aren't there?" Jennings said. "They have poisons that result in deaths that look natural. The chemicals don't always show up. It's possible that's what we're looking at."

"If all nine men had died the same way, I would agree with you," Sinclair said, before taking a sip of his coffee. "Oh, that's good. Thank you, warden."

"They have different CODs?"

"I'm hearing words like heart attack, stroke, respiratory failure," Sinclair replied. "I'll be honest with you. It sounds more like the work of a witch doctor than an assassin. Besides, where would this inmate get the poisoning agent? How would he administer it without being harmed himself? I take it there was no beef between him and the men that died."

"No direct links at all," Jennings said. "To be honest, I've never seen a concerted effort by all the major factions like this. Two of them against the third occasionally happen. The enemy of my enemy is my friend, and all that, but never three factions against an unaffiliated inmate."

Sinclair rubbed his eyes and sipped more coffee. "I'll be honest, we live in a world that doesn't want to hear many of the answers that the evidence provides. This is maybe the most clear-cut case of supernatural involvement in our world that I've ever seen."

Jennings felt a wave of fury well up inside him. He didn't want to hear mumbo-jumbo about magic or ESP or little green men. He was a good Southern Baptist, a lifetime member of the church, and he didn't believe in the supernatural. There were no ghosts. He scoffed at people who claimed the devil made them do it, even though he had an entire wing of deranged criminals who would have said that very thing. They were all sick in the head. Their wiring was crossed. Jennings was certain that there had to be a reasonable, rational explanation for what it appeared that Olson had done.

"But you can't put that into a report, can you?" Foster spoke up for the first time.

"No," Sinclair said. "And we have to report this. I won't tell you how to do your job, warden, that's not my place, and I don't have your expertise, but from where I'm sitting looks more like a medical abnormality than an altercation between inmates. The fact that it happened in the yard at approximately the same time is almost irrelevant."

"Nine inmates dying will draw scrutiny," Jennings said.

"So let them scrutinize. My understanding is that these deaths didn't have a causal agent. Further tests might change that, but for now, we aren't talking about substandard food or some chemical agent in the materials used to build this place. The only link between the nine deceased inmates is another inmate. Yet, there's no proof that that person did anything at all!"

"It might look bad then," Foster said, "if that inmate is disciplined."

Sinclair shrugged his shoulders. "If I were on the outside looking in, it would absolutely look bad."

"But Olson is involved," Jennings insisted. "We just can't say how yet."

"And if that becomes clear, then we can all rejoice," Sinclair said. "But in my opinion, the most rational thing to do is to mark this down as a strange coincidence."

Jennings knew two things at that moment. The first was that he couldn't retire. Not yet, no matter how much he wanted to. Resigning his position in the middle of an unexplained event would make him the easy and obvious target. Secondly, he knew his life was about to get much, much more complicated. Word about what happened would undoubtedly spread to outside sources. They would come looking for answers, and when they didn't find them, they would look for someone to blame. Jennings would have to use all his mental energy to make sure the hammer didn't fall on him.

"We appreciate all you've done," Jennings said.

"You'll have preliminary reports from my agents in your inbox first thing in the morning. That includes my medical team."

"How long until the official reports?" Jennings asked.

"Weeks," he said. "At that point, we'll push everything up the chain of command. I can't say who might take interest, but you've got some time to try and find a causal link."

"And if more inmates die in the meantime?"

The look in Sinclair's eyes was part pity, part fear. "Well, then, all hell is going to break loose, I would imagine. The only positive thing I can say about that is at least it's happening in the one place that no one cares about."

19

No one cared about Jude Olson. His mother had given up trying to reclaim him when he was still just eleven years old. She had other children, but he didn't know them, and they, too, were taken from her and forced to endure life without her. Jude didn't know if not having her around was better or worse. All he could say for certain was that during the brief windows of time when he did live with his mother, he took more care of her than she did of him.

He had heard that she died a few years after he was on his own. It was not a difficult loss for Jude to bear. But that left him an orphan in the world. If he had extended family, he never knew them. No one ever stepped up to help raise him when the state took him from his mother.

After giving up his powers, he had made a few friends, but he was not close to anyone. Alison had been the exception. But she was dead, and after murdering her killer, his friends had quickly abandoned him.

But despite the fact that no one outside the prison cared about him and he had been put in solitary confinement, his reputation was growing among his fellow inmates. The first real clue to his increase in status came with his dinner that night. While the rest of the prison ate peanut butter sandwiches and lukewarm tomato soup, the workers in the kitchen stole a steak from the victuals that were reserved for the administrative staff and guards. Needless to say, the quality of the food was better. Even though it was just a plain sirloin steak, it was well seasoned and expertly cooked. It was served with a side of mashed potatoes, grilled asparagus, and mushrooms sautéed in garlic butter. They even managed to make him some dinner rolls. And for dessert, he got a slice of chocolate cake that was left over from an office birthday the day before.

In addition to the meal, the kitchen staff managed to smuggle him a bottle of cold Pepsi Cola, several candy bars, and a bag of chips from the break room vending machines that were supposed to be for the guards only. All this came from an inmate named Laurie. He had long hair tied back into a ponytail and an apron.

"You Olson?" The inmate asked into the open slot of Jude's door.

"Yes."

"This is from the kitchen crew," Laurie said. He slid the tray with the lavish food on it through to Jude.

"What's this?"

There was just enough light from the slot in the door to see that he had been given a tray with real dishes, not just the normal plastic serving tray with divided segments. But it was the aroma of the rich food that got Jude's attention. His stomach growled hard as he held the tray up to the beam of weak, yellow light coming in through the door.

"We heard about what you did," the man said. "My name's Laurie. I'm one of the cooks."

"Thank you," Jude said.

"There's more," Laurie said, passing through the soda and

candy, along with several cartons of milk and a bottle of tea. "If the guards come to get you before I come back tomorrow, just hide that stuff in the corner. The guards never look in the cells down here."

"I can't blame them for that," Jude said.

"Being in the hole is hard time, man," Laurie said. "I never been myself, but I've heard stories. You hang in there. I'll be back with breakfast in the morning."

"Wait," Jude said. "What are people saying about me?"

"Heard about what you did in the yard. Can't no one deny it. I guess you're the big dog round this place now."

Laurie hurried back out of the subterranean corridor that was home to the solitary confinement cells. There was no knife to cut the steak with, but it had already been sliced into thin sections. Jude picked it up with his fingers and bit off the thin sections of meat. It was surprisingly tender. The food was much better than anything he had tasted since being arrested. And with nothing else to do, he took his time.

Jude had never been a big eater, but that night he finished his meal, washing it down with Pepsi, then ate the cake with his milk. He couldn't even touch the candy, but eventually he munched on the bag of chips.

True to his word, Officer Munson returned with blankets. There were three in total, all neatly folded, and a pillow. Jude thanked him, but the investigation was still ongoing, and he couldn't stay. The lights in the hallway went out shortly after the blankets were delivered. Fortunately, Jude had the burner phone. He didn't need to make a call, but he used the flip phone's display to see by as he spread out the blankets onto the metal platform. Even folded double, they did little to soften his bed for the night, but it was much better than cold steel or concrete. Plus, all the rich food had made him tired.

After hiding what remained of his meal in the corner, Jude fell asleep. It was his first night alone and the first night he wasn't plagued with fear that someone might come in and hurt him while he was helpless. That night, other fears haunted his dreams. He had become a death dealer, but killing people, even if they deserved it, came with a price. There was a burden on his conscience that was hard to live with. That night, he dreamed of the men he had killed in the yard. That had been part of his plan. He knew it would happen sooner or later. The prison was full of murderers, and as his reputation grew, they would want to kill him. He was more of a threat than the guards. So, it only made sense, plus he was a threat to the prison's established order. The cons who were in power would certainly want him dead, but Jude was not going to make it easy for them.

Morning came early in the prison, as it always did. Jude was not hungry, but he enjoyed the pancakes and syrup from the kitchens. They took his dishes and trash from the night before. He wasn't eating anything different from the other inmates; there was just more of it. In fact, Jude was still full from the night before and couldn't eat much of his breakfast.

A short while later, Officer Howie Pax came to get him. Jude had just enough time to stuff the candy bars from the night before into his socks.

"You survived a night in the hole," Pax said. "How about that?"

"Where am I off to now?"

"Back to your cell is all I know," the guard said.

"Really?"

"Don't be so excited. We went over that place with a fine-tooth comb. We found your smuggler's Bible."

"That was Money's," Jude said. "It even had his name in it."

"And nothing inside," Pax said. "But a little contraband is not my concern."

Jude felt a bit of relief. He could have stopped Pax from searching him, but it was better that the guard wasn't planning to.

"So, I'm not in trouble for what happened yesterday?" Jude asked.

"Should you be?"

"No, I didn't touch those men who died."

"But you're not saying you didn't kill them."

"How could I have?" Jude asked.

"Maybe the same way you had King bash his head into the wall," Pax whispered. "I don't know how you do that, but everyone knows you aren't normal. Even the warden."

"That's okay," Jude said. "I'm not trying to hide anything."

They went up the concrete steps into the passageway near the kitchens. That section of the prison was, by necessity, a much more open space. There were guards watching, but the inmates went where their duties took them without seeking permission. They weren't allowed to be alone, even in the storerooms or coolers of the kitchen. Nor could they use the bathroom without permission and supervision. One of the more significant additions to the supermax facility was a metal detector that every inmate passed through to gain entry or exit from the kitchen area.

The same corridor that led to the kitchen also led to the laundry rooms. Jude heard the big machines spinning as they washed the inmates' clothing and bedding. He also heard laughter and talking in both the laundry and the kitchen. Work was a privilege not only because it got the inmates out of their cells, but it also allowed for socialization. Jude couldn't help but wonder how many murderers and rapists enjoyed shooting the breeze while they peeled potatoes or folded bed sheets. He didn't call that justice.

At the entrance to the prison library, two black men stood glaring as Jude approached with Officer Pax. They knew who he was, and it seemed that perhaps they blamed him for old man Kelly's death.

"Hold on," Jude said as they drew near to the library.

"No trouble," Pax said quietly. It was almost like a hope, not an order.

"I need to decide what to do with the two of you," Jude said.

One of the men drew back a step, but the other hawked and spit on the floor. Then he touched the skin under one eye and glared at Jude, who recognized the sign of the evil eye.

"In exactly five minutes, the two of you will fight one another outside the guards' break room," Jude said, before strolling along.

Pax looked back at the two men, who didn't move. They might not like Jude, but the fear of him in the prison was very real.

"Why did you do that?" Pax asked once they were back in the tiers.

"You said no trouble," Jude said. "And I needed them off the library duty. This solves that problem."

"A fight is a problem," Pax said.

"The other guards will stop it," Jude said. "They deserved much worse. They're killers, you know."

"Hell yes, I know. They were part of the Brotherhood's delivery system. You don't see how much you're interfering with." Pax keyed his radio. "Open south stairwell, tier one, please."

The buzzer sounded, and Pax pulled open the gate that led to the metal staircase that was surrounded by chain link.

"I get it," Jude said. "But things are changing here."

"You know I'm part of this, don't you?" Pax said. "The Brotherhood holds my debt."

"I had a feeling about that," Jude said. "Don't you want to be free?"

"I am free. I can walk away from this place any time I want to."

"Are you sure about that? Are you sure the Brotherhood would be okay with you leaving them in the lurch without your services inside the prison?"

"I'm just saying. You could get me in a lot of hot water."

They were climbing the steps, going slowly, and talking in low tones without looking at one another. Jude was aware that almost every prisoner still in his cell was looking out the pass-through flap to watch him. Everyone knew he was capable of deadly force and that his actions in the yard the day before had radically changed the power structure inside the prison.

"I'm sure somewhere the Brotherhood have a record of your debt," Jude said. "But we already cut the head off that snake. And until they get their command structure in order, you're the least of their concerns."

"And when they do?"

"You've got a big decision to make," Jude said.

"What do you mean?"

"I mean, you have me," Jude told him. "I can help you with your problem. You just have to decide what kind of guard you want to be."

"I'm a good Corrections Officer."

"I have no doubt, but you're in debt to the Brotherhood. I'm sure your fellow officers know that, too."

"I wasn't always," Pax said. "I had ten years of seniority before they got hooks in me. I'm a sergeant, and you don't get promoted being dirty."

"So, decide if you want to be clean again, Officer Pax. If so, I can help you with that."

Pax looked at Jude without turning his head. The inmate had handcuffs on, but there was no doubt in Pax's mind that Jude could kill him. Pax hadn't been in the yard, but he had heard Jude order Devon "the King" Amon to kill himself. Pax hadn't thought such a thing was possible, not just because he had never known anyone with such a strange power, but because the king was a high-ranking gang leader. He had everything he wanted and the kind of authority within his gang to order murders or anything else he wanted someone to do. For someone like that to kill themselves was unheard of. A celebrity might climb the ladder of fame and fortune only to find that all their success was a hollow reward, but to be in control of a deadly prison gang with tentacles in the outside world that were involved in all sorts of felonious activities. That took a level of narcissism that made suicide incredibly rare.

"Then I would just be your slave," Pax said.

"I don't need slaves," Jude said. "I'm not at odds with the Corrections Officers. I need you all to do your jobs and, while I may insist at times that things are done my way, I'm not looking to own anyone. I would, however, like to be friends, Howie. I hope you don't mind me calling you that. I'll never do it in front of another inmate."

"You're a murderer," Pax said.

"That's true. I do kill people, but only those who deserve it."

"That's what every crazy person says," Pax lamented.

"I'm not crazy, I'm on a mission."

"That ain't much better, pal."

"Perhaps not. All I'm saying is that you have options. Consider that."

They reached the top of the stairs, and Pax called in the order to open the gate. Then he led Jude back to cell three-five-three. He called in to have it opened. Jude was frustrated to see the meager belongings in his cell tossed on the floor. Fortunately, the lower bunk had been cleaned, and the cell smelled of harsh chemical cleaners and not the human waste that Money had shed as he shuffled off this mortal coil.

"This is it," Pax said. "Last stop."

"You guys did a number on it," Jude pointed out.

"Not us. The FBI tossed it. No contraband though."

"Imagine that," Jude said.

"Indeed. I don't know what you're planning, Olson. And I don't want to know. Just leave me out of it. Okay? That's my one request."

"I'll do my best, Officer Pax. Thanks for the escort."

Pax snorted. The door closed, and Jude stuck his hand through the slot in the door. The cuffs were removed, and Jude was alone again. He sighed, then went to work. It only took a few minutes. He laid both rubber mattresses on the lower bunk. It didn't bother him that Money had died there the day before. He made his bed neatly, then re-stacked his books on the single bookshelf. Once his plastic cup and toothbrush were out of the little sink and arranged next to his books, he removed the candy bars from his socks and tucked them between his mattresses. The burner phone and razor blades went between the mattresses and the wall.

Finally, Jude looked at his very humble abode. It was depressing. Maybe at some point, he would have an easy chair and other trappings to make his tiny cell comfortable. Although he didn't expect to be around long enough to gather such lavish furnishings. He had shaken things up in the prison yard, but the truth was, Jude was only getting started.

20

While Jude was being escorted back to his cell, Warden Jennings was filing reports. Paperwork had become computer work, but it was roughly the same. He had eventually learned to type after resisting it for so long. When he started in the corrections industry, only secretaries typed. But eventually it was a waste of time writing things up by hand and having his secretary type them. Especially as the world sped up and everything was electronic. So, he took a course online and learned to type.

He spent the morning typing death notices. Eventually, he turned his attention to the preliminary incident report. It was the part of a very lengthy set of documents that might actually be read by his superiors and, if the incident blew up the way it had the capacity to, other government officials. The report would include the transcripts that had been created from the inmate interviews, as well as the medical findings, and the video files from the yard.

As Jennings made his report, Munson met with some of the other guards. Neil Ray was owned by the Aryan Nation gang, while Charles Crow had connections with the Cartels. Their leadership wanted to meet. But those same men were tier one inmates with long histories of extreme violence. They didn't just get put in a room together. Instead, Munson had them shackled and taken outside to their exercise space. It was nothing like the yard for the inmates on tiers two and three. The prisoners down on tier one could not be trusted not to turn violent, so they spent their outdoor time in individual cages that were lined up in a row at the edge of a concrete pad. Inside those cages was enough room for a man to do push-ups and sit-ups. The bars overhead were often used for pull-ups. Sometimes the inmates did exercises in their cages, at other times they paced like zoo animals. What they didn't do was have physical contact. The cages were close enough for conversation but too far for the inmates to reach one another. The sides were also covered in chain-link fencing. The men could get their hands through, although not their arms. It was a difficult way of life. They got sunlight, fresh air, and could have conversations, but most of the inmates from tier one were almost insane. Twenty-three hours of solitude a day could push a person past their limits, but Munson believed it was the scarring of their souls from the horrible violence they had caused that ruined most of them.

"What about the Brotherhood?" Munson asked. "Shouldn't someone be there?"

"Like who?" Ray asked. "The king is dead."

"Foley or Durell, maybe," Crow suggested.

"Here comes Pax, he'll know," Munson said.

"What's happening?" Pax asked.

"The leaders want to meet," Munson said.

"I'll bet they do," Pax said. "We gonna let 'em?"

"Might as well," Munson said. "I'm kind of curious to see what they're planning."

"Can't be but one thing," Ray said.

"The question is not what they're planning to do, it's how,"

Munson said. "You guys, move your people out. I'll monitor the communications from the box."

"Roger that," Crow said.

"Who are you taking?" Ray asked Pax.

"Durell, I suppose," Pax said.

They took their time. Moving the shot callers of the gang was always an ordeal. The men were put in shackles with leg irons, then escorted out to the cages. Hidden directional microphones picked up most of the conversations. The guards didn't always monitor the inmates, but at times of high risk, it was authorized.

The box was just a storage room where the electronics were set up to listen in on the inmates while they were outside. It had a single chair and a pair of headphones. Munson sat down, put the headphones over his ears, and adjusted the audio.

Out in the yard, Pax was the last one to deliver his man to the meeting. He put Zeus Durell in the cage to the left of Victor Cortez, and on the other side of Cortez was Forrest Sunday. They remained silent until the last of the guards was out of earshot.

"You in charge of the brothers now?" VC asked.

Durell hesitated for a moment. Looking across from his cage, he saw through VC's cage to where the General stood. He was the poster boy for white supremacy, pale-skinned and brimming with hate.

"I am," Durell said in a deep, baritone voice that resonated across the concrete yard and registered well on the surveillance system.

"Good, because we have a problem," VC said. "One that might take all three of us to solve."

"Hard to solve a problem you can't understand," Forrest declared. "Either one of you tell me how Olson killed those boys? 'Cause I sure as hell can't."

"My guys say he never touched 'em," Durell replied. "They just up and died."

"That's not possible," VC said.

"We ain't dealing with a human here, Pedro," the white man said, drawing out the Cartel leader's name so it sounded like an insult. "This fella is the devil incarnate."

"I don't believe in the devil," replied VC.

"Don't matter what we believe," Durell said. "They's a man here with real power. How we gonna stop him?"

"Can't..." Forrest said. "Not till we know how he does it. My people already pulled his file. No family. No way to leverage this beast ... and he sent us his calling card."

"How's that?" Durell asked.

"You know what he's in for?" Forrest asked.

"Murder," VC supplied the answer.

"Yeah, but how'd he do it?" Forrest asked. He paused for just a few seconds, then answered his own question. "Jude Olson burned his victim to death."

"That don't mean nothing," VC said.

"The hell it don't," Forrest growled.

"Burned him with fire? How can that not mean something?" Durell asked.

"He ain't no demon," VC argued. "He's flesh and blood. He's just a man."

"Maybe a man," Durell responded. "But I wouldn't say *just* a man."

"There's two questions that are important here," Forrest said. "The first is how he's doing the killing. My guy in the infirmary says our boys died of natural causes."

"No way," Durell said.

"They were put down, no doubt," VC said.

"But we don't know how. We discover that, and we can stop him."

"What's the second question?" Durell asked.

"Who sent him?" Forrest said. "My guys on the outside couldn't find no answers, but this guy ain't flying solo."

"We gotta get somebody close," VC said. "Earn his trust. Get the answers we can't."

"Exactly," Forrest said. "We can find out what turns him on and use that to leverage some answers."

"And when we've got 'em, we take that homeboy down hard," Durell said.

"Exactly," Forrest replied. "But you better make sure your line of succession is clear. 'Till we find out what we need to stop this beast, we're all living on borrowed time."

VC banged on the door of his cage.

"Guard! I'm through here."

Durell didn't know when he might get the chance again. He jumped up, grabbed the bars on top of his cage, and began to slowly raise himself up and down. It was a show of strength, a display for Forrest Sunday. The confab was over, and the war was back on between the gangs in the Duncan Supermax.

21

Breakfast the next morning was oatmeal. It was a bland paste, but Jude's tray was loaded with real fruit. There was a container of blueberries, some bananas, and even a few strawberries already cut up and ready to be put into the bowl. There were also several containers of butter and packets of sugar. Along with the oatmeal was more sausage links. Jude didn't know how many the other prisoners got, but he had half a dozen on his tray, along with coffee, milk, and a bottle of Simply Orange Juice. Where the juice came from, he did not know, but he didn't mind having it either.

After he ate, only finishing half of the breakfast, he sweetened his coffee with sugar and sipped it while he read. It wasn't long before his cell opened, and Pax was waiting for him.

"Time to go to work," he said.

"Is that so?" Jude asked.

"It is if you still want it?" The guard replied.

"I do. Let's go."

Jude left his tray just outside his cell and followed Pax to the stairwell. They went down to the ground floor and then back into the prison library.

"Any instructions?" Jude asked.

"Old man Kelly used to load up his carts and make the rounds, that's all I know," Pax said. "But you're to stay in here until the guards come for you."

"Sure," Jude said. "No problem."

They'll bring your assistants down."

"Oscar Miller, and Valentine Pearson."

"They're the ones," Pax said.

"The warden sign off on this?" Jude asked. He had expected to need to force it on Jennings.

"No, he doesn't bother with it. Munson and I cleared it. There's bound to be some bellyaching, but when people hear that it's you, they won't make a fuss."

Jude nodded and went to the desk chair. It was well-worn, but comfortable. Jude realized he hadn't sat in a proper chair since arriving at the prison. It felt good, and he felt more independent in the library.

His first task was putting back the books that were on the carts, which gave him a lay of the land. Old man Kelly had been the first and only prison librarian. He had set the space up himself. And the books were mostly old library books that were donated to the prison or the Bureau of Prisons. No one was buying new books. All the titles had labels on the spine, with title, author name, and the Dewey Decimal system number.

Fiction filled one entire shelf and half of another. The third shelf contained non-fiction books and biographies. It was only about two-thirds full. To Jude's surprise, there were several boxes of books that had yet to be opened. Each one needed to be catalogued and put in the card file. It was an archaic system, especially when they had access to a computer. He would update it, but there was no rush.

There were several hundred books checked out. Old man Kelly had kept a running list on his clipboard. He didn't use inmate names, just cell numbers. Every time he reloaded a book cart, he made a new list. Beside the book names he wrote cell numbers. When a book was returned, the number was marked through. Some of the books were more popular than others. Some authors as well. The Harry Potter books had a lot of cell names beside them. As did books by Clive Cussler, Stephen King and Lee Childs. But the most popular fiction titles were the John Grisham novels. Jude had read a few of them. He suspected that the underdog stories were popular because they showed the heroes getting the best of the authority figures trying to control them.

There was also a rotational schedule. The book cart made the rounds every three days. There were a hundred cells on each tier. Old man Kelly would take his time, stopping at each one and writing down book requests. He did everything by hand with little stubs of pencil. There were scraps of paper tucked in between the books and the edges of the cart. He visited tier one on Monday and Thursday. On Tuesday and Friday, he made the rounds on tier two. That left Wednesday and Saturday for tier three. Workers who weren't in the cells when he came around were allowed to stop by the library and make their requests, taking books back to their cells when they finished their shift or letting Kelly leave them with their cellmates as he made the rounds.

It was archaic, and Jude could easily update the system, but he wasn't interested in serving the prison. It was made up of the worst that society had to offer, and Jude didn't care to make their lives easier. It didn't matter that the kitchen staff favored him with choice meals or that his laundry was done well. They had stolen innocence, leaving scarred, broken people behind. They had murdered, and yet they were given the opportunity to read the latest novels? No, that wasn't right, Jude thought. It certainly wasn't justice.

Locking people away was a form of punishment, but that punishment should fit the crime. Jude knew that in some countries, if a person was caught stealing, they had their hand cut off. That seemed extreme to him. In certain places, a minor offense was a capital crime. That wasn't justice, either, and Jude had no desire to terrorize or take the lives of the innocent. But those who dealt in death, who coordinated organizations whose purpose was to profit off other people's pain, would know real fear.

Jude didn't bother changing the books in the cart. But he did update the lists on the clipboard. The first page showed all the books that were checked out. He wrote in small script. Old man Kelly had a shaky hand and a worse memory. Jude guessed there were a lot of books that never got returned. Not that he cared about the books.

The second page listed each cell number. He was going to learn about his fellow inmates and use his position to mete out justice as he saw fit.

An hour later, two guards arrived with Miller and Val in tow.

"What's this about?" Val asked.

"New jobs," I said.

"Doing what?" Miller asked.

"Helping me here in the library," he told them.

"No way," Val said. "This is the cushiest gig in the whole joint!"

"How'd you manage that?" Miller asked.

"I told the guards I wanted it," Jude replied. "Old man Kelly passed away in the night."

"Damn, he was one of the good ones," Val said.

"Was he? Do you have any idea what he did to be in this prison in the first place?"

"People change, Jude," Miller said. "Not often, but it does happen."

Jude wanted to argue the point, but it wasn't the right time. For now, the two men he knew didn't deserve to be in prison, should have the chance to relish in the fact that they had a very good job. It was probably the only positive thing that had happened to them since they arrived.

"We've got to update this place," Jude said. "Digitize the card catalog and get the rest of the books unpacked."

"There are more books?" Val asked.

"Boxes of them in a storage space in the back," Jude said. "Plus, I think there are probably a lot of books that got delivered to people without being properly registered."

"Well, I can start on the computer," Miller said. "I did a lot of data entry early in my career."

"A computer, huh?" Val said. "You think it connects to the internet?"

"I think we better not give the powers that be an excuse to send us to the laundry," Jude said. "Old man Kelly had assistants to help him move the book cart. We'll split the tasks. Val can help carry books on Tuesday and Friday. Miller, you've got the duty on Wednesday and Saturday."

"And on the off days, we work in here?" Miller asked.

Jude nodded.

"We'll have this place running like a well-oiled machine in no time," Val exclaimed.

They had to ask a guard what day of the week it was. Miller found a wall calendar with clever sayings over pictures from libraries around the world. It was a tier one day, so Jude left his companions in the library working on digitizing the card catalog. He wasn't sure how much help Val was, but that was Miller's problem.

One of the guards stayed on duty at the library, the other followed Jude, who was pushing the book cart. He pushed it back out to the tiers. Thursday was a day when he didn't need help with the cart as he would stay on the ground level. There were other guards on duty. They stayed at the corners of the big open space between the cells, which filled each side of the long building. There were fifty cell doors on each side. The worst of the worst inmates were kept on tier one. None of them were allowed to work. The showered once a week, and spent their single hour of exercise time in cages on the concrete yard.

Jude started at the beginning. He was not in a hurry. He opened his first pass-through slot on cell one-zero-one.

"Library," he said, just the way he had heard old man Kelly say as he worked his way around the tiers. But instead of asking if they wanted a book, he said, "Tell me your name."

It wasn't a request.

"Philip Culpepper," a husky voice said.

"Tell me, are you a murderer?"

"Yes."

"Give me your library books," Jude ordered.

Several books were passed to him through the slot. He took them and stacked them on the lower section of his cart.

"Hey, aren't you going to ask me if I want something?" Culpepper said.

"No," Jude told him, walking away. He stopped at the next cell, but before opening the slot, he made a note on his paper. Not the first page which any passing guard might see, but on the second. He wrote the inmate's name down and put a little box next to it. Eventually, when the time was right, he would check the boxes until justice had been served throughout the prison.

22

Warden Jennings didn't hear from his superiors right away. Not even to acknowledge that he had sent them a report. Instead, he was left to wait and wonder how the loss of nine inmates in a single day would be received.

In the meantime, there was still work to do. But it was hard to focus when the mystery of what had happened to the nine men was still unsolved. What he really wanted to do was to question Jude Olson. But he had worked in prisons long enough to know that questioning inmates was rarely productive. They might sing like a bird about another convict, but they were always cagey about opening up regarding themselves. Still, the warden had questions, and he needed answers. The only place he could think to go to was his pastor.

The First Baptist Church in Duncan County was located a full half hour drive from the prison. But no one was checking the warden's hours on site. It was assumed that he was always busy with the prison's work, and in his mind, that was exactly what his meeting with Pastor Bo Hankins was.

The church had offices outside the main auditorium. The church averaged two hundred regular parishioners on any given Sunday. There were four men on staff, three were full-time, one part-time. Jennings had called ahead to make sure he could meet with Pastor Hankins. The secretary had told him to come to the church shortly after lunch.

Pastor Hankins had an office with a big window that looked out over an empty field. There were built-in shelves on either side of the room. Bo Hankins had a large desk that was strewn with books and papers, along with a massive computer monitor. But the room was large enough for a sitting area with a sofa and two armchairs. The pastor met the warden at the door with a big smile.

"Rick, how are you?" Bo Hankins asked as he vigorously shook the warden's hand.

"Troubled, if I'm being honest," Jennings said.

"Well, come in, come in, let's talk. That's what I'm here for. How's Patricia?"

He led Jennings to a sitting chair and sat down opposite him. The two men faced each other. Jennings could see curiosity on the pastor's face. Bo Hankins had graduated from a conservative university and attended a Southern Baptist Seminary to get his Master of Divinity. He had served in various churches for nearly forty years. He was several years older than Jennings, which made the warden think he probably knew some answers to the questions plaguing Rick's mind.

"She's fine," Jennings said. "This isn't about her."

"What's it about, my friend. You can be open here. We'll keep this confidential if you like."

"It's not like that," Jennings said. "I have an issue at the prison."

"Okay," Bo replied.

"Pastor, what's the strangest thing you've ever seen?"

"I'm sorry?"

"I guess what I'm asking is, do you believe in the supernatural?"

Bo laughed nervously. "We talking about ghosts, Rick?"

"No, not ghosts... more like witchcraft or maybe curses."

"Well, the Bible warns us not to be involved with witchcraft, I know that," Pastor Hankins said.

"Have you ever seen it? Have you ever seen something happen that can't be logically explained?"

"Well, I... I'm not sure I understand what you're saying, Rick. Why don't you tell me what you've seen?"

Jennings cleared his throat. "We're confidential here?"

"That's right."

"Because I could lose my job for telling you this," Jennings said. "Maybe even get sued if it got out that I talked."

"I won't tell a soul. It's between you, me, and God."

"Alright," Jennings said, sighing as if he were unburdened and sagging in his seat. "Two days ago, nine healthy inmates died."

"What a tragedy," Bo remarked.

"These were all big, strong men, Pastor. And they were about to attack a much smaller man. He's a new inmate. But he's... different. This isn't the first time something strange has happened when he's around."

"Okay."

"So, these men that died, they're in the exercise yard, and they call this new inmate out. They're crossing the expanse toward him, and he starts killing them one by one."

Pastor Bo looked shocked.

"He didn't fight them. He would have been hurt if he had tried; there's no question of that. The men he killed were muscle for the prison gangs. I'm talking vicious men who have fought all their lives."

"How did he do it?" Bo asked.

"That's what's not clear," Jennings said. "All he did was speak to them. This convict, he's not like the others. He's not crazy. He's smart, and sometimes cagey, but he isn't insane."

"I believe you, Rick," Bo said.

"So, what I'm asking you is, do you think it's possible for a person to be able to do what he did?"

"You're asking me if it's possible to kill someone just by speaking a word?"

"That's right," Jennings said.

Bo leaned back in the chair and held his hands up. "I have no idea."

"Who would know?" Jennings asked. "I've got to understand what I'm dealing with here."

"Look, Rick, the Bible talks about some things that were strange. The story of the man with demons, who broke whatever bonds were used to restrain him, comes to mind. Or in the book of Acts, there are stories of people who died because they lied to the apostles. But I don't think there's anything in scripture about killing someone with a word."

"Nothing at all?"

"Well... I hate to bring it up," Pastor Hankins said. He lifted a worn Bible from a side table and flipped to the back. "Now, this is describing Jesus, so I don't think a man could do the same thing, but this is what it says in Revelations chapter nineteen.

"Then I saw heaven standing open, and there before me was a white horse. And its rider is called Faithful and True. With righteousness, He judges and wages war. He has eyes like blazing fire and many royal crowns on His head. He has a name written on Him that only He Himself knows. He is dressed in a robe dipped in blood and His name is The Word of God. The armies of heaven, dressed in fine linen, white and pure, follow Him on white horses. And from His mouth proceeds a sharp sword with which to strike down the nations, and He will rule them with an iron scepter. He treads the wine press of the fury of the wrath of God the Almighty.

And He has a name written on His robe and on His thigh: KING OF KINGS AND LORD OF LORDS."

Jennings was confused. "I don't understand."

"Well, there is some debate about this, but many commentators believe that the quote, 'And from His mouth proceeds a sharp sword with which to strike down the nations,' is referring to his words. That he'll speak and they'll just die."

"Yes," Jennings said. "That's what happened!"

"But that's the son of God we're talking about, not a man," Pastor Bo said. "And there are still questions about it. Many theologians consider the entire book of Revelations to be an allegory."

"But it's real," Jennings lamented. "Nine men died, presumably from natural causes. And it appears that this new inmate is the reason."

"That's not possible," Bo Hankins said. "A supernatural entity could do something like that, maybe, I don't know. I'm not a specialist in the occult."

"Who is?"

"Well, no one that I know personally. We believe the supernatural gifts ended when the Bible was completed. We have it, we don't need miracles anymore."

"But I'm not talking about a miracle, Pastor. I'm talking about a man with the power to take life simply by saying the words."

"I'll have to ask," Hankins said. "What you're talking about, well, frankly, it's hard to believe."

"It's hard to believe when you preach about miracles on Sunday morning, too, but you expect us to do it."

Hankins got up and walked to his desk. "The best I can do for you is to make some inquiries, Rick. But let me give you a warning. Things like this aren't from God. And it's best not to meddle in them. People tend to get obsessed with the occult. I've seen it ruin lives. You don't want that."

"Pastor, I have over five hundred inmates under my care. My job is to see to it that they are safely detained to serve out their sentences. I have to know what's happening."

"Then I wish you the best of luck, Rick. I really do."

Jennings knew when he was being dismissed. He felt hollow and frustrated. How could his own pastor dismiss him so easily? He had thought that of all the people he knew, Pastor Hankins would believe him.

As he walked out of the church offices with its bright banners and soft music, he realized that Pastor Hankins didn't believe him because he didn't want it to be true. Jennings felt the same way. The supernatural wasn't fair. It couldn't be controlled. And if it existed, if Jude Olson really could kill someone with the words of his mouth, what did that mean about everything they did believe?

23

Forrest Sunday had never backed down from a fight. He had faced off against men bigger than himself, against men wielding broken bottles, knives, and even guns. He knew there were men plotting against him inside the prison and without as well. Yet none of it bothered him, much less frightened him. He knew one day he would die fighting, and that was fine with him. But when he opened the flap on his door and saw Jude Olson pushing old man Kelly's book cart, he felt a shiver of fear run down his spine.

Another man he could face, even a group of men. It didn't matter their size or color, or where they came at him. A man was a man, but Forrest had his doubts about Olson. There was too much risk if the stories were true. He had heard them from over a dozen of his best people who had been in the yard. Olson had faced nine animals without a trace of fear and slaughtered them without raising a hand. It defied logic. How could a man kill with words?

Forrest sat at his desk thinking. He was a man who found great strength in thinking. Throughout his life, whenever he faced a problem, he could inevitably see ways to turn the difficultly into opportunity. Not that he wasn't a man of action, too. Sometimes, he was hasty, leaping to act before he had considered the consequences. It was how he ended up in prison, but that difficulty had become an opportunity with a little careful consideration. His mind, not his fists, had elevated him to the top of the Aryan Nation gang in the Duncan Supermax facility. He had contacts with shot callers from all over the United States and in Europe, too. The movement was spreading, growing, gaining ground in every civilized community in the West.

But Olson presented a problem he just couldn't see a way around. The movement needed a man like him, but how could he ever be controlled? How could a man even trust himself around someone with Olson's abilities? And soon, he would be speaking to the man. It made Forrest nervous, and he did not like that feeling.

When the flap in his door opened, Forrest felt a trickle of sweat run down his wide back.

"Library," Olson said. His voice was clear and unassuming. There was no malice to be detected.

"Tell me your name," the new librarian said.

The question was unexpected. He would have lied, but he answered more quickly than he expected, surprising himself in the process.

"Forrest Sunday," he said, getting up and approaching the opening in his cell door.

"Tell me, Forrest, are you a murderer?"

"I am," the General said, his face growing red with rage at himself.

Olson was scribbling something on a clipboard. "Give me your library books."

The slip of the tongue was one thing. Forrest thought that he had spoken out of nervousness, although when he found himself turning to the shelf of books across from his bed, he couldn't believe what he was doing. He tried to stop himself, but couldn't. His nerves turned from nervous trepidation to outright fear.

He gathered eight books. And began feeding them through the slot in the door. Olson took them and dropped them down into the lower bin of his cart. Forrest was shaking as he sank to his knees and watched Olson move to the next cell. He listened, hoping to glean some clue as to the man's power. Olson said the exact same thing to Luis Miraz. Whatever his power, it must have worked on Forrest. Tears stung his eyes. It was a sensation he didn't think he had ever felt before.

It took nearly half an hour to get control of himself. Dread was heavy on him. Forrest was finding it hard to breathe. There seemed to be invisible bands of iron tightening around his chest. He staggered over to his sink and splashed cold water on his face. In his desk, he kept a variety of pills, including a bottle of baby aspirin, which had gotten through a different contraband channel than his people controlled. He took one of the bitter pills, chewing it up, and moving as much of the powder as he could under his tongue. It took a few minutes for the medicine to work, but his chest relaxed, and he sat breathing ragged breaths, grateful that no one could see him in his own cell.

When he felt strong enough, he climbed up onto his bunk. Under his pillow was a black sleep mask. He put it on and tried to sleep, but fear that he might never wake up plagued him. He wondered if death would be eternal darkness. That thought caused him to pull the sleep mask off. A chill came over him, and he pulled the blanket over his body, wrapping himself in it as tightly as he could to stop the shaking. There was no way to know if the trembling was from cold ... or fear.

The pressure in his chest came back, and the air seemed too thick. It was hard breathing in and out again. Finally, the sound of crackling flames sounded in his mind. Was he going to hell? He had been a hedonistic, violent man almost all his life, but he was white. The white man was God's child. White men didn't burn in hell. No, the sound of flames wasn't real. It couldn't be real.

A booming sound began to pound in his head. Forrest was convinced he was dying. The sound was his blood bursting the vessels in his brain. He was going to be lost in the darkness for eternity, burned by the flames of hell for all his sins.

"Sunday!" A voice called, urgent but soft.

"Save me!" Forrest screamed. "I'm dying!"

Far, far away, there was the sound of voices. Then the door to his cell buzzed. The heavy metal slid sideways on its track, and two guards rushed in.

"Sunday, what's wrong with you?" Officer Ray asked.

"Dying," Sunday said in a weak voice choked with fear. "Someone's killing me."

"Emergency, I have a medical emergency in cell number one-three-three. We need a medic. I think he might be having a heart attack."

Forrest heard the words but didn't comprehend them. He wasn't dying or even having a cardiac episode. The General was having a panic attack. Fear had flooded his mind, causing his physical body to react in a way he had never experienced before.

Doctor Bill Smith came running. His assistant was a tall, white man. He carried a portable defibrillator, but it wasn't necessary. After checking his vitals, Doctor Smith determined Forrest Sunday wasn't having a heart attack. He withdrew a syringe filled with diazepam and injected it into the big man's shoulder. Forest Sunday began to relax. A gurney was brought from the infirmary. The guards helped move Forrest onto the stretcher and then strapped down his wrists while the doctor checked his pulse.

"Let's take him out of here," Smith said.

They left the cell, and the guards had the door closed behind them, as the head of the Aryan Nation in Duncan Supermax was wheeled away.

24

News that the head of the Aryans was taken to the infirmary was everywhere. Jude heard it, but knew it had nothing to do with him. The inmates thought differently, though. They expected to hear that Forrest Sunday was dead.

Jude had barely finished his tour through the ground floor cells when it was time for exercise in the yard. Just getting outside was a treat. Despite the cold weather, Jude found himself looking forward to his hour in the yard. The winter air seemed cleaner than that in the prison. And walking helped loosen up his muscles. There was tension in prison, even for Jude; it was a hostile place that found a way to creep into a person's psyche.

"You look tired," Miller said.

"I guess I am," Jude said.

"It takes a while to get used to this place," Val interjected.

"The book cart gets pretty heavy," Jude said. "I guess I'm getting soft. Would you believe I used to work construction?"

"You brought back loads of books," Miller said. "Why'd everyone return so many?"

"I thought it would be best to get them all cataloged," Jude lied. "Start fresh next week."

"Hey Jude," Val said. "Some people want to talk to you."

Jude had seen the way the other inmates were looking at him. Some were afraid. Some watched him as if he were some sort of prison celebrity.

"Who?" Jude asked.

"This here is William Adair, and Jack Sutton," Val said. "I know them. They're alright."

The two men were white and both had prison tattoos on their arms and hands. Jude knew they were Aryans, but that wasn't too surprising. Most people needed protection in prison. Joining a gang was the fastest way to get it. While he was there to dispense justice, he wasn't interested in sorting out racism.

"You guys won't hurt me," Jude told the newcomers.

"We seen what you did," Adair replied. "I don't reckon anyone can hurt you."

"What do you want?" Jude asked.

"Just wanted to say, if you're starting something, we'd be down with that," Sutton answered.

"You need anything, I'm your guy," Adair said. "I work kitchen crew, back in receiving. I gotta contact on the outside. Get you just about anything."

"I'm in maintenance," Sutton said. "We got some good hash. I can get some if you like."

"Tell me, what are you in for?"

"Homicide," Adair said. "I crashed my ride after robbing a liquor store. The other dude I ran into died."

"And you?" Jude looked at Sutton.

He shrugged. "Rape, attempted murder, assault with a deadly weapon."

"Did you do it?"

"She wanted it," Sutton said. "Begged me for it, you know. Then she changed her mind, but I was like, too late for that."

"Your genitals will swell until they burst," Jude told Sutton. "I don't need anything, Adair, and I'm not starting something. Go back to your racist gang and tell them we aren't interested."

By the time Jude finished his sentence, Sutton had stopped walking. He was holding his crotch with both hands; his eyes open wide with fright.

"Screw you, Olson," Adair snapped.

Jude just walked away. He wanted to do more. Both men deserved justice, but Jude wasn't ready for that. He hadn't even cataloged the second and third tiers. At some point, when people started dying, the authorities would come in and send people away. If it happened too soon, many of the worst criminals in the prison would go on living without the true consequences of their actions ever coming due. So, Jude walked away, but Adair was having none of it. If Jude's reputation frightened him, he didn't show it. Maybe his anger was just greater than his fear. He followed after Jude and kept shouting at him.

"Man, you ain't nothing. You're a hack, a fraud. You ain't got no juice, man!"

Jude whirled around and said, "Choke on your own tongue."

Adair sneered at Jude and was just about to call him out again, but he suddenly started to cough. His eyes were bulging, and he struggled to breathe. Jude turned around and walked away.

"Come on," he told his friends. "Keep moving."

The entire conflict lasted less than ten seconds, but by that time, Sutton was screaming. Had he turned and looked, Jude would have seen bright red blood staining Sutton's pants. He dropped to his knees, then flopped onto his side, still holding himself with both hands and screaming.

Adair couldn't scream. He was coughing and sputtering. Jude was angry. People were pointing at him, and a warning siren sounded. His refreshing walk in the sunshine was being rudely interrupted again. The guards ordered everyone on the ground. Sutton and Adair were carried away, and everyone else was ordered back to their cells.

"This is getting old," Miller said.

"People have to learn not to bother him," Val suggested.

Other people were talking too. There were questions of whether Sutton and Adair would survive. Jude thought that depended on the doctor and his inmate assistants. If they acted fast, both men could be saved. But in Jude's mind, both men deserved what they were getting; only things were starting to spin out of control. Jude had expected that people would be frightened of him and give him a wide berth. The time would come for justice in the prison, but he wasn't ready to dispense it yet. He couldn't deal death indiscriminately. And it was possible there were more people like Miller, who were wrongly convicted for crimes they hadn't committed.

Back in their cells, the inmates settled down. While others gossiped about Jude, Van scribbled a message and gave it to the guard outside his cell.

"Get that to Sunday."

"He's in the infirmary, moron," the guard sputtered. But he took the note. Van didn't have a lot to report, but he was getting closer. Eventually, he would have the answers the Nation needed. The only question was whether he could get those answers before everyone in the prison was dead.

25

The prison infirmary was full. There was an outbreak of panic attacks from various prisoners like Forrest Sunday. The slightest ache or pain was enough to throw the desperate prisoners into a panic like they were cursed to die. Doctor Bill Smith was giving out anti-anxiety meds like it was candy at Halloween.

Meanwhile, locked in his office, the warden was ignoring everything else as he did a deep dive online into the occult. He eventually landed on the website of a man called Alford Dillon. He had a podcast and talked about all sorts of strange, fringe phenomena from UFOs to Bigfoot. Dillon also did coaching to help people sort through strange experiences. For seventy-five dollars, the warden could schedule a video call with Dillon, and he couldn't get the appointment booked fast enough.

While he waited, he arranged his computer so that his certificates and awards from the Bureau of Prisons showed behind him for the video call. When his computer chimed with the invitation from Alford Dillon, he hurriedly clicked the icon. On his screen, the image of an older man with gray hair and rimless glasses appeared. He was sitting in front of a bookcase with several of the books he had written prominently displayed.

"Mr. Jennings?"

"Yes," the warden said. "That's me."

"It's a pleasure to meet you," Dillon said. "I'm excited to hear more about you."

"Okay, yeah, that's alright," Jennings said. "But I need your advice, Mr. Dillon."

"Call me Al, we're friends now."

"I've got a real situation here. You see, I'm the warden of a prison. And we're experiencing some things I can't explain."

"Prisons are notoriously haunted, I'm afraid. And havens for unclean spirits."

"That's not the issue," Jennings snapped. "I don't believe in any of that stuff. I'm a Christian."

"So am I," Dillon said proudly.

"Please, Mr. Dillon... Al, I... I don't know what I'm dealing with."

"Tell me about it, then. I'll just listen until you're finished."

It was like someone had pulled the plug on a heavy container of liquid that the warden had been forced to carry. The incidents with Jude Olson came tumbling out of him, including the latest victims, William Adair and Jack Sutton. Adair had recovered quickly after his frenulum ruptured, causing him to swallow his tongue and nearly choke to death. Jack Sutton was in worse shape. Blood had somehow pooled in his groin and the surrounding tissue. The swelling had caused his scrotum to split apart and pinched off his urethra. Surgery was required to allow his bladder to empty, with no guarantee that he wouldn't need a permanent catheter.

Dillon listened without interrupting. He did occasionally scribble a note, which made Jennings feel like the man he was paying for the consultation was really engaged. When Jennings finished, he was sagging in his chair.

"That's an incredible story," Al said. "Are you the only person who has witnessed this inmate... calling down curses on these men?"

"No!" Jennings replied, sitting up straighter in his chair. "The prison guards have seen it. And the FBI was here after the nine men died. They're conducting an investigation. I'm not just making this up."

"I didn't think you were. It's too strange for that," Dillon said.

"Can you tell me what I'm dealing with?"

"Well," Dillon sat back in his chair and folded his hands across his stomach, "I have some ideas. Honestly, Mr. Jennings, I've never heard of anything like this. It's got to be some sort of mind control. I've read about mentalists who could steer an entire room of people into believing things that didn't happen. Hypnosis, maybe, that could explain some of the physiological reactions, but honestly, in my extensive research, the only thing that comes close to the effects you're describing is the Bible."

"The Bible?" Jennings asked worriedly. He could feel his blood pressure rising.

"Absolutely," Dillon said. "Most people sort of gloss over it, but the Bible is full of strange, supernatural events. Fire coming down out of the sky, the dead coming back to life, telling the future, demonic attacks including possession, the interaction of divine beings with mortal men, the Bible is chock-full of that kind of stuff."

"Mr. Dillon, please excuse my skepticism, but I've been a Christian all my life. My wife volunteers at our church. I don't think any of the things you're talking about are in the Bible."

"Do you read the Bible?" Dillon asked in a calm, supportive voice that had no condescension in it.

"Of course, I do," Jennings snapped. "I read a scripture every morning with my coffee."

"Okay, well, do you believe that Jesus was born of a virgin?"

"Yes."

"Think about it, Mr. Jennings. We're talking about a young woman who never had sexual contact with a man getting pregnant. You believe that's possible."

"It was Jesus," Jennings declared.

"That's right. We're talking about divine DNA. A man who was fully human, but also God. Do you believe that?"

The words were starting to penetrate into Rick Jennings' mind. He had always believed in Jesus, but he rarely thought about him the way that Alford Dillon was describing him.

"Do you believe that he worked miracles? The Bible says he turned water into wine, that he knew things about people that no human could know, that he could heal all kinds of diseases and even raise people from the dead."

"But..." Jennings felt like his world was spinning out of control. "Aren't all those things just sort of... I don't know... Bible stories."

"If you mean are they in the Bible, yes. If you mean they're fiction, then no. They weren't just stories meant to illustrate some kind of life lesson. Wild things happened around Jesus, but not just him. The Bible is full of supernatural interactions, miracles, and demonic activity."

"And you believe it literally?"

"I wasn't planning to have a theological discussion with you, but yes, sir. I do believe it. The Bible is historical and prophetic. In the past, archaeologists scoffed at the history in the Bible. But over time, artifacts have been found proving it is reliable history. And none of the predictions in the Bible have ever not been true. In fact, some of them are so accurate that skeptics try to say the prophecies were postdated, or written after what they supposedly wrote came to pass. But there's proof that the Bible you and I have in our homes is the same as when it was first written. The Dead Sea Scrolls are excellent proof of that."

Jennings didn't know what the Dead Sea Scrolls were, or how the Bible factored into what was happening in the prison. There were prisoners who were clearly demented. Crazy, out-of-touch individuals who acted so wild that some people thought they were possessed by demons. Rick Jennings had always just assumed the devil and demons were a way for people in the past to explain the unreasonable things that happened in the world. He wouldn't go so far as to say the Bible was a myth, but then again, he didn't realize it talked about the things Dillon was describing.

"Look, I can tell this is all news to you, Mr. Jennings. So, let's set the authenticity of the Bible aside for a moment. Either what's happening is a very clever illusion ... or a very powerful supernatural ability. If it's the first, then I trust the experts in your field will uncover it. But if it's the second, if it really is supernatural, then you've got an entirely different problem on your hands."

"How do I fix it?" Jennings said.

"I suppose that depends on the source," Alford said thoughtfully. "If it's demonic in origin, you should be able to exorcise it from the person. Again, there is good source material for that sort of work in the Bible."

"And if it's not demonic?" Jennings asked.

"Then I see two possibilities. The first is that it's from God, and you had best just stand back. If this is God's judgment, no one can stop it, albeit you might get caught up in it yourself."

"God's judgement?" Jennings asked. "Isn't that like earthquakes or something?"

"It can be," Dillion said. "It can also be much more personal. Think about Moses when he faced Pharaoh."

"I don't..." Jennings felt a flash of embarrassment. The thought of Moses brought back flannel pictographs of a baby in a basket floating down the river and an old man holding up stone tablets with the Ten Commandments on them. He didn't recall much about Pharaoh from Sunday School, which he had stopped attending when he was a teenager.

"Look, before Moses led the nation of Israel out of bondage to Egypt, Moses confronted Pharaoh. God enabled him to perform miraculous signs that would convince the King of Egypt that Moses really was doing God's work."

"Okay," Jennings said.

"He threw down his staff and it became a snake."

"That's... terrifying."

"Sure, but the Bible says that Pharaoh's court magicians could do the same thing. They turned their staffs into snakes, but Moses' snake attacked and killed theirs. It says his snake ate their snakes ... and when Moses picked it up by the tail, it became a wooden staff again."

"I'm not sure what you're driving at here, Mr. Dillon."

"Al, please, I don't stand on conventions, warden. I'm reminding you of these stories because they illustrate that at times God uses supernatural signs to get our attention."

"My attention?"

"Maybe. I don't know for sure. But don't forget, the court magicians also worked powerful spells that had supernatural results. In our enlightened age, we've lost some very potent knowledge and abilities. I said there were two possibilities. One was God's judgement, the other is a little more out there."

"Go on," Jennings said.

"How familiar are you with Genesis chapter six or the Book of Enoch?"

"I'm not," Jennings confessed as his face flushed with some shame.

"Well, just sticking to the Bible here, in Genesis chapter six, we have the story of angelic beings that left their natural realm and came to earth. We don't have time to get into all the nuances and interpretations, but suffice it to say that those beings came to Earth and married human women. It says they had children who were heroic figures."

"Okay, what does that have to do with my situation?"

"It's possible that these semi-divine offspring had supernatural powers. Some scholars believe these beings were recorded in various myths from around the world. We might know them best in Greek mythology. The demigods like Hercules. He had super-natural strength."

"Are you saying my problem inmate is a demi-god?"

"No, but there are literally tens of thousands of reports of unexplained abduction phenomena. Are you familiar with it?"

"No," Jennings said. "Should I be?"

"Not necessarily, but there have been studies by well-respected academics about these cases, Mr. Jennings. They all follow a similar pattern. Men and women are taken. They experience phys-ical and mental issues such as sleep paralysis, episodes of lost time, and brain fog. Those who can remember what happened to them report medical probing that is almost always tied to their sexual organs. They have sperm and ovum removed. The women sometimes report implantation that results in real, documented pregnancies, but they never go to term. Almost all of them are abducted, usually in the second or early days of their third trimester. When they are returned, the child is missing. There's no evidence they were ever pregnant in the first place."

"I'm sorry, but I'm lost again."

"What I'm trying to say is that it appears that beings not from the world are still creating offspring, or at least genetically modi-fied offspring."

"Alien babies?"

"Hybrids of some sort or another, just like the stories in Genesis chapter six. If this is happening, these hybrids could have supernatural powers."

"But... why..." Jennings stammered.

"I'll leave you with one last passage from scripture. It's in the Gospel of Luke, chapter 17. Jesus is speaking of his second coming. Do you believe that Jesus will come back like he promised, Mr. Jennings?"

"Well... I don't... know..."

"I believe it," Dillon said. "I believe all of the Bible. And Jesus said, 'Just as it was in the days of Noah, so will it be in the days of the Son of Man.' Do you know why God sent the flood in Noah's day, Mr. Jennings? It was because the earth had become overrun with the offspring of the Nephilim."

"The who?"

"The fallen angels who left their domain and had hybrid children on Earth," Dillon said. "So, it's possible that's what you're dealing with now."

"A hybrid?"

"Yes," Dillon said. "But let me warn you, Mr. Jennings, you won't be able to deal with this person unless you believe."

"I... well, I really don't know... what I believe about all this."

"That's fair. And there are more and more voices in this space talking about the supernatural. They claim to have secret knowledge of ancient writings and the like, but let me assure you that the Bible has all the knowledge we need. There are just too few theologians willing to open up and teach what the Bible says about the supernatural."

They ended the call, and Jennings was left feeling as though everything he knew - and believed in - had come undone. He was still contemplating what he believed and what Alford Dillon had told him when his intercom buzzed.

"Warden, there's a man here saying he needs to speak to you right away."

"I'm busy. Have him leave a name and number, and I'll reach out when I get a chance."

The door to his office suddenly opened, and a man with platinum blonde hair and eyebrows stepped in. He wore a three-piece suit that looked to have been tailored for him, and he had a wicked grin.

"You need to see me now, warden," the man said.

"Who the hell are you?"

"Lucas Barnes," he said proudly. "And I'm here to take over your prison."

26

The buzzer sounded on cell three-eight-five. Valentine Pearson shared the small space with Hector Ispanza, an older convict in his early sixties who rarely spoke. As the cell door began to open, Val rolled off the top bunk. He was excited to get back down to the library. He had been in the Duncan Supermax for eleven months and twelve days. He never lost track of the time. Initially, he had worked in the laundry. It was hard work. Hot, physical, and exposed to harsh chemicals. Needless to say, he hadn't lasted long, and the Aryans had passed him around, forcing him to do the worst jobs, until he was on the verge of suicide.

And then Forrest Sunday had pulled some strings. He saw potential in Valentine that Val didn't even see in himself. Forrest got Val moved to the maintenance crew, where he spent his days scrubbing floors. It was dreary work, but not as physically taxing as the laundry had been. It wasn't long before Val was serving as Forrest Sunday's message runner. The job gave him just the tiniest bit of authority within the Nation, and Val had milked it for all it was worth.

But the library job was even better. He got to be with his friends. The labor was simple. Move a few books around, and help with the data input in the computer system. There were times when he could even sit in a real chair and put his feet up on the desk, while the Screw in the hall who was there to keep an eye on him had to stand. The library felt like the one place in the prison where the guards didn't intrude. Val was certain his life was finally moving in the right direction.

Unfortunately, Forrest Sunday had been sent to the infirmary. He was being monitored for a severe panic attack and given diazepam to help combat the uncontrollable fear. Among his lieutenants in the Nation, the General's malady was their chance to rise up and seize the throne. Instead of Officer Neil Ray escorting him to the library for his work detail, the guard had opened the cell for two of the Aryan Nation's enforcers to get their hands on Valentine.

As soon as Val saw them, he knew what was going to happen. There would be no stopping it. He had been working on a shiv for personal protection before becoming a runner for Forrest Sunday, but it was hidden under his mattress and only half finished. Besides, even if he had the weapon, it wouldn't be enough to stop either of the big men crowding into this cell.

"Not so high and mighty now, Pearson," one of the intruders said.

"We're here to send a message to your boss."

Hector didn't speak. He simply raised his feet up onto his bunk, wrapped his arms around his knees, and kept his head down.

Val tried to dodge the first punch, but failed. It missed his face but landed hard enough on the side of his head to knock him into the metal platform the upper bunk was made from. The edge of the unforgiving steel split the flesh above his right eyebrow. But before Val could react to the pain, he was hit in the stomach. The punch lifted him off his feet and sent the air exploding from his lungs.

"Things are changing," the first intruder said. "Sunday's out. He's too soft. You're living proof of that."

"For now," the other man said.

"That's right. Don't worry, Valentine, you won't be able to feel the pain much longer."

Val was on his knees, his head bent forward as blood flowed into his eyes and dripped onto the concrete floor. One of the men spat on him. He felt the saliva hit the back of his neck. The enforcers didn't bother lifting him back to his feet. Instead, they used theirs, kicking and stomping on Valentine, who could only manage to get his head under the lower bunk. That one move undoubtedly saved his life. But the rest of him was exposed. He was left with a broken arm, both hands broken, one wrist crushed, one shoulder dislocated, nine broken ribs, a punctured lung, internal bleeding, and a torn meniscus in his right knee. The men hadn't stopped there either. They stomped his groin until both testicles were ruptured and one of his epididymides was severed.

They left him there, weeping and retching. He vomited up his breakfast and then blood. Hector never moved and didn't lift a finger to help. The two Aryan Nation enforcers left the cell, and Corrections Officer Ray ordered the door closed without radioing for medical attention. Valentine was left to die simply for being one of Forrest Sunday's trusted lackeys. Rebellion was underway within the Aryan Nation at Duncan Supermax, and the contenders for the crown had just sent a very powerful message. The General's days were numbered.

27

Jude had been in the library for almost two hours when Miller arrived. He had spent the first hour just looking at the books on the shelves. There was something calming about the library. The books were so well organized, the colorful titles drew his eye, and he let his fingers play across the neatly arranged spines. The shelves had gone from sloppy and disorganized to a neat display that left the books easy to find in just a single day. There were more books to add to the system and place on the shelves. The prison had been supplied with dozens of boxes of books, and only about half of them had ever been opened. Organizing the prison library appealed to Jude's passion for fixing things and creating order from chaos. It was one of the reasons he had become a carpenter and contractor. He especially loved restoration work. Bringing a structure or space back to life filled him with a sense of fulfillment he had never experienced in his young life.

He had given all that up in his quest for justice. Once he had done his job at the Duncan Supermax, he felt certain he would have the chance to do the same at other prisons, which was why he was at the computer researching state and federal prisons when Miller arrived.

"Where's Val?" Jude asked.

"He's not coming," Miller said.

"What? Why not?"

"Sick," Corrections officer Ray said from the hallway. "You'll have to get by without him."

There was almost nothing that Jude couldn't do in the library all by himself. The only task that actually required a second person was carrying the book carts up to the second and third tiers. But it was only their second day to work in the library, and Jude had hoped he would be able to back off from hurting the other inmates so that things could settle back down before he made his big move.

"Sick?" Jude asked. "What's wrong with him?"

Even as the words came out of his mouth, he saw Miller give a tiny shake of his head. But it was too late, and CO Ray charged into the prison library. Jude was grateful the desk was between him and the savage guard.

"That's none of your damn business, convict! Keep your mouth shut and do your job, or I'll feed you to the wolves and there won't be enough left of you to fill a mop bucket!"

Miller wisely stepped between the shelves of books and stayed quiet. Jude was shocked, at first, and frightened. His power wouldn't stop him from getting hurt if he was attacked. It had certainly happened often enough as a child in the foster homes and boys' facilities he grew up in. But Officer Ray didn't come around the desk, and he didn't draw his baton. He just glared at Jude, who quickly took control of the situation.

"You won't hurt us," Jude said. "Now, take a step back."

Officer Ray looked surprised as he did what he was told. The guards weren't used to taking orders from the inmates. But Jude's commands weren't optional. His ability forced the guard to back up.

"Tell me what's really wrong with Valentine?"

Ray had to answer, and he had to tell the truth, but he didn't have to be nice or polite in the way he did it.

"Your little friend got a visit from the Aryan Nation this morning," Ray said with a sadistic glare. "I guess he pissed off the wrong people."

"They hurt him," Jude said, realizing suddenly what must have happened.

"That's an understatement."

"Did you call for help?"

"What's the point? If the Nation wants him dead, he's dead."

Jude glanced at Miller, who looked horrified.

"Take me to his cell," Jude insisted.

"Come on then," Ray said.

Miller stepped close to Jude and whispered, "Is that a good idea?"

"We have to help him.'"

"You a doctor?"

Jude realized there wasn't much he could do. So, he nodded and looked back at Officer Ray.

"Call in help for Valentine Pearson right now."

The CO frowned, but he reached up and triggered the transmit button on his radio. "Emergency medical assistance to tier three, cell three-eight-five."

"Copy that," a voice crackled through his radio. "Rolling medical to tier three."

"Do you need to be up there?" Jude asked. "Can the doctor get into his cell?"

Ray clamped his mouth shut so tight his lips compressed into a thin line across his face.

"You will answer me," Jude told him.

"They need a guard to call it in."

"Go and do everything you can to help Valentine Pearson. You will not hurt him or allow anyone else to hurt him."

"Whatever!" Officer Ray snarled, but he turned and hurried away.

"What is happening?" Miller said when they were alone in the library.

"I don't know. I guess Val stepped on some toes in the white gang."

"I'm not talking about Val. What did you just do? How can you make people do what you want them to?"

Jude realized he had never talked to his friends about what he could do. Before Alison died, he never told anyone. But losing her had seemed to change the way he felt about his own personal safety. He didn't really care what happened to him or who knew what he could do. It wouldn't change what he was able to do.

"It started when I was a teen," Jude confessed. "I was in the foster care system. It wasn't much different than this place. Children's homes can be brutal places."

"I'm sorry," Miller said.

Jude was a little surprised. Miller had always been reserved and careful. He seemed like a tough guy to Jude, like the sort of man who could snap if he was pushed too far. Yet, he was being kind and compassionate. His concern touched Jude in a place that he thought had died with Alison.

"Thanks. You can imagine how much you want people to stop when you tell them not to hurt you in that kind of environment. I think I was fourteen the first time someone actually did what I told them."

"What do you mean by that?"

"I mean it literally. I told someone to stop. They were coming to hurt me, egged on by a group of followers who took some kind of perverse pleasure in seeing others suffer."

"I can relate to that," Miller said as he waved a hand to represent where they were.

"Exactly. Only when I told the guy to stop, he did. When I told him to leave, he did. The rest of the boys were shocked. I was, too. But from that point onward, I could make people do whatever I wanted by simply telling them to do it."

"Show me," Miller said as he picked up a copy of *American Gun* by Chris Kyle. "Make me give you this book."

Jude chuckled. "Can I have the book?"

"No," Miller said, with a smile that was real. Jude hadn't seen his friend smile since they had arrived at the Duncan Supermax.

"You know you want to," Jude said.

"I do not."

"Are you sure?"

"One hundred percent."

"Okay. Give me the book."

Miller looked shocked, almost like someone had suddenly slapped him in the face. He wasn't hurt, but he was caught completely off guard. He held out the book, and Jude took it.

"That's what I mean," he said. "When I tell someone what to do, they can't resist doing it."

"That's how you got the guard to call in help for Val?" Miller said.

Jude nodded. "That's how I got him to tell me the truth about what happened. And how I forced him to get help."

"Alright, but that doesn't explain what you're really capable of."

"No," Jude said. "Over time, the ability to tell others what to do grew more powerful. I could make more than one person at a time do what I wanted. I could command entire groups of people."

"Wow."

"Yeah," Jude said. "When I was seventeen, I left the foster care system and never looked back."

"What did you do?"

"I got money?"

"How?"

"Telling people to give it to me," Jude said. "I could tell a perfect stranger to give me all the money in their wallet, and they would do it."

"Just like that?"

"Just like you gave me this book," Jude said, holding it up.

"Why didn't they call the police?" Miller asked.

"And tell them what?"

"That you forced them to give you their money?"

"But had I? If I had a weapon, or even if I had taken their wallet, they could say I robbed them. I got asked about it a time or two by the police. But in most cases, there was evidence that they took out their billfold and handed me the cash. No harm, no foul, just a chagrined person who had been targeted by a teenager with an incredible ability to persuade people."

"What'd you do with the money?"

"Whatever I wanted," Jude said. "I ate good food. Bought nice clothes. Traveled. I stayed in ritzy hotels and went to clubs. I could do anything, and I could convince people to do anything. I would see a pretty girl and go up to her and tell her to hang with me for the night. They would. Their boyfriends would come around, and I told them to get lost. For a few years, it was all fun and games."

"So, what changed?"

"Who says it changed?"

"I do," Miller said. "You're not a spoiled man-child."

"No, I guess not," Jude replied. "I could have the prettiest girl in the bar, but I could see in her eyes that she didn't want to be with me. I had money and cars, and even a few boats by the time I was twenty-two years old. I was living it up and completely miserable. I had no friends. Every relationship I was in was temporary. It's like catching a butterfly and putting it into a bottle. You can name it and even love it, but all it wants is to get out and fly away. And the first chance it gets, that's exactly what it does.

"Then my power took on a new facet. I was in a club, drinking of course, and I saw a pretty girl walking across the bar. I stepped off my stool and told her to come have a drink with me. She did. She also told me her boyfriend was a professional fighter and the jealous type. I just laughed. We were halfway through our drinks when the boyfriend arrived. He made a beeline for us. This guy was a monster. Not huge, but just a knot of pure muscle. There were scars on his face, and his ears had that puffy, swollen thing wrestlers get."

"Cauliflower ears," Miller said.

"That's it. He grabbed my shoulder and slung me around. I immediately told him he couldn't hurt me. I could see him trying, but his body just wouldn't respond. So, I pushed it. I told him that I was taking his girlfriend home and there was nothing he could do to stop me. I told the girl to cling to me. I told her she wanted me real bad, and it was working. The guy was going crazy as I started to walk away with her. And then I did something I had never done before. I looked over my shoulder at this dude and told him to drop dead. You know, just like dismissing a person who doesn't matter to you. Only he really did. Right then and there. He dropped to the floor and stopped breathing. It really rocked my world, Miller. I killed an innocent man. It was truly an accident, but that didn't make it any less real. I sent the girl home and spent the night trying to understand what I could do. The next day, I walked the streets, trying to figure out my life. I saw a homeless man attacking another. I told him to stop breathing, and he did. I didn't kill him, but I could have. I tried to help people after that. I went to the hospital and found a man in a coma. I told him to wake up, although he didn't. I found an old man with emphysema and tried every way I could think of to get his lungs working correctly, but nothing helped. I could harm, but I couldn't heal. I could take life, but not give it. That was my lowest point.

"I had a realization that if I wanted anything real, any kind of authentic bond with another human being, I needed to change. I had this power, but I wasn't using it for anything good. So, I walked away from everything. The money, the cars, the big apartment, I let it all go. I bought myself a set of tools and a used pickup and started driving. I wound up in a nice town with plenty of opportunities. I started working with my hands. I've always been pretty good with my hands, and I picked up carpentry fast. I got a little apartment and started making a few real friends. A few years later, I had enough money that I had actually earned to start a business. You know what I discovered in those years?"

"What?" Miller asked.

"I came to realize that earning something from utilizing a skill was incredibly rewarding on an emotional level. It felt better to build something, even the smallest thing, a shelf or a bookcase, than it was to party with the prettiest girls or buy the flashiest cars. And then I met Alison."

"You loved her?"

"Oh, yes, and she loved me."

"Did you tell her?"

"I told her how I lived, not how I was able to live. I hadn't used my ability to force people to do things I wanted them to do in years. When I landed a client, it was because they believed I was the right man for the job. And when a friend asked me to hang out or get a beer, it was because they wanted to spend time with me, as an orphan; that was the best feeling in the universe. People liked me, you know. If you don't have that as a child, it feels like you never will."

"I can't imagine that, Jude."

"Alison and I started dating, and I knew right away, I didn't want to be with anyone else. She was sweet and very old-fashioned. She made me promise we would wait until we were married to be physically intimate. I agreed, of course. I thought we had the rest of our lives."

"But you didn't?"

"I proposed," Jude continued. "I wanted to elope. But she had the dream of a nice little wedding with family and friends. We compromised, and we were on track to be married just two months after the engagement. I bought us a little house and was remodeling it. She picked out everything, and I worked nights and weekends to get it finished by the wedding. We were three weeks out, and I was finishing up the kitchen when she got hit by a drunk driver."

"Oh, no," Miller said.

Jude was in a kind of trance, recalling the details. "I got a call from her mother. She had been run down less than half a mile from the new house."

"That's tragic."

"Yeah, we were all devastated. To make matters worse, the police stopped the guy who did it. It was dark; the police stopped him because the passenger side headlight was busted. But the cop was in a hurry. The guy hadn't been driving erratic. He claimed he hit a deer, and the cop believed him, despite the open container of whisky in the vehicle. Worse still, because the cop took pity on the guy and let him off with a warning, he didn't file a report. It was days later before anyone thought to check up on the guy who supposedly hit a deer. By that time, the guy had his car fixed. There was no physical evidence. They questioned him, but he stuck to his story, and the prosecutor wouldn't move forward with the case. The bastard got away with murder."

Miller didn't say anything. Jude was struggling with the emotions of it all. He leaned back in his chair and ran his hands over his stubbly hair.

"You have to see it from my point of view. We all knew the

guy was guilty, but no one would do anything about it. For weeks, I despaired. I thought about ending it all. I thought about moving away and starting over. But then I had an idea. I couldn't heal people, and no one deserved to be forced to do something against their will under most circumstances, but what about people who were really guilty? What about the Alex Metfords of the world?"

"Who is Alex Metford?"

"The guy who killed Alison."

"Why not just tell him to go to the police and confess. He could be in here instead of you."

"That's just it, Miller. This is not justice. This is where people are sent so that the rest of society doesn't have to deal with them anymore."

"I'm not sure I follow."

"Look, the justice system is deeply flawed."

"You're preaching to the choir," Miller said.

"Yes! You're the perfect example. The innocent get punished, the guilty go free. The police are just looking for the path of least resistance. Truth plays no part in the criminal justice system."

"I'm not sure I would agree with that."

"Look, if I had told Alex Metford to confess to the police, he would have done it. But then he would have lawyered up. That lawyer would have argued that he was coerced, that he didn't mean what he said, that he was a distraught man whose wife had left him and whose children wouldn't speak to him. So, then it's about the evidence, right? Only there is no evidence. Everything can be explained away, and once again, the murderer goes free. Even if he somehow got convicted, the lawyer would say it was an accident, he didn't mean to do it, and he even turned himself in. They would have given him a light sentence in a minimum security prison that's more like an extended rehab clinic than a jail. He would sleep a lot and play games, and maybe take a turn in the facility kitchen, but in a few years, the parole board would release him. How is that justice?"

"It's not," Miller said. "But you don't know that's how it would have gone."

"I know that I have the ability to know if a person is truly guilty," Jude argued. "I can make a person tell the truth about their crimes. And if a person is guilty, not just beyond a reasonable doubt, but absolutely without any shred of doubt, then justice is to carry out the sentence immediately."

"And who determines the sentence?"

"It's not rocket science. The punishment should fit the crime. An eye for an eye."

"That's from the Bible, and it's to keep people from overreacting to an offense."

"Maybe," Jude said. "But it's just common sense. That Sutton guy raped someone. Probably several people before he got caught. He also hurt them. He said he was guilty of attempted murder. So, I made sure he would never have the ability to rape anyone ever again."

"That's not your decision to make, though."

"I can make a pretty argument that it is," Jude said. "Perhaps that's why I have the power to do what I can do."

"Just because I can do something, doesn't mean I should," Miller said. "Society makes the laws, and we have a system for how to determine if a person is guilty or innocent."

"But they convicted you and you're innocent."

"My situation isn't normal," Miller insisted. "But even when we get it wrong, there are appeals. It's an ongoing process, which is why an immediate death sentence isn't right. People should have the chance to continue trying to prove their innocence."

"Even if they aren't innocent."

"Who can say they aren't?"

"Me," Jude said. "That's my point. I can compel people to be honest."

"Okay, but still, that's no reason to dismantle the entire system."

"At the very least, it should be shaken up," Jude said. "People are smart. We can come up with a better way to ensure that justice is served. Even as terrible as this place is, a person can carve out a life here. Should a murderer who takes an innocent life be allowed to live? I don't think so. And most of the people in here are guilty of many crimes they were never convicted of."

"You're a good man, Jude. You believe in fairness and justice. Those are admirable qualities, yet the prison system takes into account that people can change. Forgiveness can be had."

"Not for those who are murdered."

"Do you know where we get these ideas of justice and mercy, and second chances?"

"After school specials?" Jude said. He was only half joking.

"It's from the Bible. The same book that lays out an eye for an eye also advocates that we forgive those who hurt us and that we pray for our enemies."

"Sounds like it contradicts itself."

"It doesn't, but you have to be willing to look at it with an open mind, Jude. If you do that, God will show you the truth."

They were interrupted when Munson stuck his head in the library door. "Pearson is in the infirmary. He's busted up pretty bad, but he's alive."

"Is he talking?" Jude asked.

"Not yet. The doctor has him sedated. He'll be going to the hospital for surgery."

"Is this my fault?" Jude asked.

Surprise broke across Sergeant Munson's face. "No, he was attacked by enforcers from the Aryan Nation. Their top man is one of the inmates in the infirmary suffering from a panic attack. It looks like his lieutenants are in a scramble to take his place. No rounds today. You two just work in here, and we'll escort you back to your cells at the end of your shift."

Jude was frustrated and thankful at the same time. He was also worried about his friend, but Miller asked the question on Jude's mind before Jude could.

"Will Valentine be okay?"

"I guess that depends on how he handles surgery. He's been through a lot. And I'll be honest with you, the Duncan County Hospital isn't known for world-class surgeons."

Munson hurried away, leaving Officer Crow watching the two inmates in the Prison Library.

"When I find out who did this..." Jude said.

"Can't you just get your justice now?" Miller said. "Tell their hands to fall off or something?"

Jude shook his head. "It doesn't work like that. People have to be in earshot. They have to hear what I tell them to do, or it doesn't work."

"Oh," Miller said.

"But we'll find them. In a place like this, secrets don't stay secret for long. Justice will be served."

28

L ucas Barnes loved his job, even though officially it didn't exist. But it came with power, and that was the important thing. The money was nice, too. He wore expensive suits and traveled in a private jet, although the part he loved the most was stepping in and taking control away from the bureaucrats who normally ran things, such as the Duncan Supermax Prison.

"Excuse me?" Warden Rick Jennings declared. "I don't know who you are, but I am the warden of this prison, and its operation is my exclusive purview."

"Sure," Lucas said. "Still is, but the Bureau of Prisons is under the purview of the United States government, which I'm sure you already know. I've been sent to get things under control."

"By who?"

"By the President of the United States," Lucas said.

He had buried the lead on purpose. Just as he had waited to send the email that established his authority until right before he walked into the warden's office, it made for a more dramatic scene, and Lucas Barnes enjoyed being center stage. He knew that within seconds, Jennings would roll over and give him total control of the prison—a few seconds after that, Jennings' secretary would have quietly messaged her coworkers with the news.

The look on Jennings' face when Barnes lowered the boom was so sweet that Lucas actually almost forgot his next line. Then it came back to him.

"You should have the email now," Barnes said, and he waited.

Jennings hesitated. Then he looked at his computer and clicked his mouse. Barnes saw his eyes moving as he read the email. His lips moved a little, too, and when Jennings looked up, he seemed absolutely terrified. Which was exactly what Barnes was going for. He had to utterly destroy the warden's sense of security if he was going to win the man over. And for his job to be successful, he needed Jennings to be unreservedly on his side.

"Am I... fired?"

"Should you be?" Lucas asked.

Jennings's mouth moved. He didn't want to say it ... and who could blame him? It wasn't like they were discussing the weather or world politics. If Jennings admitted the blame that was rightly his as the prison's highest administrator, then he was facing a very bleak future.

"I... well, I'm..."

"Don't worry, Warden," Lucas said. "You're not fired."

There it was. The relief that came from knowing his life hadn't just imploded. It might not be the way he wanted it. There were certainly some uncomfortable days ahead, but Jennings knew he deserved to be fired. Once he was reassured that his job - and more importantly - his retirement pension wasn't going away, he would join team Barnes.

Jennings leaned back in his chair, a wide smile on his face as he caught his breath. The man must have felt like he just dodged a bullet. Lucas couldn't relate to nearly losing his job. He had only ever excelled in life. But he had actually been in life-or-death situations, and he understood that Jennings was probably intoxicated by the rush of hormones that followed his sudden terror and quick relief.

"But we do have work to do here," Lucas said, quietly closing the warden's office door. The rest of the staff didn't need to hear how the sausage was made. Mystery was part of the fun. Let them wonder exactly what was going on behind that closed door.

Barnes sat down and stared hard at Jennings. "You have a problem here, warden. I wouldn't have been sent otherwise, but fortunately for you, I can accomplish my purpose and save your prison at the same time."

"How's that?" Jennings asked.

"Let's just say that our goals are aligned. The powers that be are still invested in this prison working out. It's pretty rare to have state and federal prisoners in one facility. Yours happens to have some very big fish. Unfortunately, things are starting to come apart. I couldn't care less, really, but prisons are like economies; they are delicate. I don't have to tell you that the status quo inside a penitentiary depends more on the inmates than the Corrections Officers or the facility administrators. Prisons work because the inmates make it work. We set the conditions, they do the heavy lifting, and most of the self-policing, making it possible for a security force that is a fraction of the inmate population to control the facility. But the facility - and by that I mean the walls and gates - are really just an illusion aren't they?"

"Well... I wouldn't put it that way," Jennings replied, still shaky from believing he had just been fired.

"Be that as it may, we don't want anarchy even in the prison system," Lucas continued. "And short of every prisoner being assigned two or three guards to ensure they follow every rule and carry out every desired activity we give them, the inmates have to play along. They accept their role and, within it, carve out a pseudo-society. Gangs, shot callers, enforcers, it's all very organized. Even those who don't make the cut in the gangs have a hierarchy, don't they? But there are inmates in your facility with a say in what the inmates in other facilities are doing. If we aren't careful, the entire stack of cards could come crashing down."

"I suppose," Jennings said.

"And we can't afford to deal with the fallout," Lucas pressed. "I don't have to tell you how many prisons are currently operating in the United States."

"One thousand, forty-seven confinement facilities," Jennings said. The man knew his statistics. Lucas's respect for Jennings inched upward slightly.

"And do you know how many adults are incarcerated in those facilities?"

"Over one million," Jennings said.

"That's right. The crooks have a million-man army. We can't afford to let them gain the upper hand. But I've seen the reports on your facility, warden, and while you may not know this, I am an expert in prison viability. I hate to be the bearer of bad news, but you are on the cusp of a very, very bad incident here. But don't worry, I'm going to keep that from happening."

"I guess that's good then," Jennings said.

"It's very good. Now, let's get started. Tell me all about the incident that occurred on February third. And don't leave out a thing."

29

Jude was still new to prison life. So, it didn't strike him as worrisome that the entire facility was on edge. Since arriving at the Duncan Supermax prison, he had lived under a sense of impending doom that muted most other emotions. A little more anxiety just felt normal.

But things weren't normal. The Brotherhood was leaderless, and the word of Devon "the King" Amon's suicide had incited uprisings both in the prison and in other facilities. It affected the gang's operations in the free world as well.

The Aryan Nation was not as organized and certainly not as public. Most of the members hid their true feelings about race and used the gang's network as a way to circumvent those they did not like or to promote things they approved of. But in the Duncan Supermax, there was a civil war brewing over who was going to take the General's place.

Then there was Jude Olson. He wasn't aware of most of it, but his presence in the facility was sending shock waves through the residents. Fear is an uncomfortable emotion. Most people avoid it when necessary. Many even utilize things such as horror movies to help them gain a sense of control over their fear.

For those people who live outside the bounds of civilized society, fear is dealt with in a straightforward manner. Young men combat their fear through violence until they are desensitized to it. In prison, fear is so great that it must be constantly held at bay. An inmate must be ready to fight at any moment. They will fashion weapons from just about any object in order to have a slight edge over their adversaries. They will demean themselves in order to earn a place within a gang, from hiding contraband inside their bodies to committing acts that would be repugnant to most people. If a shot caller requires something of his followers, they do it, no questions asked. The alternative is too frightening to contemplate for most convicts.

Facing fear also means defying the guards despite the fact that Corrections Officers are armed with serious weapons. Inmates often stand nose to nose with the possibility of a severe beating from the prison authorities. Fear must be met head-on, but to quell its power over the individual, as well as to show rivals that it isn't a factor.

The problem in Duncan Supermax involved the introduction of a new type of fear. The power that Jude Olson appeared to wield left the rest of the prisoners terrified. A vindictive guard could be isolated and taught a lesson ... or even killed under the most extreme situations. A rival could be bested in combat or eliminated through betrayal. Loss of self-dignity was a given and could be coped with. But the power that Jude held couldn't be seen coming. It had no cure, no counterattack, no way to avoid it. Every prisoner who felt any sort of physical ill was instantly terrified that they were going to be murdered by the invisible power of the new prison librarian.

There was no escape. They were locked inside a large cage with the very thing they feared the most, which was weakness.

For his part, Jude was oblivious to the way he made the other inmates feel. He wanted them to respect what he could do simply because he didn't want to be attacked himself. Yet, he was oblivious to the effect he was having on the prison.

After taking his hour's worth of exercise in the prison yard, Jude was returned to his cell. He spent the evening reading a travel book about the Polynesian islands. He was beginning to think that maybe he would go. Miller's argument against Jude being the bringer of justice to the inmates in the prison had resonated with Jude. He didn't want to admit it, but he could sense his resolve wavering. Perhaps it was the thought of killing so many people that frightened him. There were times in the middle of the night that he dreamed of Alex Metford's screams. They left him feeling sick and weak, although he managed to shake it off.

Killing the nine men in the yard had not been physically or mentally taxing. When he was conscious of the act, he recalled that they initiated the conflict with the intention of hurting or killing him. Self-defense was a legitimate reason for lethal force, yet at night, alone in his cell, he was starting to have doubts. And the nine enforcers weren't the only men he had killed since arriving at the prison. He had murdered the king simply because the opportunity had arisen. Sure, Jude wanted to develop a reputation as someone the other inmates didn't want to mess with, but that did nothing to soothe him in the night when his sleep was filled with nightmares. And then there was old man Kelly. Sure, he had been a bad guy. As a young man, he had murdered an innocent child, shattering a young family forever. But the truth was, Jude had murdered him because he wanted the old man's job. Jude tried to justify the killing by claiming it was justice and that it was a path to more justice. But his arguments were starting to ring hollow in his own ears.

Dinner that night was meatloaf. The meat was questionable, the ketchup sour, and the instant potatoes tasted like cigarette ashes. Maybe it was just Jude's state of mind, but he couldn't eat it. Even the tea was bitter despite the fact that Jude had poured an entire sugar packet into his paper cup.

As Jude languished in his cell, the prison around him simmered.

Sergeant Tyler Munson could sense the tension. He prided himself on having his fingers on the pulse of prison life. Some guards tried to manipulate or even force their will on the inmates. Others were unnecessarily cruel and sadistic, which seemed to come from some brokenness in their own past. The majority just wanted to survive. They were facilitators, some even tried to befriend the inmates in the vain hope that if trouble popped off, they would be spared. Munson knew an authority figure in a penitentiary would never survive if they were afraid. Not that any person in their right mind wasn't afraid at times. The inmates at Duncan Supermax were all extremely violent, both in the free world and in prison. They had earned a place because they showed a willingness to harm others. But like any penitentiary, the social dynamic had to be stern but flexible. The inmates needed to feel like they had some control over their lives. Officer Munson believed it worked best when the Corrections Officers showed the prisoners dignity and respect. Sometimes that respect was due to fear of an inmate's capacity for sudden, unprovoked violence. Sometimes it was just the recognition that a convict was also a human being.

He had found a balance and tried to lead the way by example. At times, it cost him with the other officers. At times, the inmates disappointed him. But he held out hope. He was a religious man who took his beliefs seriously enough to view the inmates as he believed God saw them. But he was not a blind follower or a foolish prison guard. His faith colored his work, not the other way around. He was not oblivious to the temperament of the prison.

He could sense it as a whole; the fear and suspicion of the inmates were elevated and rising.

He had planned to tell his immediate supervisor, Lieutenant Foster, of his concerns. Yet, when he got to the admin center, he found a stranger questioning some of the other guards.

"What's going on?" Munson asked.

"This is Lucas Barnes," Jennings said. "He's with the Bureau of Prisons."

"Here to help us out with our little problem," Foster said.

Munson knew his boss well enough to catch the note of suspicion in his voice. The newcomer smiled and held out a hand. He was dressed in a nice suit, but there was something almost unsettling about his albino features. The short hair was cut and styled perfectly, the icy blue eyes unwavering, but his smile seemed insincere.

"Lucas Barnes," he said. "And you are?"

"This is Sergeant Munson. He's one of our best."

"Excellent, I'm almost finished with these guys, if you wouldn't mind to wait in the other room, I need to speak to every guard who was on duty during the incident on February third."

"Sure," Munson said. "Happy to."

It wasn't the truth. Prisons were no different than any other workplace; no one liked an outsider coming in and questioning things. But Tyler Munson was not the type to buck authority. Plus, he knew that none of the guards had done anything wrong. Of course, that didn't mean that someone wouldn't end up as the warden's scapegoat. Jennings had been all smiles and cooperation with Barnes, which probably meant his job was safe. The man at the top rarely ended up taking the heat. Most of the wardens Tyler had worked for were experts at dancing around the facts to avoid the blame for any situation.

The odd thing about the incident on the third, while tragic, had no direct links. No one had laid a hand on the deceased inmates; no guard had even challenged them. It would be hard to bring charges against the Corrections Officers, but not impossible. The officials in the Corrections Department were just as susceptible to lying and corruption as anywhere else. Records could be altered, testimony recanted, and evidence twisted to fit a narrative. The fact that an outsider was there to question them seemed like evidence enough to Munson that the powers in the Bureau of Prisons wanted someone to blame.

He walked into the Admin break room, which was much nicer than the one in Cellblock A near the prison library. There was the obligatory table and chairs, but also two sofas. Instead of vending machines, the Admin break room had full full-sized refrigerator and a bank of cubbies where employees could store their personal items. Munson removed his walkie-talkie and put the base into a charging cradle, then stepped into the break room. He found Sergeant Howie Pax munching on someone's leftover popcorn while Officers Ray and Crow were sitting side by side on one of the sofas, staring at their cell phones. Personal phones weren't allowed anywhere inside the prison other than the administration building, which was usually the guards' first and last stop on each shift.

"Isn't this a sorry state of affairs. What are you guys doing here?"

"Waiting to talk to the fed," Pax said.

"What's he want, Sarge?" Ray asked.

"I don't know," Munson said. That was the truth. He had no idea what the guy was after, and until he did, his suspicions wouldn't help anyone.

"Can only be one thing," Howie said. "We've got the grim reaper on tier three."

"Man, you're crazy," Crow argued.

"Crazy like a fox, maybe," Howie said before stuffing a handful of popcorn into his mouth.

"He's probably right," Munson said.

"Right about having the angel of death in the prison?" Crow asked.

Munson shook his head. "No, but it's probably about inmate Olson."

"What's he got to with us?"

"Our watch, our responsibility," Munson said. "You know the drill."

"And you know we had nothing to do with anything," Ray growled.

"Sure, I know it," Munson said. "Don't mean the feds know it."

"They questioned us when they were here," Crow said.

"Not this guy," Munson said. "I would remember him."

"We gonna lose our jobs?" Ray asked.

"How should I know?" Munson said. "Everything is upside down right now. There's no way to know what the brass will say about it."

"Or who'll they blame it on?" Pax said.

Before Munson could point out that it would be hard to prove they were responsible for the nine dead inmates, especially when the medical examiner's initial finding was of natural causes, Foster knocked on the door frame. Everyone knew who was responsible, but how could you blame someone when you couldn't explain how they committed the crime?

"You jokers are up next," the Lieutenant said. "Shoot straight and you've got nothing to worry about."

"I already checked in my sidearm," Ray said, getting to his feet. "I didn't know I needed it."

"That was a joke," Munson said.

"Sort of," Pax added, which earned him a stern look from his best friend.

"Hey, LT, do we need our union rep for this?" Crow asked.

"Negative, this guy isn't after us."

Munson felt guilty for having a wave of relief wash over him.

The sad truth was that he liked Olson. The guy was calm and cooperative, but that didn't give him the right to kill people. And his rationalization wasn't enough either, not in Munson's book. But true to his word, Olson hadn't made trouble for the guards. If his power worked the way he claimed, he could be more than a problem. He could be a clear and present danger.

Munson led the way back into the conference room. Jennings was there making coffee. The outsider, Barnes, wasn't."

"Don't worry," Jennings said. "Mr. Barnes just went to relieve himself. He'll be back."

"Hope he washes his hands," Pax said.

"Don't be crass, Sergeant," Jennings said. "Trust me, things could be a lot worse."

"Who's this guy with?" Munson said. "I've never seen or heard of him before?"

"Bureau of Prisons has a large staff. We wouldn't necessarily have seen him in the past," Jennings said.

That got an eyebrow raise from Foster, but he kept his mouth shut, and the other Corrections Officers followed his lead. They were waiting quietly when Barnes came back in. He had his jacket off and hung it carefully on the back of a chair.

"Let's start with names," Barnes ordered.

"Sergeant Tyler Munson."

"Sergeant Howie Pax."

"Corrections Officer Neil Ray."

"Corrections Officer Charles Crow."

"Outstanding," Barnes said. "You three, I know. Brotherhood, Aryan Nation, and the Sineola Cartel," he said, pointing at Pax, Ray, and Crow in turn. "Don't worry, I'm not here to look into you three."

"Who are you here for?" Munson asked.

Barnes pretended to chuckle, and he pointed at Tyler. "You, I don't know," he said.

"Sergeant Munson is clean," Foster said.

"A boy scout, eh? Well, that's alright. I prefer my COs a little dirty. It's easier to see where they're coming from." Barnes looked at the other three men. "I mean, when a guy is in bed with the enemy, he really only cares about one thing... saving his own skin."

"Do you have questions for us, sir?" Munson prompted. "We're off the clock, and it's been a long day."

"I won't keep you long, but I need some help. You see, it's my job to stop inmate Jude Olson from killing everyone in the prison, including the Correctional Officers."

"What makes you think something like that would happen?" Pax asked.

"It's not my job to think of what might happen, but to plan for what could happen," Barnes said. "What we have here, gentleman, is a special case. That's what I do best, special cases. In fact, we have a unique facility built just for them. And I plan to transfer Jude Olson there, but we all know what will happen if I try that."

"What's that got to do with us?" Ray asked.

Barnes wagged a finger. "I need information. What's Olson like?"

"See for yourself," Pax said. "The guy's pretty open."

"Open to you," Barnes said, leaning against the edge of a table. "But he'll clam up with me around."

"I should hope so," Crow said.

Barnes sighed. "Officer Crow, this is not an inquest, but it can become one. Would you like that? Whose side are you on, anyway?"

"He didn't mean it like that," Munson said.

"Don't get me wrong," Crow spoke up again. "It's just that when Olson talks, bad things happen."

"Like nine heavies who suddenly die of natural causes?" Barnes asked.

The Corrections Officers all nodded together.

"I've heard. It's what makes Olson special. The question is, what kind of special are we dealing with?"

"No one knows," Munson said. "I don't think he knows."

"You're close with him?"

Jennings broke into the conversation, "Sergeant Munson has a good rapport with all the inmates."

"You're the fair screw, I get it now. Walk softly and carry a big stick, is that it?" Barnes asked. "I'll bet you're the CO everyone cries to when they're offended."

Barnes made it sound as if it was an insult for Tyler to be good at his job.

"This ain't about him," Foster said.

"No," Barnes replied. "It isn't. Has inmate Olson shared with you any of his secrets, Sergeant Munson?"

"He's told me about his crimes," Tyler said.

Barnes assumed Tyler was referring to what got him sent to prison, which was exactly what Munson had hoped.

"But not about what makes him special," Barnes said. "He's smart."

"He's a killer," Foster said. "Don't forget that."

"I never do," Barnes said.

"I heard him say something," Crow volunteered.

"What?" Barnes asked.

"In the library today. He was talking about what he does that hurts people, using his words," Crow explained. "Anyway, he said it only works if the person hears him. If they're out of earshot, he can't do anything."

Barnes actually threw back his head and laughed. Munson felt a lump form in his stomach. For some reason, he felt like Crow had given away too much to Barnes.

"That's it! I should have realized it, but sometimes you can't see the forest for the trees," Barnes said. "You see, all these exceptional people have a weakness. We all do, I suppose. But now we know how to get to Olson. Thank you, Mr. Crow. You have a bright future here at Duncan Supermax. Warden, give this man a day off with pay. He's earned it."

Charles Crow glanced at the other COs, then turned his attention to the floor by his feet. Munson didn't know what to say, but Foster spoke up.

"What does that mean? You know how to get Olson?"

"It means we can use a deaf CO, and Olson will be powerless to stop him."

"There are no deaf Corrections Officers," Jennings said. "Standard hearing is mandatory for all personnel in the Corrections industry."

"He's right," Foster said. "Sounds like you're out of luck."

"Actually, I'll come at this from another angle," Barnes said. "If we can't get him through official channels, we'll use the back door."

"What's that mean?" Pax asked.

"It means we'll use another con," Foster said.

"A deaf convict should be easy enough to round up," Barnes said. "You know, they won't rat their fellow prisoners out, by and large, but give them the opportunity to stab one another in the back and they jump at the chance."

"You can't be serious," Munson said.

"As a heart attack," Barnes said. "Excuse me, gentlemen, I have a call to make."

Tyler Munson had a sinking feeling as he followed the other COs out of the conference room. It felt like he had just sold out the good guys, and despite the fact that he hadn't actually said or done anything, Tyler knew he would have to warn Olson before it was too late.

30

The next day was one of Jude's two days to get a shower. His first experience in the shower room had not been all that bad, but the next was a completely difference experience. Jude and nineteen other prisoners were escorted to the showers. There was nothing pleasant about a cold shower in the chilly prison. It was best to get finished as quickly as possible, which was why Jude didn't notice the guards stepping out of the room and some of the other inmates surrounding him.

He was rinsing the shampoo from his stubbly hair when he noticed that no other prisoners were showering on the spots to either side of his nozzle. He quickly swiped the water from his eyes and turned around. Of the twenty other prisoners, four were black, and another five were Hispanic. Those nine prisoners were busy at the showers that were as far away from Jude's as they could get. The other ten inmates were white men. Three of them were cowering behind six others who looked very intimidating. A few of the six menacing individuals even had small, sharp objects. How they got them into the showers, being completely naked, was a mystery that Jude had no desire to look into.

"You will not hurt me," he said in a loud voice.

"Ain't no one looking to hurt you," the tenth man said. He was tall, thin, and covered with tattoos including a spread Nazi eagle on his chest. "But we need to talk, so I sent the guard out for a smoke."

"There's no smoking in the prison," Jude said.

"True," the tattooed man said.

Jude knew his ability to command obedience was enough to keep the white supremacists from attacking him. But the speaker with his racist tattoos was a surprisingly frightening individual. His voice was strangely deep with a heavy southern accent.

"My name is Merle," he said. "Course, I know your name. Everybody does."

"What's this about?" Jude asked, shivering slightly as the cold water from the shower sprayed across his back.

And if he was honest, he trembled slightly from fear as well. He was naked after all, dripping wet, and surrounded by killers who were all naked. It was a shockingly vulnerable situation to be in.

"It's about loyalty," Merle said. "See, everyone 'round here is up in arms cause they are all nervous about you. Can't nobody seem to figure out whose side you're on."

He stepped between two of the menacing figures until he was close enough to Jude that he could have reached out and touched him.

"I'm not interested in joining your racist club," Jude said.

"Well, don't be so quick to judge. You're a new fish 'round here. And between you and me, there's a lot of dangerous cons in this joint. Them negroes over there are watching every move we make. The spics too, even though they're killers. You know what they want?"

"To be left alone?"

"Oh, hell no," Merle said with a chuckle. "They want what we got."

"And what's that?" Jude asked.

"We're the advanced race, see. Been that way since our great, great, grandparents built this country. That's when everyone understood their place, but things change. They damn sure do."

"For the better."

Merle laughed again. "You been drinking the liberal Kool-Aid, brother. They ain't no such thing as equality between the races. History proves it. The white man is naturally superior, and we built this country and made it prosperous. Then the race traitors began pushing their lies about how the negroes are our equals, and how the wetbacks should just come right into our country. Why don't the blackies just go back to Africa? Why are the spics all trying to get into America? Because they want what we've got. They think if they can take over, they'll be the top dogs and live the good life. But just look around, brother. If they're so equal, then why is it they all come from places that are so terrible? Cause they ain't our equals."

He tapped the side of his head.

"Not up here. They don't make anything, see. They don't invent cures, or develop new technologies, or do anything worth a damn. They're users, every last one. Just parasites, really. And ain't a one of 'em worth anything. You can try and educate 'em, send 'em off to fancy schools, but they don't develop, see. They don't start businesses, or advance science, or nothing. They just cling on to what we've already built and siphon off as much as they can."

"That's a sad way to look at things," Jude said. "I'm not interested."

"That's a shame," Merle said. "There's new leadership in charge 'round here, and a fella like you ain't really welcome if he ain't willing to accept the truth."

"That may be so," Jude said. "The truth is, I don't think too much of anyone in this place. You're all liars and killers."

"Might better keep that in mind, seeing as how you're all alone in this lion's den with no one to watch your back."

"I'll take my chances."

"That's a shame. I coulda used you. A man needs a good watchdog. But it seems like you're just a mongrel. The type that bites the hand that feeds it. Know what my people do with a dog like that?"

"I can imagine."

"You won't have to imagine it, Jude. You're about to find out."

Merle turned and made a slashing gesture across his throat. But no one moved. Jude could see them trying, but their body wouldn't respond to the commands their minds were making.

"Looks like things aren't going your way," Jude said. "Tell me the truth, are you the one who ordered the hit on Valentine Pearson?"

When Merle turned back around, there was rage on his face. His cheeks were red, and veins were bulging in his neck.

"Damn right I did," Merle said. "Sent that little weasel straight to hell. And you're about to join him. Kill this moth—"

"No!" Jude said in a loud voice. "All of you but Merle will go and shower right now. None of you will ever hurt me, or allow anyone else to hurt me."

The group split around the two men. They went to the pillars where water sprayed in a cold stream from tiny nozzles that were designed to save water and increase water pressure. Merle stood staring at Jude, who moved out of the cold spray and stood dripping beside the racist convict.

"Tell me," Jude said to him. "Are you a murderer, Merle?"

"Yes," the man growled. "And one way or another, I'm gonna find a way to break your demonic power and make you my next victim."

"I don't think you'll get the chance," Jude said. "The next time you get water in your mouth, you are going to choke to death. Now, go take a shower."

Merle stepped toward the spray of water Jude had just left. It only took a few seconds for the water from the fine, almost misty spray to get into Merle's mouth. He started to choke, and Jude stepped to the wall where a clean towel hung on a series of hooks. He took one and called out for the guards.

"Guards, get in here! Merle's choking."

It was true. There was no reason for it. Only a tiny bit of water had gotten into the inmate's mouth, yet it seemed to be filling his lungs. As the guards rushed in, they were calling in the emergency on their radios. Merle fell to his knees, the cold shower water pouring over him.

Another guard entered and ordered everyone back. The inmates, most of them finished washing, but a few still dripping with soap, stepped to the edges of the shower room.

"What happened?" the new guard demanded. Jude didn't recognize him and shrugged.

"Beats me, he just started choking," Jude said.

The first two guards carried Merle out by his arms. The choking inmate left a trail of water on the floor as they rushed him toward the infirmary. Jude knew it was a worthless gesture, but he kept his thoughts to himself.

"The rest of you move to the wash basins," the third guard said. His name badge said Allen. He grabbed Jude's arm and said, "Not you."

"You will not hurt me," Jude told him.

"Maybe, maybe not," Allen growled in a low voice as the other inmates shuffled to the next room. Jude could see them through the opening. A low wall separated the wash basins and toilets from the shower room. "What the hell really happened in here?"

"Nothing," Jude said.

"Don't lie to me!" Allen said.

He shifted his weight and was on the verge of pushing Jude into the wall when he froze. There was a look of surprise on his face.

"I wasn't lying," Jude said calmly. "Now, let me go and do your job."

"Go," Allen said, releasing his grip on Jude's arm.

By the time Jude was back at his cell, news of Merle's death was spreading through the prison.

31

"We've had another incident," Corrections Officer Lieutenant Foster said as he entered the warden's office.

"Really?" Lucas Barnes asked.

Warden Jennings was at his desk doing paperwork. The newcomer, Barnes, was sitting in a chair with his feet up on the edge of the warden's desk, studying his phone.

"What now?" Jennings said. He looked up and pulled off his reading glasses.

"Merle Lott choked on water in the shower," Foster said. "He just died in the infirmary."

"No?" Barnes said, his eyes open big in surprise.

Foster thought the man sounded excited, which struck the Lieutenant as completely inappropriate.

"Choked on water from the shower?" Jennings said. "Is that even possible?"

"That's the report," Foster said. "Murray and Wendell were on duty. Allen came to assist when the emergency call went out. They carried him to the infirmary. Doc Smith tried to suction his lungs, but..."

"How'd he get that much water in his lungs?" Barnes asked. "The other inmates would have needed to hold him down."

"There isn't a mark on him," Foster. "Lott was on his knees when the guards went in. Said no one was around him."

"Remarkable."

"No, it's a black mark on this facility," Jennings said. "We have a rash of deaths. How long can we go on like this before word gets out?"

"That's not important," Barnes said. "What is important is who was in the shower with this Lott character."

"I'd think the bigger issue is why the guards weren't in the shower room," Foster pointed out.

"Let's not pretend that we don't all know how the system works," Barnes said. "There's only two things that mean anything in a penitentiary like this: fear and money. It's true of the inmates and the guards. This Lott, was he some kind of boss here?"

"That's one of General Sunday's captains," Jennings said. "A lifer named Merle Lott. If ever there was a true believer in the white supremacy cause, it's him."

"Was him," Foster said.

"This works," Barnes said. "I take it Forrest Sunday is out of the infirmary?"

"He should be," Foster said. "Although I think he's enjoying a change of scenery before returning to his cell."

"What happened to him?" Barnes asked.

"Panic attack," Jennings said. "Presented like heart failure, but turned out to be psychosomatic."

"That can't be good for his reputation," Barnes said.

"Blood in the water," Foster said. "All the sharks are circling. Lott was the first to make a move, but the others will soon."

"Sunday will undoubtedly try to take credit for Lott's death," Barnes said. "It could reestablish his dominance over the Nation. My guess is once we take care of Olson, things will settle back down here."

"And when are we doing that?" Jennings said. "I've lost thirteen inmates in less than a week. At this rate, we won't have any prisoners left in a few months."

"You have to admit it's an interesting problem to have," Barnes said. "Inmates dying, all with natural COD. Personally, I think we should send Olson to every prison in the nation."

"Why not just line the prisoners up and shoot them?" Jennings said.

"Too messy," Barnes said, as if the suggestion was a serious one. "A situation like this is delicate. But you're right about one thing, warden. If people keep dying, you'll have a lot of interlopers trying to figure out why, from medical specialists with lots of letters after their names, to environmentalists trying to find mold or some other cause for the rash of deaths."

"Any of which would be enough to shut us down," Jennings said.

"Not if they don't find anything," Barnes said. "If there really is no other cause of death, no drugs, no toxic exposure, or chemical in the water, then they have no case."

"All they'll have to do is talk to one inmate to learn about Olson," Foster pointed out.

"True, but that's merely conjecture," Barnes said. "No one will believe in a supernatural explanation. Anyone who does could easily be discredited as a conspiracy theorist or a crackpot. No one wants to believe that there are people with abilities that set them far apart from the rest of humanity."

Foster looked over at Jennings, who had an uneasy expression on his face. The Lieutenant was not the type of person who believed whatever he was told. But he had seen things in his almost thirty years of Correctional work. He had seen criminal masterminds, charismatic inmates who could recruit followers willing to do anything they were ordered. Moreover, he had seen inmates with alternate personalities. Some people called them demons that possessed the convict, which Foster didn't really understand, but he had seen those same inmates do things they shouldn't have been able to do, like break handcuffs and shackles. At times, they knew things they had no means to have learned, like what transpired in a private conversation outside the prison or what was going to happen in the immediate future.

Foster didn't know exactly what got into those poor souls, whether it was an outside influence or the price they paid for their seemingly supernatural abilities, but he was certain it happened. But it didn't happen often. Most of the convicts were at least partially insane, despite what the courts said about their mental acuity. Not that Foster was a big believer in mental health services either. C Block was full of inmates who were responsible for atrocious murders that were being treated by health professionals. Foster didn't think the treatment was worth two cents or that the inmates should ever be released, no matter how much they seemingly improved. Nor did he think they should have more privileges than the killers on the first tier of cellblock A. But that was above his pay grade.

Barnes continued, "What's really interesting about your situation is why Olson is here in the first place."

"He murdered a man," Foster said. "Burned him to death with a propane torch."

"Oh, heavens," Jennings said softly.

"That may be true, but how did he get arrested? Have you really thought about that? Olson can tell the inmates what to do. He can tell them to die, and they do it."

"I still find that hard to accept," Jennings said.

"My point is, why not tell the cops who arrested him that he wasn't their guy, or that they should arrest someone else. Why not go to trial? He could have told the jury to believe him and gotten away with it. They wouldn't have been able to convict him."

"Maybe," Foster said. "We don't really know the extent of what he's able to do."

"I'd say murder was the extent," Barnes said. "But consider this, at any time he could tell your COs to escort him out the front gate, and they would do it."

"I'm not sure I like what you're insinuating about my people," Foster said.

Barnes chuckled. "Your people. We really aren't much different from the inmates inside these walls, are we, Lieutenant? Don't get offended. I'm just saying that the possibilities of what Jude Olson can do make the question of why he would choose to stay behind bars interesting."

"Maybe we should isolate him," Jennings said.

"On what grounds?" Foster said.

Barnes shook his head. "That won't stop him."

"From what? What do you think he's got planned?" Jennings said.

"I don't know, but I'd like to find out," Barnes said. "I think I'll speak to him."

"He's on work detail right now," Foster said.

"Who approved that?"

"My Sergeants signed off on it."

"They may not have had a choice," Barnes pointed out.

"What's he doing?" Jennings asked. "It better be scrubbing stains out of prison underwear or someone's going to get fired."

"He's in the library," Foster said.

"Unbelievable!" Jennings declared.

"Don't worry about it, warden. He won't be your problem

much longer," Barnes said. "Set it up when he's through. I can wait."

Foster didn't like it, but he didn't have a choice. He nodded and went to set things up.

32

Carrying the book cart up the stairs wasn't easy. The cart was made of hard polymers, but the wheels were metal with a band of thick rubber for tires, and the books were heavy. Jude only loaded books on top of the cart so that it appeared he was carrying out his duties. He would have required the inmates to give up their library books the same as he had on tier one, but he didn't want to have to make the climb up and down with the cart.

Officer Tyler Munson was assigned to watch the pair and required Miller to stay with him near the stairs while Jude made his rounds with the cart. He took names and forced confessions from the prisoners in their cells. The doubts he had wrestled with after his conversation with Miller the day before had vanished after the confrontation in the shower. It wasn't just that the inmates were all guilty of heinous crimes, but they continued to threaten and hurt people.

In particular, Jude reflected on Valentine Pearson. The man was small, maybe a bit too talkative, but harmless. Jude couldn't imagine Val as a threat to anyone. The fact that he wasn't liked was understandable, but he didn't deserve to be killed. Officer Munson told Jude the specifics about the attack. What frustrated Jude the most was that it wouldn't have happened had a guard not let the assailants into Val's cell. Yet nothing was being done to the guard. It was just another day in prison for the officials in charge. Jude was beginning to wonder what kind of justice would allow them to do as they pleased at the expense of inmate safety. The two guards who had escorted Jude to the shower room had conveniently been occupied with something else when Merle confronted Jude. He wondered briefly if they would be penalized for their lack of attention, but then he realized that guarding rapists and murders was not a highly sought after career. It was probably difficult to get reliable help that was willing to put themselves in harm's way as a Corrections Officer. It would probably take a gross dereliction of duty to get them into real trouble.

When he finished making his way around tier two, there was still time before they would be sent out to the yard for their daily exercise. Back in the library, Miller saw Jude's convict list.

"What is this?" He asked.

"Call it due diligence," Jude said.

"Seriously, man, what are you up to?"

"I'm here for a reason, Miller. You know we're surrounded with real-life monsters, right?"

"I know there are a lot of people here for a lot of bad reasons," Miller said. "But people aren't all bad. They can't be summed up by their worst decisions."

Jude was in the chair behind the desk, and Miller was leaning against a nearby bookshelf. There wasn't a lot of work being done in the library. Perhaps Jude could have put in more effort and made the place something that the inmates really enjoyed, but he wasn't planning on being around that long. Nor did he feel like the murderers and rapists deserved to enjoy anything.

"Their worst decisions ended lives and destroyed families,"

Jude said. "Maybe you don't know what it's like to lose someone you love, but I do."

"You think I didn't lose people I loved?" Miller said, his voice suddenly thick with emotion. Jude shrugged. He didn't want to hash out the ethics of what he planned to do with Miller again. "Do you know why I'm here, Jude?"

"I know you're innocent."

"I'm innocent of the crime I was convicted of, but I'm not innocent. The truth is, no one is innocent. We've all done things we're ashamed of. We've hurt people, failed people, fallen far short of our potential in many cases."

"That's not what I'm talking about," Jude said. "There's a big difference between having an affair or missing a child's music recital, and murdering someone."

"You have no idea," Miller said. "I know it was crushing to your soul to lose your fiancé the way you did, but we've all lost people. You murdered the guy who killed the woman you love. If someone asked if you're guilty, you'd have to say yes. Yet, you don't think of yourself as being just like the murderers and rapists in this prison."

"I'm willing to take the weight of bringing justice to an unjust world," Jude said.

He felt pretty good about saying it. In his mind, the prisoners in the highest-level security facilities all deserved death. Why the government felt compelled to lock them away rather than carry out justice seemed arrogant in a sense to Jude. How dare they say that some murderers could live long lives, supported by the state, while their victims lie cold and moldering in their graves? He couldn't stomach the thought of it. But what Miller said next made his blood run cold.

"Then you should start your revenge tour with me," Miller said. "I didn't kill my wife and children, but I'm responsible for it."

"What are you talking about?"

"I'm not a good person, Jude. I failed my family many, many times. I gamble. I used to think I was good at it, too. Not sports betting or playing the ponies, I was a poker player with my sights set on being a world champion."

"You were that good?"

"I was that deluded, yeah," Miller said. "Truth was, I didn't know when to quit. Pathetic, isn't it? I sound like every gambling addict. My wife and I had two kids, a boy named Griffin and a little girl named Summer. They were the most amazing people in the world, Jude. But I was too busy either working or playing cards to really spend time with them. I think my wife could have made things work if I hadn't gone off the deep end, but she left me when I gambled away the money we had set aside for Griffin to go to private school. That was the last straw."

Jude didn't know what to say. It was obvious that Miller was reliving the nightmare of his life.

"That was three months before the... before..."

His words stuck in his throat, and he couldn't finish the thought. Jude could see how much his friend was hurting. All the moral grandstanding suddenly evaporated.

"I'm sorry," Jude said, but Miller forced himself to keep going.

"She didn't want anything but the kids," Miller said. "I was so mad, but the truth was I felt guilty. I was guilty of doing terrible things. And we were in a fix financially. I had a decent job, but I took out a second mortgage on the house. Our credit cards were maxed out. My wife cut coupons and found ways to save money every place she could. When her parents passed away, they left her some money to send the kids to a good school. I wasn't supposed to touch it, but I was so certain I could turn things around."

Jude felt the blood running cold in his veins. There was nothing so terrible as a man trying to fix his situation and only making it worse. Miller's voice trembled as he continued his confession.

"When she found out the money was gone, she packed up and left. I begged her to stay, but she refused. She said she had given me as many chances as I was going to get. By the time she got the kids to the car, we were screaming at each other. It was probably my lowest moment. The kids were crying. I saw the neighbors peeking out their window shades while my wife drove my children away.

"There was no money for support. I couldn't sell the house; the market was too soft, and I was overextended. I should have insisted they stay. I could have left, but I was so angry. I hated the whole world, but mostly I hated myself. My wife got a job and rented a crappy apartment. It was too small, just one bedroom. She got a little bit of furniture second-hand. I told her she could come back home as long as she didn't file for divorce. She never even considered it. I knew the place she was living wasn't safe, Jude. But I let them stay there. I made it impossible for her to come home. I could have let the bank take the house and given them my money, but you know what I did instead?"

"You gambled," Jude said softly.

"Yeah, I gambled. You want to know why the cops thought I killed them? It's because the night my wife and two children were murdered in their crappy apartment that I had pushed them into, I was playing cards in an illegal poker game. You know the kind, big money. And you know what? I won big. It was the biggest night of my life. I played all night long, cleaned out everyone. It was enough money to pay off the second mortgage. I finally felt like I had turned things around. I had wads of cash in both pockets. I remember walking out into the sunlight of a new day feeling like I had vanquished all my foes, and all I wanted was to tell Sienna."

"I was sure she would come back to me once she realized I was a winner. What kind of fool thinks that way, Jude? I was such a fool. After stopping at the bank and paying off the second mortgage with cash, I went to her apartment. I should have known something was wrong when the door wasn't shut. The front door to this place, Jude, it was just terrible. How could I let my wife and children live in that rat's nest?"

"What happened?" Jude asked. He knew, but he needed to hear the rest of the story. His heart was pounding, and tears were stinging his eyes, but he needed to hear.

"I went in, calling out my wife's name. There was no answer. The place was tiny, just two rooms. The front room was half kitchen and half living space. It was so old the linoleum on the floor was peeling and it had shag rug that was probably older than I am. And then the bedroom. My wife never shut that door, but it was shut, and I felt my guts go ice cold. When I pushed that door open, my worst nightmares didn't compare to what I saw."

"You don't have to say more," Jude said.

"The killer used a knife. It was still in my wife's chest. You can't imagine the horror. Seeing your babies slashed up like that. Blood everywhere. They were lying on the bed. It was all saturated. I rushed in, but I was too late. I had failed them, Jude. I failed them in a way no man should ever fail his family. I pulled the knife out of my wife's body. The neighbors heard me screaming and called the cops. Why no one called when they were being killed still haunts me, you know. How does that happen? I don't know."

"And that's how your prints got on the knife," Jude said.

"Yeah. When the cops showed up, I was covered in their blood. They hauled me in, but I was a complete wreck. I don't even remember what happened initially; it's all just a blur of gut-wrenching pain. But eventually, I told the cops everything. The poker game, where I had been, why I went to the apartment that morning instead of going to work. Of course, they always suspect the spouse in those types of cases ... and there was plenty of evidence of a breakup."

"And your alibi?"

"It was an illegal game. It's not like I was at poker night with my buddies playing for nickels and dimes."

"No one would vouch for you?"

"Maybe they would have if I hadn't cleaned the floor with them that night," Miller said with a rueful chuckle. "I never should have been there," he said, emphasizing each word.

"You couldn't have known," Jude tried to rationalize.

"Of course, I knew," Miller said. "That crappy place, in the worst part of town. I knew. Everyone knew. Her friends begged her not to stay there. But she was proud, you know. She felt like marrying me had been a mistake. She had trusted the wrong guy, and it really cost her. So, she was going to fix it. I could have moved out of the house and let them live there, but I needed cash to get into the good games, you know. I didn't want to spend money on an apartment. And I told myself she was the one who decided to leave, not me. Not me..."

The tears were flowing down his cheeks. Jude couldn't speak. There was nothing he could say.

"They wouldn't let me go to the funeral," Miller said.

"Who, the cops?"

"No, her friends," Miller said. "They all thought I did it. Her parents were gone, so her friends took charge. I tried to get into the funeral home, and a few of the husbands beat the hell out of me. I didn't even try to stop them. I was already hurting so bad, you know? I wanted to die."

"But you didn't."

"No. The cops filed their charges. I got a lawyer, but the evidence was against me. I didn't have a chance."

"You take a deal?"

"No," Miller said. "I fought it. But by the time the trial rolled around, I had no friends, no money, the house was gone, and my car had been repossessed. My lawyer dropped me after the initial hearing when bail was denied. I was stuck with a legal aid rep who didn't have the time or energy to track down the other members of the poker game. Not that he could have gotten them to talk."

"I'm so sorry."

"It felt like justice in a way," Miller went on. "I deserve to be here. I deserve everything about my wretched life except the happy memories, and the fact that, because I was the easy, obvious target, the real killer is still out there. A person who does that sort of thing won't stop. He'll kill again. That shouldn't be put on me, but I suppose it will."

"You're too hard on yourself," Jude said. "You didn't kill your wife and kids. That's on the person who did it."

"I'm just as guilty as the guy with the knife," Miller said. "And ironically, that's the one piece of evidence the prosecution couldn't explain."

"What kind of knife was it?"

"Ka-bar, military issue. You can get them at any military surplus, but this one had someone's initials carved into the handle."

"There was no way to track it?"

"My current lawyer is another legal aid guy. He says he's going to run the initials through the military database and see if there are any records that might give us a clue, but it's a long shot."

"You just need someone to believe in you," Jude said. "Ever think about trying to escape?"

"From this place? No, I'm not that creative. Besides, that would kill any chance at overturning the verdict."

"That's more important than freedom?"

"All I want from the rest of my life is for Sienna's friends to know I didn't kill her."

Jude nodded. It was a long shot, but he believed that the truth was out there ... and that justice would prevail. Not because of the justice system, but because of something higher. A force for good that wouldn't allow a man like Miller, flawed of course, but innocent of the crimes he was convicted of, to spend the rest of his life in prison. Especially a prison as terrible as the Duncan Supermax.

33

While Jude and Miller were talking, the guards were accepting a new transfer. Kiner Grossman was in his late fifties, but carried himself like a younger man. Life in prison can weigh heavy on most people, but there are some who thrive in the joint. Some find a kind of success they never had on the outside.

Lieutenant Foster was part of the intake team, as was Lucas Barnes, who happened to be the only person that Kiner could communicate with. The man was deaf. Foster observed while Pax, Allen, Ray, and Crow took the prisoner from the bus into the facility. They stopped him and unshackled his chains in the intake room.

"Tell him to strip out of his clothes," Pax said.

Barnes gave the instructions in sign language. Ray and Crow stood to either side of the new prisoner. And Pax remained directly in front of him, while Allen lingered by Foster.

"What the hell, LT? We aren't prepared for this," Allen complained.

"Not our call," Foster said. "Barnes ordered the transfer. Warden Jennings signed off on it."

"Why?"

"Beats the hell out of me," Foster said.

"You know we can hear you, right?" Ray pointed out.

"So? The convict can't hear anything," Allen snapped. "Does he read lips or anything?"

"I believe he does," Barnes said.

Grossman undressed. He moved slowly. The swagger he had getting off the bus and walking into the supermax prison was gone. He moved very slowly.

"He's milking this," Allen grumbled. "Tell him to hurry up."

"You tell him," Barnes replied with an icy grin. "Oh, that's right, you can't. Maybe you just shut up and let the adults work here, Officer."

Foster felt Allen tense up beside him. Allen was not the cream of the crop when it came to Corrections Officers. He tended to have a temper and obviously took no joy in his work. In fact, he could be cruel. The man had a dozen reprimands in his personnel file, although nothing that would get him fired. He seemed to know there was a line he couldn't cross, but he enjoyed getting as close to it as he could.

"What the hell?" Crow said.

Kiner had a broad chest, with long, sloping pectoral muscles. Across his chest was a series of lines or hash marks, like the type used when keeping track of something. Four lines would be horizontal and close together, with a fifth line slashed diagonally across the others. There were over fifty individual marks, and they looked as though they had been cut into the convict's flesh with the intention of leaving a scar.

There were other marks, too. Most were livid scars from wounds that Kiner had endured.

"This guy's been through the wringer," Ray said.

"What do you think those scars on his chest mean?" Crow asked.

"Ever hear of the Barbosa Eight?" Barnes asked. The COs all shook their heads. "It's an elite group in the United States prison system. They are unaffiliated with any other gang. It's pretty rare to have more than one in any facility. They're just too dangerous."

"Dangerous how?" Allen asked.

"They're killers," Barnes said. "Usually, contracting with the gangs to carry out hits inside the prison. They keep track of every kill. This is how Kiner does it." Barnes waved as the deaf convict's chest.

"Over fifty people?" Allen said quietly.

"I suppose so," Barnes said. "He hasn't been officially named in any prison murders, but you really just never know, do you?"

They took Kiner through the intake process. He was eventually locked up in cell three-five-four, right next door to Jude Olson.

Dinner that night was Salisbury steak, which consisted of a meat patty that consisted mostly of gristle. It was swimming in a dark gravy that was too salty. There were boiled potatoes that had no salt at all, a stale roll, and the pudding cup, which was served with every lunch and dinner in the prison. Kiner wasn't alone in his cell. It was occupied by a white man in his early twenties named Mason James. He was responsible for the deaths of six people who were killed in a home fire that James set in an insurance scam. The authorities were fairly certain Mason James was guilty of starting at least a dozen other fires, three of which had claimed innocent lives. Still, they couldn't put together enough evidence to convict him of the other charges.

Kiner had looked around the cell when he was led in, and when the door clanged shut behind him and his handcuffs had been removed, he immediately attacked Mason James. The fight was fast and vicious. Kiner didn't intend to kill his cellmate, although he knocked several teeth loose and broke three of

Mason's ribs. When dinner arrived a short time later, Kiner ate the food from both trays while his cellmate lay unconscious on his bunk, barely able to move.

The note taped to the bottom of one tray was easy to find. Kiner felt it as soon as he picked up the tray. But he waited until the food was consumed to remove the note and read it. It said simply: *Jude Olson. Maim, don't kill.*

Kiner had no idea who Jude Olson was, but he knew he was being moved for a reason. He existed for only one reason: to hurt and kill. He was a bullet, and he had just been aimed. Once he found the target, he would carry out the job the only way he knew how, with extreme violence.

34

After dinner, Jude was surprised when the buzzer sounded and his door opened. Officer Munson was waiting just outside his cell.

"On your feet, Olson," Munson said. "You know the drill."

"What's going on?" Jude asked as he put his book down and sat up on his bunk.

"You've got a meeting with someone."

"Who?"

"Hands behind your back. Approach the line," Munson said. "All your questions will be answered soon enough."

Jude faced the back of his cell and walked in reverse to the edge of his cell. Munson stopped him there and snapped handcuffs on his wrist. Then he took hold of Olson's elbow and led him away from the cell.

"Close three-five-three," Munson said in his radio.

The cell closed behind them, and Munson took Jude to the gate that led to the stairwell.

"Open south gate, tier three," Munson radioed.

Jude stayed silent. He knew that some of the COs didn't like him. Others were fearful of him. But Munson always treated him fairly. He never worried that Sergeant Munson was going to hurt him or lead him into a dangerous situation.

They were halfway down the stairs when Munson finally started talking. He whispered quietly, his eyes straight ahead, but Jude heard every word, despite the shouts and occasional screams from the inmates in their cells.

"I can't tell you who this guy is," Munson said. "He's a 'high up' in the Bureau of Prisons. Has the warden by the short hairs, I suppose. I get the feeling he's dangerous. Not directly, but be careful what you tell him."

"Got it," Jude said softly. "Thanks."

Munson didn't say anything else as they reached the bottom of the stairs. He paused, radioing in to have the gate unlocked. Then he led Jude outside. It was winter, and snow was falling softly. The prison lights were on, but beyond the prison walls, Jude could see the darkness that was all around the facility.

"You mind if we slow down?" Jude said.

"It's cold out here," Munson said.

"Been a while since I've been outside at night. I hate not to savor this snow."

"You okay without a coat on?"

"I'll be fine. I can deal with some cold. It's not the first time I've been uncomfortable since I got here."

"I suppose not," Munson said. "We can go as slow as you like."

"How come you're so nice, Officer Munson? You aren't like the other guards."

He smiled. "I guess I have a different point of view," he said. "Working here is my job, but I believe God put me here for a reason."

"God?" Jude asked. "What for?"

"To remind the inmates here that there is still hope."

Jude stopped walking and put a hand on the chain-link fence. The cold and snow were forgotten as he stared at Munson.

"Hope for what?"

"Forgiveness," Munson said.

"God will forgive murderers and rapists?"

"Yes."

"Well, that's nice. I'm not so magnanimous, personally."

"Forgiveness is not the same thing as clemency," Munson said. "No one is talking about relieving the guilty of the consequences of their actions."

"I think the consequences are that they should burn in hell forever," Jude said.

"We're not the judge of the human soul."

"Maybe we should be," Jude argued. "Why should anyone who murders someone, or ruins a person's life through violence, be allowed a second chance. The people they killed don't get a second chance."

"Are you sure about that?" Munson said. "Do you really believe this life is all there is?"

"You don't?"

"No," the guard replied. "I believe we were made for eternal life with God."

"Even murderers?"

"We're all sinners," Munson said. "And sin was what Jesus died for. In that regard, we're all murderers."

"Now you're just talking in philosophical circles. What I care about is what I see in front of me, not myths and fairy tales."

"Do you know God's story?"

"I know enough. There's too much suffering in the world to believe in a loving God."

"That's a shame," Munson said. "You've got so much potential to help people."

"No, I really don't."

"You could use your ability to help."

"I tried that. It doesn't work. I can't heal people. My talents are the total opposite of that."

"So, you say," Munson countered. "But you can keep people from hurting you, right?"

"Yes," Jude admitted.

"I'm thinking you could probably keep people from hurting one another. You could probably give the inmates a lot more hope than you realize."

"That's…" Jude began, but he had trouble finishing his sentence.

"I'm not trying to tell you what to do with your life," Munson cut in. "I'm just saying that you have options. And in my experience, a little positivity goes a long way. Especially, in a place like this."

They continued walking. Jude was silent, but not angry. He wasn't a religious person. Growing up, no one had taught him about God. He heard snatches of conversations about Jesus and God's love, but nothing substantial. In the meantime, he was busy just trying to survive. Growing up in foster care wasn't easy, and there was no one to comfort him in the night when bullies had threatened him, frightened him, stolen from him, and hurt him. Jude had been forced to rely solely on himself. That had changed with Alison. His entire universe had been changed by her love, and then she was cruelly snatched away with no warning. One minute, she had been going for a jog. She was beautiful and funny and full of life. The next thing Jude knew, there were police cars and an ambulance racing past the house, and he was filled with dread. When Alison didn't come back when he expected her to, he knew something was wrong, yet he told himself she was distracted, maybe even helping whoever the ambulance was racing to save. Then the call came from Alison's mother. It shattered his world and left his heart in pieces.. Jude didn't think that Alex Metford deserved forgiveness or a second chance.

But he couldn't deny that there was something different about Munson. He was a guard and did what guards did, but the way he did it was different. It was like he wasn't touched by the horror and danger of the prison. He had some kind of invisible shield and, in a place built for despair, he let the light of hope in. Jude wasn't sure if that was a good or a bad thing. He was still planning to bring justice to the Duncan Supermax. There were a handful of innocent men in the facility, but they were less than one percent of the total prison population. The rest were guilty and waiting for their lives to end. Jude was planning to speed that end along.

When they reached the admin building, Munson opened the door but didn't go inside. It was the same room that the warden had questioned Jude in, the parole review space. Jude glanced at Munson, who gave him a reassuring nod. Then he stepped inside and found Barnes waiting for him. Jude was a little shocked at the man's appearance. Unlike the warden, he was in a clean, well-tailored suit. The man's colorless hair and icy blue eyes made him seem different, too. There was a wide smile on his face, but it wasn't sincere. It was part of a mask that Barnes was using to hide his true nature. Jude felt a shiver run down his spine that had nothing to do with the cold weather outside.

"Inmate Olson, welcome. I'm sorry to pull you from your cell. You probably have a routine that keeps you sane in a place like this."

"It's no problem," Jude said.

"Good," Barnes said, before waving to a chair. "Here, sit down. Let's have a conversation. I hear that you are a very interesting man."

Jude didn't respond verbally, but he sat in the chair. The cuffs on his hands rattled a little as he rested them on his lap. Barnes pulled a second chair over and sat a few paces away from Jude.

"You're probably wondering what this is all about?"

Jude nodded, but didn't speak. The warning that Munson had given him was fresh on his mind ... and Barnes was the type of person that made Jude nervous. He seemed to know things that Jude didn't. Barnes was angling to get something from Jude that he probably didn't want to give up.

"It's just a friendly conversation," Barnes said. "You've got a lot of people talking."

"How's that?" Jude asked.

"How about we cut out the part where you act like you don't know what I'm talking about. I've done my homework. And you're not the first person with special abilities that I've met. In fact, that's why I'm here, Mr. Olson. You can think of me as a specialist in those with unique talents. Yours is interesting, given your current location."

"I'm not sure I understand what you mean," Jude replied.

"Okay, let me put it another way. The fact that a man who can coerce people into doing whatever he wants simply through the power of his voice is unique. There are people who have doubts. I mean, how powerful can your gift be if you ended up in prison?"

"Maybe I wanted to be here," Jude said.

Barnes laughed. "Now we're getting somewhere. Why would anyone want to be in a hellhole like this?"

"That's my business," Jude said.

"Actually, it is literally my business. My job is managing people like yourself."

"What's to manage? I'm an inmate in a supermax prison. I'd say that's the very definition of a person being managed. I can't even take a piss without permission."

"And why is that, Mr. Olson? I believe you would walk out of this place right now if you wanted to."

"Are you offering to let me leave?"

"No," Barnes said, his fake smile returning. "But you don't need my permission, do you? When did your talent for persuasion manifest? From my work with other individuals of your stature, I'd guess it came along with puberty."

Jude didn't say anything. He felt like he was playing high-stakes poker. Barnes was staring hard at Jude, and the only thing the inmate felt certain of was that he couldn't trust the man in the suit.

"Don't clam up on me, now, Mr. Olson. We're just getting started."

"I feel like I should have my lawyer present."

"Oh, I assure you, the time for civil rights is far in the rear view mirror. What we're dealing with now is how best to put your talents to work. But first, I need a little clarification about your abilities. I know you can kill people. Is that all you can do?"

"I don't know what you're talking about."

"Yes, you do. By my count, you're at thirteen. Not that anyone who understood who your victims were would blame you."

"I haven't touched anyone," Jude said.

"Doesn't mean you didn't kill them. You spoke, they died. Is it some kind of verbal curse you put on them? Is there more to it than just your voice?"

"I really don't know what you're talking about."

Barnes sighed. "I've been watching. Killing people is one thing. That's easy. Anyone can do it, really. A child can point a gun at someone and pull the trigger. It isn't the killing that interests me, Mr. Olson. But how did you manage to get the job as the prison librarian? You see, that takes a completely different level of skill. It's more useful. You are one of the newest prisoners here, and there's a system in place for moving inmates through the work programs. It starts with the laundry, followed by the indoor maintenance team, then the kitchens, and then the outdoors maintenance team. At the pinnacle of the prison job hierarchy is the library. It's not just an easy job, but it comes with privileges, most

namely access to every prison cell in the facility. In this penitentiary, there are many inmates who never come out of their cells.
So, I'll ask again, what can you really do with your abilities?"

"You don't believe I have any abilities," Jude said. "You believe
I'm just a regular inmate. You want to go home, Mr. Barnes. You
are tired of this place, and you want to leave right now."

There was a look of mild confusion on Barnes' face for a
moment, then he stood up.

"I've had enough," he said. "Guard!"

The outside door opened, and Jude felt cold air wafting in.
"Take him back to his cell," Barnes said. "I've got better things to
do than to waste another minute here."

The albino in the nice suit turned on his heel and stormed out
of the parole room. Jude stood up and walked slowly toward the
door where Officer Munson was waiting. He was wearing a heavy
coat, but it was wet from the snow. The ground outside was beginning to turn white.

"How'd it go?" Munson asked as he closed the Admin building
door and led Jude through one of the long enclosed walkways.

"Hard to say," Jude replied.

"He didn't seem happy."

"I guess he didn't get what he wanted from me."

"And what was that?"

"Answers, I suppose."

"You didn't answer his questions?"

"Not if I could help it."

Munson nodded. There was no judgment from the guard. It
might have been reasonable for the Corrections Officer to side
with Barnes, but he hadn't. In fact, it was Munson who warned
Jude to be careful with Barnes.

They passed through several gates and wound their way
through the open-air walkways and corridors. Jude enjoyed seeing
the snow in the bright prison lights. He could make out a few

shadowy figures on the walls as well. It seemed like a miserable duty in bad weather. The guards on the walls would be wet and cold. There would be no protection from the wind up on the high walls. Jude could think of much better ways to make a living. But his own choices had led him to a very uncomfortable place with an unsavory purpose. Still, it was something he believed in. Justice needed to be served, and he was going to make sure it was.

35

The following day was a Saturday. Normally, Warden Jennings didn't come into work on the weekends. None of the regular administrative staff worked, and the Admin building was usually only used by the Corrections Officers. But Jennings was at his office by seven and shocked to find that Barnes had left the night before with no word about when he might return.

Inside Cellblock A, life went on as it did every single day. There was no difference between one day and the next: no weekends or holidays. If the inmates wanted to keep up with them, they weren't disciplined for it, but they were given no special treatment. The only exception was Thanksgiving, when they got cold turkey and stuffing that came from a box as their meal. It was no better or worse than their regular fare, just different.

Jude had a double helping of eggs and some type of meat that was supposed to be bacon, but fell well short of the mark. At the library, Jude and Miller loaded the book cart and carried it up the two flights of metal stairs. On tier three, Jude made his rounds, labeling every cell and the occupants inside. Many of the prisoners were assigned to work details and not in their cells. They would be the lucky ones, Jude thought. They would thank God in heaven for the job they were assigned, no matter how lowly, when he brought justice to the Duncan Supermax prison.

When the hour for their daily exercise arrived, Jude was ready for it. It was one of the milestones for the repetitive days in prison. Like the meals, it marked the passage of time. The inmates were given long wool coats. They weren't washed between shifts, which meant someone else had worn the jacket, perhaps many people, since the last time it had been cleaned. It was still damp from the last user, both inside and out. Jude would have preferred not to wear the smelly garment, but it was cold outside. The yard was a mixture of frozen mud and dirty snow. The inmates continued to wear their thin, canvas shoes that had no waterproofing abilities. It didn't take long for Jude and Miller to fall into a comfortable silence. They walked with their heads down and their hands tucked under their arms to help hold the coat closed. The thick wool garment had no pockets or buttons. And despite the less-than-pristine condition of the garment, Jude was thankful for it as the hour wore on.

Kliner was in the yard too. He stayed close to the Aryan Nation gang, masking his presence. He had been in his cell the day before when Jude came by with the cart. After being alerted as to who the librarian was by his cellmate, Kliner had watched him out the pass-through in his cell door. He had a good memory for faces, and Jude wasn't hard to find. He walked with one other inmate a little apart from the other prisoners, who were giving the pair a wide berth.

Kliner knew nothing about Jude Olson except that his cellmate feared the librarian. There were strange stories about the inmate. None of that meant anything to Kliner. He was a man with a singular focus. Violence was his specialty, and killing was the pinnacle of his craft. But the note indicated that Olson was to be injured, not killed. Kliner had taken a shiv from his roommate. Mason James had stolen a piece of metal from the laundry or maintenance space. What it had originally been wasn't clear, but it had a sharp point that was ideal for thrusting.

With his weapon tucked inside his sleeve, he began moving forward. The other prisoners were content to trudge through the muck. They noticed Kiner, yet didn't speak to him. No one tried to stop him. When he was only a dozen paces behind his target, he let the shiv down into his hand but held it close to his coat. The guards were oblivious, as usual. And then he made his move.

Jude and Miller had no clue what was coming. They would have been completely caught off guard if Kiner hadn't stepped into a puddle behind them. The splash made them both turn their heads, and something in the newcomer's dead eyes gave his violent intentions away.

"Stop!" Jude shouted. Half the prisoners in the yard stopped, but not Kiner. "You won't hurt me!"

Little did he know that Kiner couldn't hear him. Miller, however, saw the shiv and threw himself in front of Jude. It was a completely selfless act. Kiner was already in the process of thrusting the shiv at Jude, and instead, it punctured Miller's stomach.

"Stop him! Stop him!" Jude cried out.

Miller sagged, and Kiner flung him aside. Jude, not normally given to fighting, saw his friend being thrown to the muddy ground, and he flew into action. His first punch landed hard; a straight right hand driven hard into Kiner's nose. The hired assassin was pushed back two steps. Blood exploded from both of Kiner's nostrils. He blinked back tears, the natural reaction to having one's nose broken. Had Jude been a fighter, he would have known better than to punch his opponent hard in the face with a closed fist. The blow did little to stop his attacker but broke two of the small bones in Jude's hand. He staggered back, grabbing his punching hand with his empty left hand.

Kiner regained his balance and, despite the blood pouring from his nose, advanced toward Jude, the shiv held ready to strike again. But Jude's call to stop Kiner had set the other prisoners in motion. Several surged forward, sprinting through the mud. They grabbed the assailant from behind. Kiner struggled, managed to flip one over his back. The prisoner fell into the mud at Kiner's feet, but the deaf assassin couldn't fight everyone. The other prisoners grabbed his arms; some wrapped their hands around the collar of his coat. Someone even grabbed him by the ear. They tugged him backward until he fell. Then they began kicking and punching.

It all happened fast. Within seconds, Kiner was down, and the guards were rushing to stop the melee. Jude stumbled toward Miller, who lay in the mud, his hands on his stomach. The dark wool coat had fallen open, and bright red blood was staining the front of his shirt.

"No! Don't die!" Jude shouted at his friend.

"You don't... have... to do it," Miller said, his voice a tremulous whisper.

A guard grabbed the back of Jude's coat and spun him away from Miller. "Get on the ground!" The guard screamed.

"You won't hurt me," Jude shouted. "Save him! Save Miller!"

Doctor Smith wasn't scheduled to be at the facility on weekends. A nurse covered the infirmary, handing out meds, changing bandages as needed. He was a small man with thick glasses named Emory. When he came out, he immediately ordered the guards to call for an ambulance.

"He needs to get to the hospital right away," Emory said. "Keep pressure on the wound."

Turning to Kiner, who was lying on his back unrestrained, the shiv nowhere in sight, but spitting the blood that ran into his mouth. The nurse turned him onto his side.

"Are you hurt anywhere else?" He said.

"That one can't hear you," a guard said. "He's deaf."

Jude could feel his broken hand swelling, and the cold mud was seeping through his clothes. His eyes blurred with tears. He felt the same, terrible sense of loss knowing that Miller was hurt, maybe dying. And there was something else too, a new feeling. He didn't recognize it at first. It was love.

His friend had sacrificed himself to save Jude. It was something Jude couldn't quite grasp. The selflessness just didn't make sense. Sure, Jude had helped Miller and even gotten him into the library, which was a cushy job, but that was a far cry from saving the man's life. And Miller didn't agree with Jude about justice. Yet he had selflessly flung himself in front of Jude, taking the brunt of the deaf man's attack.

Jude lay numb in the cold muck like all the other prisoners. Kiner was taken to the infirmary, and Miller was placed on a stretcher and carried out of the yard. Fury and sadness mingled inside Jude. Then guards arrived, yanking him to his feet.

"You won't hurt me," he ordered.

"Not going to hurt you, but the warden wants you in the hole!" The guard named Allen said with a sadistic grin.

"My hand is broken," Jude said as they pushed his arms behind his back. "Take me to the infirmary."

"Got orders," Allen said, but he didn't move.

"You will take me to the infirmary right now," Jude ordered.

"Take him," the guard named Allen snarled. "He ain't going anywhere. The hole will be waiting for you, convict."

The guards began to lead Jude away. They half-carried, half-dragged him along. The moment they reached the door leading into the prison, Jude ordered them to stop. "Let me walk," he said. "Don't touch me."

"Keep moving," one of the guards said.

Jude didn't recognize them, but he didn't think that really mattered. He hurried through the corridor as water and mud dripped from his clothes and the stinking wool coat. When they reached the infirmary, Jude saw two rows of beds. There were no dividers between the patients. They were all strapped to the beds, and most were sleeping even though the lights were on and the room was bright.

The guards stayed by Jude as another pair stayed by Kiner. The assassin was in no shape to be a threat. He wasn't seriously injured, but he had taken a beating from the other inmates who had kicked, punched, and stomped on him in the few seconds they had before the guards arrived on the scene. That wasn't something that Jude had ordered them to do. He had simply said *stop him,* and they did that the way they naturally would. But Jude didn't mind the fact that he was in pain. The man had tried to kill him.

Emory, the nurse, had gone with Miller, helping him as much as possible until the paramedics arrived. Jude wished he could be with Miller, but they would never let him leave the prison. To yell orders at the nurse would only slow down Miller's journey to the hospital. So, Jude let his friend go and focused his wrath on the man responsible.

"Get him out of those wet clothes," said one of the volunteers. It was a young inmate who worked with Doctor Smith five days a week and knew as much or more about triage as Emory the nurse.

"I can do it," Jude said. "You don't touch me."

One guard got Jude a towel, the other found fresh clothes. Jude stripped down, used the towel to clean himself up one-handed, then got slowly dressed in the clean clothes.

"Is he going to make it?" Jude asked.

"No reason he shouldn't," the young volunteer said.

"Tell me your name," Jude said.

"Frankie Donaldson," the volunteer said without looking up. He had a pair of angled scissors that he was using to cut Kiner's clothes off.

The deaf assassin moaned. The sounds were oddly frightening. The quick clot bundles that had been thrust into his nostrils were already saturated and beginning to drip. The exam table was big, with separate sections that Jude guessed could be angled upward, but they were all laid flat. There was no padding, and no sterile paper to cover the table as Kiner bled onto it.

It was ten minutes before Emory returned. In that time, Frankie had set up the X-ray machine. It was on a big, articulating arm coming out of the ceiling. The film was in a tray that loaded into a compartment on the exam table.

"What have we got?" Emory asked as he came hurrying into the infirmary.

"Broken nose, maybe a few ribs," Frankie said.

"How's his breathing?"

"Seems fine. He's in a lot of pain."

"Play stupid games, get stupid prizes," Emory said. "We'll give him some ibuprofen when we're done with the X-rays. He'll have to learn not to fight if he doesn't enjoy pain."

Jude watched. They didn't bother with a lead apron. The X-rays were taken, and a guard held Kiner's hands as Emory probed the ribs.

"I think they're just bruised," he said. "Doctor Smith can follow up with him when he comes back on Monday."

Jude knew Kiner wasn't going to live that long.

"Why's he making that sound? Are you okay?"

"He can't hear you," Frankie said. "Deaf."

The nurse nodded. They gave Kiner some pills and a cup of water, then a guard led him to a bed and used thick straps to secure him to the bed. Kiner lay back on the thin, stained mattress and groaned.

"Next up," Emory said.

Jude held out his swollen hand. "Can you do anything for this?"

"You the reason the last guy's nose is broken?"

Jude nodded. The nurse sighed, but took Jude's hand and began gently probing it with his thumbs.

"Can you move all your fingers?" Emory asked.

"Yes," Jude said.

"It'll be fine in time. Don't be going punching anyone else, and I'll bet it will heal on its own. If it's still bothering you Monday, you can come see Doctor Smith."

That seemed to be his prescription for everything. Not that Jude minded. But he wasn't going back to the hole. He was sick of prison, sick of the constant stress, the lousy food, and the cruelty. It was time for him to act, and he knew that. Although his hand was aching and he wanted some rest.

"You are going to keep me here in the infirmary," Jude said. "And give me some ibuprofen, too."

Emory didn't even look up from the incident report form he was filling out. "Frankie, get this man some anti-inflammatory pills and put him in a bed."

"For a broken hand?"

"Just do it," the nurse said.

Frankie rolled his eyes but waved for Jude to follow him. A guard went along as well. Just as Jude lay back on the bed, the guard took hold of his uninjured arm and began strapping it down.

"Don't do that," Jude whispered, "but if anyone asks, tell them you did."

The guard wrapped the straps around Jude's wrists but didn't work them through the buckles to tighten them down.

Frankie gave Jude a pair of small pills in a small paper cup. He tipped the cup back over Jude's open mouth, then held a larger cup of water with a straw to his lips. Jude caught the straw in his mouth and sucked down enough water to swallow the little pills.

Across the aisle, created by the two rows of beds, Kiner was grunting in pain with every breath he took. Frankie walked over, pulling on a rubber glove, and plucked out the absorbent pads from his nostrils. Kiner grunted, his hands jerking upward but held in check by the restraints. Frankie didn't even seem to notice. He pulled two fresh cylinders from a box on a tray next to the bed. Then he slipped one into each nostril. The material expanded as it got wet from the blood until it filled the nostril and stopped the bleeding.

"That'll do you for now," Frankie said.

He turned to start back toward the exam area, but Jude stopped him. "Tell me how long your shift is," he said.

"Six more hours," Frankie said with a sigh.

"Wake me in five," Jude ordered.

Frankie gave a curt nod, then went on about his business. Jude looked at Kiner and thought, *enjoy breathing while you can.*

36

It was shortly after lights out when Frankie woke Jude up. He had more ibuprofen, which Jude took, and then, when the inmate volunteer stepped back, Jude got up from the bed.

"What are you doing?" Frankie asked in shock.

"Getting justice for Miller," Jude said. "Follow me."

They walked over to where Kiner was sleeping. "What now?" Frankie asked.

"Get me a sharp object," Jude ordered.

He turned, pulled a shiv made from several tongue depressors that were taped together. One end was whittled down to make a point.

"Will this work?" Frankie asked.

"It's perfect," Jude said.

The lights in the infirmary ward were off, but there were smaller lamps above each bed that cast light upward. It was a dim glow, enough illumination to see by, but not so much that it would make sleeping difficult. Jude reached out with his good hand and pinched Kiner's nose. The deaf man came awake with a squawk of pain.

"Hey!" Jude said in a whisper, but exaggerating his lip movements. "Remember me?"

There was a look of intense fury in Kiner's eyes. His hands shook the restraints, and his legs thrashed on the bed.

"You can't hear me," he said slowly. "But I'm betting you read lips. Is that right?"

Kiner just glared. Jude started to reach for the deaf man's nose again. Kiner jerked and turned away. Jude grabbed his chin and turned Kiner's head back to where the deaf man could see him.

"Answer my question or I'll pound your nose with my fist."

Jude held up his fist in front of Kiner's eyes, which narrowed. Then he nodded slightly.

"Do you read lips?"

Kiner nodded his head up and down.

"Good," Jude said. "Tell me who sent you."

Kiner shrugged. Jude reached up toward the deaf man's face. He jerked away, then said in a loud, moaning voice, "I don't know. I swear. Got a note."

"You got a note to kill me?"

Kiner nodded. Jude was pretty sure he knew who sent such a note, but he would worry about that later. He turned instead to Frankie, who looked nervous.

"Use that thing," Jude said. "Make it quick."

He turned away as Frankie leaned over Kiner. There was a small screech, but it had barely begun when it was abruptly cut short. Jude walked down the aisle back to the exam area. There was a door with a bolt lock and a name plate that said Doctor Smith. Jude pointed at the door and turned back. Frankie was coming quickly up the aisle. One of his hands was covered with blood, the other was cradled under it to catch any drips.

"The doc have a computer in there?" Jude asked.

"Yeah," Frankie replied.

"You got the key?"

"Emory has one."

"Where's he?"

Frankie pointed with his chin to a passageway that led to a dark room.

"He sleeps in there," the inmate volunteer said.

"Thanks. Go get cleaned up and forget what happened to the deaf man."

Frankie hurried to a nearby sink and started scrubbing the blood from his hands. Jude went into the dark passageway. It was short and dark, but enough light came in for Jude to see the nurse's lab coat hanging on the door. Emory was snoring. Jude checked the coat and found a set of keys in the pocket. That was convenient, maybe not so safe in a prison, but Jude wouldn't complain. He went back to the doctor's office and started trying keys. The door opened with the fifth key he tried. Frankie was watching him closely.

"When the guard comes, tell him that the nurse is in here," Jude instructed him.

Frankie nodded, and Jude went into the little office. It was the size of a closet, with a minuscule desk just large enough for a laptop computer and a phone. Jude woke the computer. A security screen appeared that required a passcode. There were no Post-It notes or scraps of paper. Jude leaned out and looked at Frankie, who was perched on the side of the exam table.

"Tell me the password to the computer," he said.

"I don't know it," Frankie replied. "We're not allowed in Doc Smith's office."

Jude searched the drawers but didn't find anything. He was about to give up when he lifted the computer up. There was nothing under, but taped to the bottom was a scrap of paper with the word *BobDillion*.

Jude set the computer down and typed in *BobDillion* in the password slot. When he hit return, the security page vanished, and the prison's mainframe icons appeared. It was exactly what Jude was looking for. It only took a few moments to find the intake files. His was there, along with Miller's. The only newer file belonged to a Kiner Grossman. Most of the information was of no use to Jude, but one thing stood out. The transfer was initiated by Agent Barnes, SAD. Jude had no idea what SAD was, but it sounded bad. And it confirmed what Jude had surmised. Barnes had brought in someone who Jude couldn't control for the express purpose of killing him. But Barnes hadn't counted on Miller.

Jude picked up the phone. It felt heady to think of making a call out of the prison, but that's what he intended. The local hospital was on the phone's speed dial button. Jude pressed it and waited. Soon, someone picked up.

"Duncan County Regional Medical Center, how may I direct your call?" A woman's voice said.

"This is Doctor Smith at the Duncan Supermax. I'm calling for an update on a convict that was taken there this afternoon."

"I'll transfer you."

Soft music played for nearly a minute before someone picked up.

"ICU, how may I help?"

"I'm Doctor Smith from Duncan Supermax," Jude lied again. "I'm calling for an update on Oscar Miller."

"He just came out of surgery. Doctor Farage did the surgery. The wound punctured the patient's diaphragm and stomach. It was repaired, but there was extensive blood loss. We transfused, and we're keeping him on close watch for any signs of infection."

"Will he live?" Jude asked with just a hitch of emotion in his voice.

If the nurse heard it, she didn't mention it. She seemed busy, almost put out by the call.

"He's expected to make a full recovery."

Jude felt a flood of relief. His friend would make it. That was important to him. Jude would have to see to it that Miller got out of prison as soon as possible.

"Thank you," Jude said.

"You're welcome," the nurse said. Then the line went dead.

Jude hung up the phone and leaned back in his seat. His hands were shaking, and tears brimmed in his eyes. Miller had a long road of recovery ahead, but he would make it. Jude felt guilty that his friend had been hurt. It wasn't Jude's fault, but Miller had stepped in and took Jude's punishment. It was the kind of sacrificial act that no one would have ever done for Jude in the past. Jude knew he would never forget it.

There was another inmate volunteer brought in after Frankie. It was an older inmate named Lane Pointer. He didn't seem surprised at all that Jude was in the doctor's office. He did a quick tour of the beds, either not noticing or not caring that Kiner had been killed, then settled on a stool in the corner and read a book he had brought along for the occasion.

Jude spent the entire night looking into Miller's file. Oscar had been railroaded, of that there could be no doubt. It wasn't so much about the evidence against him as the lack of evidence exonerating him. An online search showed lots of articles that gave the details of the attack. They all listed Miller as the prime suspect. Anyone on the jury who kept up with the local news would think he was guilty before the trial even started. Jude wasn't sure how, but he knew he had to get out of the prison and get his friend some help. That was the most important thing, even more important than the justice he had gone to prison to mete out.

Jude found Miller's new attorney in the file, a Kevin Newfield. He was approved for visits by the prison board. But Jude didn't expect to meet him on the inside of Duncan Supermax. It was time for him to leave. There was just one more thing he needed to do first.

At dawn, he left the infirmary and found a guard. It was
Sergeant Howie Pax who looked exhausted after a long night shift.

"Come with me," Jude ordered.

Pax never said a word. He just followed along, staying close to
Jude. They went immediately to the prison library, where Jude got
the book cart. He unloaded everything but a few books for show
on the upper section. Then he began pushing the cart into
tier one.

"What's going on, Howie?" Corrections Officer Allen said in a
loud voice that echoed off the metal and stone.

Jude turned around. The sun was up, and breakfast trays were
already being collected from the cells. The new day had started,
and soon prisoners would be sent to their work assignments. Jude
needed to work fast.

"You don't care what we're doing. You think it's unimportant,"
Jude said.

"Oh, hell, I don't even care," Allen said.

"Not too close," Jude told Pax. "I don't want you to hear me."

Howie nodded and took up a station by the stairs. He stood tall
and stiff, his thumbs tucked into his belt. His eyes stared straight
ahead.

Jude nodded and made his way to the first cell. It was occupied
by a huge brute with tattoos, brands, and scars over most of his
body. He had a bald head and big ears. Jude checked his list, then
bent down to the pass-through. It opened with a squeak, and Jude
gave the command.

"Your heart stops beating," he said quietly.

Inside the cell, the Brad "the Butcher" Stevenson lay on his
bunk. He had been snoring, the thick chest rising and falling.
Suddenly it stopped. Stevenson never knew what happened. One
minute he was dreaming, the next he was in Hell.

Jude moved to the next cell, checked his list, gave the
command, and kept going. It took nearly ninety minutes to stop at

every cell. There were no innocent people on tier one. And when Jude approached Pax at the foot of the stairs, there was no one left alive in the cells of tier one.

"You don't have to do this," Pax said.

"Do you care about them?"

"Not really," the guard confessed. "But you seem like a pretty good dude. Why do this?"

"Justice."

"For who?"

"For the victims. For the people whose lives were forever scarred by the rapists and killers in this prison."

"I doubt they'll see it that way," Howie said. But he didn't stop Jude, he just opened the gate to the stairs and helped him carry up the book cart.

On tier two, the process took longer. In many of the cells, there were two inmates. Jude gave each of them the same order. At one point, CO Neil Ray went to retrieve one of the dead convicts, but Jude intercepted him. There were nearly three hundred dead convicts by the time Jude was ready to proceed up to the third level. Only two innocent men were left alive, and only because Jude could force the inmates to be honest about the crimes they were accused of committing.

On tier three, Jude started again, but his time was running out. The highly restricted inmates on the ground floor still got yard time. They went in shifts that started at ten o'clock in the morning. Sergeant Tyler Munson was with three other COs on their way to start retrieving the inmates. Jude abandoned the book cart and hurried to the next cell. Down on the ground floor, an emergency was called in. It took Nurse Emory two minutes to reach the slain inmate's cell. Fortunately, the group hadn't moved on to the next convict yet. Jude carried out his style of justice to five more cells before the next death was discovered. One dead inmate was strange; two dead inmates warranted suspicion. Munson immediately checked the next cell and found another dead prisoner. He started barking orders and calling for an immediate lockdown.

"Stay where you are," Jude ordered Pax and Ray when the order came to secure all prisoners.

Jude got through eight more cells, about half of the total on the tier three, when Munson started up the stairs with two other officers.

"What are you doing?" Munson shouted.

"What I came here for," Jude replied.

"Stop him. Howie, Neil, what are you doing? Stop him!"

"They can't," Jude said. "And neither will you. All of you, stop climbing the steps. Secure tier two and don't let anyone else come up here."

Munson and his fellow officers complied. Jude continued going from cell to cell. There was no need to be creative any longer. There would be no doubt as to who was responsible for the deaths of the inmates in the Duncan Supermax. Jude had become an executioner.

There might come a day when what he did tore his soul to pieces. But at the time, he was so consumed with getting the task done that he didn't have time to contemplate his actions. People can debate the concept of capital punishment, but that's not what Jude was doing. He was murdering people. They were criminals, the most violent kind. They had all earned their place in Duncan Supermax by harming others, breaking rules, and threatening the innocent. Perhaps they deserved to die, but they were like mice in a cage with no way to escape the carnage that was coming for them.

He had only a handful of cells left when the sound of helicopters approaching was heard. By the time he was finished, there were calls on the radio for all officers to prepare to breach the prison and shoot him on sight.

"There's no way out of here," Pax said.

"I've got a plan for that," Jude said.

"They've got a SWAT team out there. Snipers. You won't get ten feet."

"Let me worry about that," Jude said. "Open the gate."

"Can't," Ray said. "The entire prison is on lockdown."

"But you have a physical key. Unlock the gate, now."

Pax muttered a curse under his breath and unlocked the gate.

"See, that wasn't so hard, was it?" Jude said.

He was still looking at them when he took the first step. Only it wasn't there. Jude's arms windmilled, and his feet scrambled for purchase on ice, but there was none. He was falling, and there was no way to save himself.

37

J ude woke up gasping in his bed in the prison infirmary. It was still night. Frankie was on a stool with wheels, cruising up and down the aisle between the rows of beds.

"What?" Jude asked.

His mind seemed foggy, and his hand was throbbing. He reached out to rub it and discovered that his hands were bound tight on either side of the bed.

"Hey!" He said in a loud voice. But Frankie didn't respond. "I'm talking to you, Frankie!"

The volunteer still didn't respond. He was bobbing up and down. When the stool rolled past Jude's bed, he saw the earbuds he had in. There was no doubt that he had the music cranked up. Across the aisle, Kiner was sitting up, staring at him. The deaf man had cold, dead eyes.

"That's end of shift!" Officer Tyler Munson called out. He appeared at the main entrance to the infirmary and waved his hand at Frankie. The volunteer jumped off the stool and pulled the earbuds from his ears. He discreetly stuffed them into his pockets.

Munson pushed the swinging door to the infirmary open and held it as Warden Jennings walked in. He looked tired and angry.

"Where's Emory?" Jennings said in a loud voice. Several of the other inmates were stirring on their beds.

"He's in the back," Frankie said. "Would you like me to get him?"

The young volunteer slipped into the darkness of the back room before the warden could answer. Jennings turned and glared down the ward to where Jude sat propped on his good elbow, watching. Emory came out rubbing his eyes.

"Is something wrong?" The nurse asked.

"I think so, yes," Jennings said. "What grounds do you have to keep a prisoner I ordered to the hole in your ward?"

"What?" Emory said.

"Inmate Olson. I want him in the hole. Is there some medical reason you're keeping him here?"

"The guy with the broken hand," Frankie said.

"Oh, riiiight," Emery said, drawing out the word. "I just thought it best to keep him here until the doctor could check his hand. It might need surgery."

"He won't hurt it anymore being in the hole. I want him moved. Right now!"

Jude could have spoken up. He could have changed the warden's mind. Instead, he remained quiet and waited.

"Fine," Emory said.

"See that this gets straightened, Munson. And I mean right now!"

"Yes, sir," the sergeant said. "I'll do that."

Jennings spun on his heel, and Munson started down toward where Jude lay. To his surprise, as Frankie was escorted out, the same older volunteer Jude had seen in his dream came in. The man checked the log for instructions, then sat down in the corner and started to read.

"You okay, Olson?" Munson asked.

"Not really," Jude said. "I just had the worst nightmare."

"Sorry to hear that," the guard replied. "I wish I could say things are going to get better for you."

"I heard," Jude said. "Back to the hole."

"Yeah, no getting out of it now," Munson said.

Jude disagreed, but he was still reeling from his dream. He had bad dreams before. And there were times when he woke up shuddering from dreams that he was back in a foster care facility. But they were never so vivid. It was like he had lived the entire night and was back to do it all over again.

Kiner was still staring daggers at Jude as Munson unfastened the buckles and helped Jude off the bed.

"I won't cuff you if you promise to cooperate," Munson said. "That hand looks pretty bad."

"Not as bad as his face," Jude remarked.

It was true. The bridge of Kiner's nose was black, and so were both his eyes. His cheek bones were puffy and eyes were mere slits between them and his forehead. Red bundles of quick clot stuck out of his nostrils, and his mouth was covered in dried blood.

Munson took Jude by the arm, and they started back toward the main doors of the infirmary. The prison wasn't quiet. There were still shouts and curses in the main area that echoed back through the long corridor past the prison library and kitchens. The place seemed so alive after he had slayed the entire prison population in his dream.

"We got word about your friend," Miller said. "He's going to make it."

"Let me guess," Jude said. "The shiv punctured his diaphragm and stomach. They're watching him for infection."

"That's right," Munson said. "You a doctor?"

"No," Jude said. "I dreamed it."

"You dreamed it?"

"I dreamed that I broke into the doctor's office and called the hospital," Jude said.

"That could just be a coincidence," Munson said. "But I believe sometimes God gives us dreams."

"This was more of a nightmare," Jude said.

"Yeah? Maybe it's a warning."

That thought resonated with Jude. And he hadn't felt so much turmoil in his conscience since losing Alison. Fatigue was clinging to him. His hand was throbbing with pain, and he just wanted to close his eyes again, to make the whole world go away.

When they reached the row of solitary cells, Munson opened the first one. It was dank and smelled of urine and chemical cleaners.

"Hard to get the smell out of concrete sometimes," Munson said. "I'll try to reason with the warden next chance I get."

"Thanks," Jude said.

He went inside, and it felt like the weight of an entire mountain was pressing down on him. The metal slab was cold, but Jude didn't care. He was tired, bone tired. He lay down, used his good arm for a pillow, and fell asleep.

"Pssst! Hey man, you awake in there?"

The strange voice roused Jude. He didn't want to wake up, but he was cold. His entire left side was hurting almost as much as his broken hand. He had to move and work out the soreness.

"Am now," Jude grumbled.

The voice chuckled. "Well, well, I kinda thought you was dead," the voice said. "Been hollering at you for a while now, yes, sir. A while now."

Jude moved to the door and leaned his back against it. "I half wish I was."

"Bad day, eh? Yeah, I know all 'bout that right there. I've had a string of 'em for a while now, yes, sir."

"You got a name?"

"Sure do. My momma gave it to me. She called me Ritchie Lyon."

"I'm Jude. What are you down here for?"

"Don't really matter, does it? We all end up down here for the bad things we done. Ain't no body righteous, you hear what I'm saying?"

"Yeah, I hear you," Jude said, rubbing the back of his neck with his good hand.

"I heard about you, though. Everybody round here done heard about Olson. They say he speaks life and death. I don't know 'bout that, but I know a person pick up a bad rep, it can kind of warp 'em, like untreated wood left out in the wet and cold."

"I feel like I was left out in the wet and cold. It's freezing down here."

"Shor'nuff is," the voice said. "Stays cold down in the hole. The only thing worse is the fire that don't stop down in the pit, you know what I'm saying?"

"You religious, Ritchie?"

"We's all religious in the joint, man. Ain't no doubt 'bout that, right there, see. But not like them folks getting all dressed up to go to church on Sunday, no, sir. We the people of true religion. We live what we believe in here every single day."

"I don't know what I believe."

"Come on, now, Convict. 'Course you do."

"I thought I would get some justice here, but all I end up doing is getting people I care about hurt," Jude admitted.

"Them's that live by the sword, gonna surely die by the sword, now that's some hard, cold truth right there, yes sir."

"Some people die for no reason at all," Jude said, his voice brimming with emotion as he thought about Alison.

"Don't get it backward, sir. Death ain't the tragedy, it's them that live for no reason, no purpose, that's tragic. Truth is, we all die and that's no lie right there. But now, we all got a little something that we didn't earn, we didn't find, we didn't make, and we can't explain. We's just born with it. And that little something can lead to more, or it can lead to less. But it's what we do with that thing can't nobody make, can't nobody take away, that we's gonna hafta give an account for. You hear what I'm saying in there?"

Jude did hear, and he felt the words breaking up the fog in his mind. He thought about his own gifts. They were few, but powerful. And what did he have to show for it? Nothing good. He had abused his gift at first, then ignored it. And worst of all, he had gone to prison with the plan to use his gift in the worst way possible.

"I think it's too late for me," Jude said. "I'm too far gone."

Ritchie laughed again, then said, "Way I see it, you still breathing, yes sir. And long as you be drawing breath, you get to choose. Ole Joshua done said it best: Choose this day who you gonna serve. Man can't serve God and mammon, but you already knows that I think."

Jude didn't remember where he had heard the word mammon before, but somehow he knew it meant money.

"And maybe you been dancing around the edges with death herself. She's a crafty old heifer. Spins plenty a people right out their dancing shoes, they ain't careful. But it ain't never too late to turn yourself around, Ole-son. No, sir, it ain't never too late."

"I don't know how?" Jude said.

"That's cause you ain't supposed to do it all by your lonesome. No, sir! We got a friend; his name is Jesus. Now, all you gotta do is believe. And when you do, things will change."

Before Jude could respond, the bolt on the door to his cell slid back with a clang. Jude took a step forward. He was cradling his broken hand. Letting it hang at his side caused the blood to build up in and the throbbing was worse.

A guard that Jude had never seen before was just outside. He was bigger than any guard and any inmate, for that matter, that

Jude had seen. His shoulders were broad, and his hair was a golden color even in the dirty light of the subterranean bulbs outside the cells.

He didn't speak, but he had two blankets neatly folded, a pillow, a sling for Jude's arm, and on top of all that, a tray with a tall bottle of water, a bundt cake on a small paper plate, and a condiment cup with some medication. He held out the blankets, and Jude took them. Then the guard closed the door. Jude heard the bolt slide home.

He stood waiting for a few minutes, then he said, "Ritchie, did you see that guy?"

There was no response. Jude called out again, and then a third time, but there was never an answer. Confused, he went to the steel slab that he had slept on. He took the pills and drank a good bit of the water. He hadn't realized how thirsty he was. Then he began to unfurl the blankets. The fatigue was back on him. It seemed to weigh him down. To his surprise, between the blankets was a glow stick. He bent it until it snapped, and the chemicals inside began to glow. He could finally see inside the cell. To his surprise, there was writing on the wall. It was in black letters that looked like cave art, as if someone had a piece of charcoal and used it to write on the walls. It said:

And Elijah was afraid and ran for his life. When he came to Beersheba in Judah, he left his servant there, while he himself traveled on a day's journey into the wilderness. He sat down under a broom tree and prayed that he might die. "I have had enough, LORD," he said. "Take my life, for I am no better than my fathers."

Then he lay down under the broom tree and fell asleep. Suddenly an angel touched him and said, "Get up and eat." And he looked around, and there by his head was a cake of bread baked over hot coals, and a jar of water. So, he ate and drank and lay down again.

A second time the angel of the LORD returned and touched him, saying, "Get up and eat, or the journey will be too much for you." So, he got up and ate and drank. And strengthened by that food, he walked forty days and forty nights until he reached Horeb, the mountain of God.

It was odd, and Jude certainly didn't understand it, but on the tray was a little bunt cake. He ate it and drank some more water, then, with the mystery of the message on the wall, he fell asleep.

When he woke up, he couldn't tell how long he had been sleeping. In the hole, there was no difference between night and day. But unlike the last time, he wasn't in pain. He got up and moved around. The glow stick had barely any glow left. Still, he picked it up and went to look for the bottle of water. He found it, and to his surprise, there was more medicine in the cup and another little cake.

"I must be delirious," he thought.

He took the pills, ate the cake, and drank the rest of the water while he read the words on the wall over and over. He had to use the glow stick, holding it close to the wall to read the words, but they were there. And felt like he could hear them in his head, even after he lay back down. It was the part at the end that stuck out in his mind. *And strengthened by that food, he walked forty days and forty nights until he reached Horeb, the mountain of God.*

The cell door opened while Jude was still sleeping.

"On your feet!" An angry voice shouted at him. "Move it, convict!"

Jude sat up. His arm was in the sling and didn't hurt nearly as badly as before. As long as he didn't move it too much, the pain was bearable. He turned on the blanket that covered the steel slab. Looking down, he saw the tray and the empty bottle of water, even the glow stick that wasn't glowing anymore. And the words echoed in his mind, *...strengthened by that food, he walked forty days and forty nights until he reached Horeb, the mountain of God.*

All thoughts of vengeance were gone from his mind. Instead, he felt compelled to walk. So, he stood up and stretched.

"Get moving, you lazy oaf," the guard said.

Jude stepped to the door, saw that his tormentor was Officer Allen.

"You make trouble and I'll use leg irons on you, Olson," Allen threatened. "Just because you've got a busted arm doesn't mean I won't crack your skull if you try me."

"No," Jude said. "I won't. Who is Ritchie Lyons?"

"Who?"

"The other inmate in the hole."

Allen drew his baton and pushed Jude toward the stairs with the end of it. "You're losing your marbles. There are no other inmates in the hole."

"I heard him," Jude said. "Kind of a folksy guy. Ritchie Lyons."

"You're daft," Allen said. "Inmates can't talk to each other in solitary confinement, you idiot. Now move along!"

Jude was too afraid to ask about the big guard who brought the blankets and pillow. Not that he feared Allen. The man was sadistic, but Jude could control him easily enough. He was afraid of what the big guard really was. Could it have really been a messenger from... God? Jude didn't know what to think. He had never really believed in God. His own power was supernatural and proof that there was more to life than what could be seen and explained by naturalistic causes, and yet he had never given God a chance.

Why that was, he suddenly couldn't remember. He felt foolish, both for considering that God had spoken to him and for not giving God a chance. But the blankets had been real. The food, the medicine, and the water were real. Even the writing on the wall. He didn't know where it came from or why it was there, but the words had burned into his soul. And without another thought, he knew what he needed to do. God had strengthened him for a journey. And it was time he got a move on.

38

"Tell me," Jude said as they walked down the wide corridor past the prison kitchens. "Is Officer Munson on duty?"

"He is," Allen snapped. "No more talking."

"Radio for him to meet you at the Officer's break room," Jude said, ignoring the order for silence.

Through clenched teeth, Allen made the call. They reached the prison library, and Jude looked inside. He felt sorry that he hadn't done more for the place. He could have done a lot. He and Val, and Miller could have made the prison library a well-stocked, easy-to-operate section of the prison. His feelings about what the convicts deserved had changed. He still felt a sense of anger at the crimes that had been committed by the inmates, but he also could see Miller's point of view that people deserved a second opportunity to turn their lives around. It was possible, he realized. Under the right circumstances, it really was possible.

"You want me?" Munson asked.

"I did," Jude said.

"I told you to shut your trap!" Allen barked.

"You go take a break and forget about me," Jude said.

"I'm taking a break. Deal with this meat puppet, would you?" Allen said.

Munson shook his head and said, "I guess."

Jude waited until Allen was in the break room before explaining himself to Munson. "I've got new marching orders," he said.

"What's that mean? The warden wants to see you?"

"No, it's not the warden," Jude said. "What time is it?"

"Just after midnight," Munson said. "I think you'd better get back to your cell."

"No, you take me to the Admin building," Jude said.

"Or I can take you to the Admin building. Let's go."

They passed through Cellblock A. Despite the late hour, there were inmates yelling and cursing. Jude knew he wouldn't miss it.

"What's gotten into you?" Munson said.

"I think maybe you were right," Jude said. "Maybe my dream was a warning."

"Is that right?" Munson said, opening the doors to the cold, maze-like pathway that led to the Admin building.

"I think so," Jude said. "You're a religious man, aren't you?"

"You know that I'm a man of faith," Munson said.

"There's a message down in the hole."

"What did you write?"

"It wasn't me, but I think it was meant for me."

"You aren't making much sense, Olson."

"Don't I know it?" Jude replied.

They passed through the gates. It was dark and cold, but the snow had melted the day before. When they reached the admin center, Jude told Munson to wait for him. The computers in the Admin Center didn't have security passcodes. It only took Jude a few minutes to erase his files. They weren't gone forever. He knew they could be tracked down through the cloud, and there were hard copies somewhere, too. But it would slow down the hunt.

"I know what you're making me do," Munson said when Jude met him by the guard's entrance. "This isn't the way to do things. You'll just get caught, and there's no telling where they'll send you next.

"You guys occasionally have to run out and get something from the car that you forgot to bring in, right?"

"I won't help you escape, Jude."

"Call it in. Tell them you're running out to grab your lunch from your car."

"I drive a pick-up truck."

"Then tell them it's in your truck. Do it now."

Munson was conflicted, and for a moment, Jude thought the righteous guard might defy him. But then he reached up to his uniform mic and made the call. The outer door buzzed, and Jude pushed it open. He looked back at Munson.

"When this closes, make the call to open the staff gate," Jude said. "And you will forget you ever knew me."

"I won't forget," Munson said.

"You will, but I won't."

He closed the door to the admin building and walked to the metal gate in the wall of the prison. It wasn't the main gate, just a man door with a big metal bolt that suddenly slid back, and the door popped open. Jude stepped through and into the darkness on the outside of the prison walls.

Inside, Munson looked around, trying to remember what he had gone to the Admin building for. He lingered a few minutes, getting his lunch from his locker in the break room, then heading back to work in Cellblock A.

Outside, Jude moved quickly. The bright prison yard lights reflected off the low clouds and bounced down outside the prison walls. But the guards weren't looking outside the penitentiary. And even if they had, the big lights lit the interior so well that they had no night vision at all. Everything outside the prison was shrouded in gloom.

Jude could have taken someone's keys and stolen their car, but he didn't want to steal. He didn't want to break any laws, even though he was breaking the law just being outside the prison. He was a criminal, a murderer, after all. It wasn't justice that he was roaming free. He had taken a man's life. That man had children, even if they were estranged. It hadn't been Jude's right to take that life. But for some reason only God could fathom, he had other plans for Jude Olson.

He walked through the night. It was cold, but he stayed warm. He was moving through the woods and came upon a hunter's cabin. From the looks of it, no one had been in the little shack in a very long time. It didn't take much effort to get inside, and when he did, he discovered a chest with some hunting clothes inside. Camouflaged pants, green army issue tee-shirts, and a camouflage jacket. He removed his prison clothing and put on the camos. There was even a pair of army-style lace-up boots. They were too big, but with the extra socks he found in the chest, they worked just fine.

He carried his prison clothes into the woods and eventually tucked them under a fallen tree. At some point, the prison officials would figure out what happened to Jude Olson in cell three-five-three. They might send out search parties and eventually discover the prison clothes in the forest, but that felt like a long shot to Jude.

Around noon, the following day, he came upon a farm. The couple that owned it were elderly. The husband had a load of lumber in the back of an old pickup truck. Jude didn't need to use his gift to convince them he could help. They declared him to be a gift from God. The old man was trying to build a wheelchair ramp for his wife, who couldn't get around very well and couldn't climb stairs at all. It took the rest of the day with Jude's injured hand, but he remembered how good it felt to make something useful from a pile of lumber and do something for others. They insisted he spend the night. They had a big supper with fried chicken, mashed potatoes, green beans, sweet corn, and freshly made buttermilk biscuits.

The next day, the couple gave Jude a hundred-dollar bill and a Bible. He thanked them, but they insisted that he had helped them more than he could know. His walk continued for three more days before he ended up in a small town late in the afternoon. He was being careful with who saw him and how he spent the money the couple had given him. There were still three twenties and a few ones left in his pocket. He was walking down the street when he came to a Greyhound Bus terminal. People were boarding, and there was an agent at a little window taking tickets and handing out boarding passes. Forty dollars got Jude the one hundred and twenty miles he needed to travel.

It was nice to ride instead of walking. He sat by the window and looked at the scenery. Eventually, the bus reached Springdale. It was late at night, but Jude easily found a diner where he could get a late supper and kill most of the night sipping coffee. There was only one thing that Jude felt he had to accomplish: That was to help Miller in some way. When the sun rose, Jude found the lawyer in Springdale who was working on his case pro bono. Jude had to wait in the office for a while, but eventually the busy lawyer had time to see him.

"Hello, Mr. Price," the lawyer said, using the phony name that Jude had given him. "Welcome to legal aid. I'm Willie Parson. How can I help you?"

"I'm hoping I can help you," Jude said. "I'm an acquaintance of Oscar Miller."

"Is that so? I haven't been able to find too many people who will admit that around here."

"Which is why I'm here. I want to help."

"Do you know about his case?"

"Via Miller, yes."

"But you don't know the men who played cards with him the night his wife died? I really need their testimony to prove Mr. Miller's innocence."

"I don't, but I can find them," Jude said. "I can convince them."

"I'm not sure how," the lawyer said. "His first lawyer tracked them all down. They all denied knowing him or playing cards on the night of the murder."

"But you have other evidence, right?"

"We have the knife. I did manage to find the list of former soldiers whose initials were a match. There was one person of interest. Lewis Holms, who was released with a medical discharge, although I haven't been successful in getting copies of his medical file from the military. He was homeless at the time of the murder and got picked up, a few weeks later, ranting and raving. The police put him in the hospital, which held him in the psych ward. Again, they are not forthcoming with medical records, but I have reason to believe he had violent compulsions and acts out stabbing people quite often."

"That could be the guy," Jude said.

"It makes sense, but no one ever looked into him. Mr. Miller was the low-hanging fruit. His alibi didn't pan out, and there was trouble between him and his wife."

"Yeah, he told me as much. Give me the names and let me see what I can do to get you the testimony you need. Meanwhile, file a petition to retry the case."

"Under what grounds?"

"New evidence," Jude said.

"It would have to be very compelling evidence," the lawyer said.

"It will be. How quickly can we get a hearing?"

"Well, as you may know, Mr. Miller was stabbed in prison. He's recovering, but that may be enough to get us in front of a judge by the end of the week."

"Do it," Jude said. "I'll get the evidence we need."

With less than twenty dollars in his pocket, Jude needed a way to earn some money. He could have just compelled someone to give him funds, but he didn't want to do that. Instead, he found an ad on Craigslist for a construction laborer. The contractor took Jude on for site cleanup and paid him in cash. At night, Jude tracked the poker players down. He used his ability to compel them to tell the truth. They made statements to the legal aid lawyer. By the end of the week, he had an entire file of new evidence.

"All we have to do now is convince a judge," Parson said.

Jude bought a suit at the Goodwill store for just twenty dollars. It was old and not in style, but it fit, and with his hair growing out, Jude looked and felt like a new man. The motion before the judge went well in Jude's eyes, yet it quickly became evident that the judge had no intention of granting the appeal for a new trial. She was just about to make her ruling when Jude stood up.

"May I speak, your honor?"

"Who are you?"

"I'm a friend of the accused, your honor. You want to hear what I have to say."

She blinked several times as if she was confused, then nodded her head. "Go ahead then," she said with a sigh.

"You know the new evidence in this case is very compelling," Jude said, putting all the force of his will into every word. "You believe in justice and that sometimes the system fails. You want to see this case brought back before the court, and you are willing to grant the defendant a limited release to help prepare the case."

The woman on the bench was fifty years old. Her dark brown hair was sprinkled with gray, and she had large eyes. She blinked hard several times. When she spoke, she sounded a bit odd, as if she couldn't believe the words coming out of her own mouth.

"I'm granting the defendant's appeal for a new trial," she said. "I believe that sometimes the justice system fails the innocent. We can't let that happen here. In light of the attack that Mr. Miller suffered, I'm also granting him bail so that he can assist with his defense when he is physically able."

She wrapped her gavel on the bench, then left the courtroom. The legal aid lawyer dropped into his chair. He looked at Jude with utter disbelief.

"How did that just happen?" He asked.

"Sometimes the justice system gets it right," Jude said. "Are you going to see Oscar?"

"Yes!" The lawyer exclaimed. "Come with me. I have no idea how you got so much done so quickly, but you should see Miller. I'll take you. It's only about two and a half hours to the hospital in Duncan County."

"I'd love to see him," Jude said. "But I can't. Please tell him that I wish him well, and give him this letter for me."

Taking an envelope from his coat pocket, Jude handed it to the lawyer.

"Are you sure?"

"Positive," Jude said. "I've got other people to help. That's my purpose, and I don't want to waste another minute."

EPILOGUE

"We have him, sir."

"Good, don't lose him," Barnes said. "This slippery eel got past me once. Let's not let that happen again."

"No, sir," the agent in charge of the FRT said. His name was Todd Nix, and he had been part of the Fugitive Recovery Team of the FBI for over a decade. In all that time, he had never seen someone like Lucas Barnes. The man had an almost psychic knowledge of the fugitive. Jude Olson had secretly been placed on the most wanted list after his escape from the Duncan Supermax prison.

Nix understood why the Bureau of Prisons wouldn't want word to get out about the escape. The joint venture between the state and federal Corrections Departments had been plagued with difficulties. How an inmate managed to escape was not something the powers that be were willing to talk about. The entire case was classified. All Nix knew was that the fugitive had been found ... and not very far from the scene of the crime. He was in the same state and in a legal courthouse to boot. Nix thought it took real moxie to do something like that. Somehow, Barnes had known about the case and the very strong possibility that the fugitive would be in attendance.

"He's heading down that side street by the old department store," one of Nix's agents said.

"Good, we'll take them there. Hogan, get the van into position."

"Copy that", the agent behind the wheel of the vehicle they called the capture van said.

"Murphy, tell me you have this guy in your sights," Nix said.

"Plain as day. Just waiting on your go, no go, order," the sniper said.

"Take him down," Nix said.

The van drove quickly to the far end of the side street. Agents from either side of the street followed several yards behind the target. The long-range tranquilizer dart flew over their heads and hit Jude Olson in his left back shoulder. He cried out in pain, stumbling several steps forward just as the capture van rolled into view.

The pair of agents charged at Jude, who fell to his knees as the tranquilizer worked through his bloodstream, making him drowsy.

"You don't... want... to hurt...me," he managed to say before falling face down. His head was turned slightly. His cheekbone hit the pavement and split open. The agents grabbed his unconscious body and flung him into the van. Then jumped in after him.

"He's bleeding," Nix said, pulling the dart from his back.

They rolled him over and poured quick clot powder into the cut on his cheekbone. It was already swelling. Nix squirted super-glue into the wound and pinched it closed. They ran plastic restraints over his wrists and ankles. Then the agents sat back and 'high-fived' one another.

"Nice work," Nix said, congratulating his team. "Beer's on me tonight."

"That's what I'm talking about," the driver said.

"Pick up Murphy. We'll have this guy on a plane before he wakes up. Someone notify Barnes. This fugitive is his problem now."

Barnes was waiting in a hangar at the airport. The van pulled in next to a mid-sized private jet. The side door of the van slid open, and Nix jumped out.

"Here's your fish," the special agent in charge said. "Back in your net where he belongs."

"Is he conscious?" Barnes asked.

"Not yet. He'll be down another ten, fifteen minutes."

"Good, get him on the plane and we're done here."

The FBI agents loaded the fugitive onto the plane, strapping him into a seat and then heading back to their field office. As soon as they were gone, Barnes ordered the plane to take off. It had to get clearance from the flight tower and taxi into position. While the pilots did their job, Barnes used the power controls on the side of the seat Jude was strapped into. Once he was reclined back, Barnes took out a fat syringe full of pink liquid from a bag, along with a plastic tongue compressor. He opened Jude's mouth, pressed his tongue down with the plastic instrument, and squirted the liquid into his mouth. It immediately turned to foam, filling Jude's mouth and sealing it off even though it was open as wide as possible.

Five minutes later, the plane was climbing into the air. Barnes had already fixed himself a scotch and strapped in across the aisle from Jude, who was just starting to wake up. He sipped his beverage and gave the groggy fugitive a little more time. When the plane reached altitude, it leveled out, and Barnes leaned over toward Jude.

"Don't puke," he said. "You'll choke to death, and neither of us wants that headache."

Jude couldn't speak. He tried to move his mouth and work out the obstruction, but couldn't. He started to raise his hands, but he couldn't raise them.

"Oh, I tied down the restraints. We can't have you pulling that foam out of your mouth. You and I both know what you're capable of when you're free to speak."

Jude groaned, turning his head from side to side, but it was no use.

"It's the same foam they use when making a mold for your teeth," Barnes said with his evil grin. "Not toxic, but very effective in sealing off your mouth, and precluding your tongue from moving. It won't come free unless we pull it out, and that might take your teeth too. We'll find a more permanent solution back at the facility where I keep people like yourself. We can always have your tongue, teeth, and lips removed. It might be easier to just clip your vocal cords. I'll have to talk to our physician and decide, but you know, it is possible to have a permanent feeding tube. We can pump your stomach full of a nutrient solution, think of it like baby formula. It can keep you going for decades."

He got to his feet and went to a bar at the back of the airplane and sat down heavily in the seat with another scotch.

"I've got to say, I really thought you had bigger plans than just running away," Barnes continued. "But hey, to each his own. You managed to slip past the assassin I brought in, and he's a heavy hitter. Kiner has over fifty kills. I'd put him up there with any spec op goon. He's not quite talented enough to be in my program, but he's close. I'm glad you didn't kill him. He's bound to come in handy down the road."

Jude struggled against his bonds, but they were too strong to break. His heart was pounding, and it was hard to breathe just through his nose. He felt like he was going to gag, but he knew Barnes was right. If he threw up, it would kill him.

"You're going to like it at my place," Barnes said. "We built it especially for unique individuals just like you. It's quiet, not like a regular prison. And more comfortable too. Good food, oh, but that probably won't matter to you, will it?"

Barnes laughed. It was an evil cackle, almost maniacal. But Jude closed his eyes. He knew there was a reason he had been led from the Duncan Supermax. He wasn't going to panic just because Barnes had tracked him down. There was something out there, something bigger than himself. It was something worth believing in. Jude felt certain it had a purpose for him. So, he forced himself to relax. He slowed his breathing and stopped fighting. The time would come for him to act. A tiny opportunity would be all it took, and he would be ready when the time came. Barnes had the upper hand for the moment, but he wouldn't always. When the time came, Jude would help him shuffle off this mortal coil. All it would take was a few simple words.

AFTERWORD

I love writing books like these. Sometimes they come all in a rush. In fact, this book came tumbling out almost all at once. There is more to this story in my mind; in fact, there is a series of stories with other people of power. We'll just have to see how this book fares. If you liked it and would enjoy more of Jude's story, you can help by rating and reviewing the book. And telling your friends about it, too.

If you liked *Sons of Perdition*, you might also really enjoy *Blood Moon*. Continue reading for a preview.

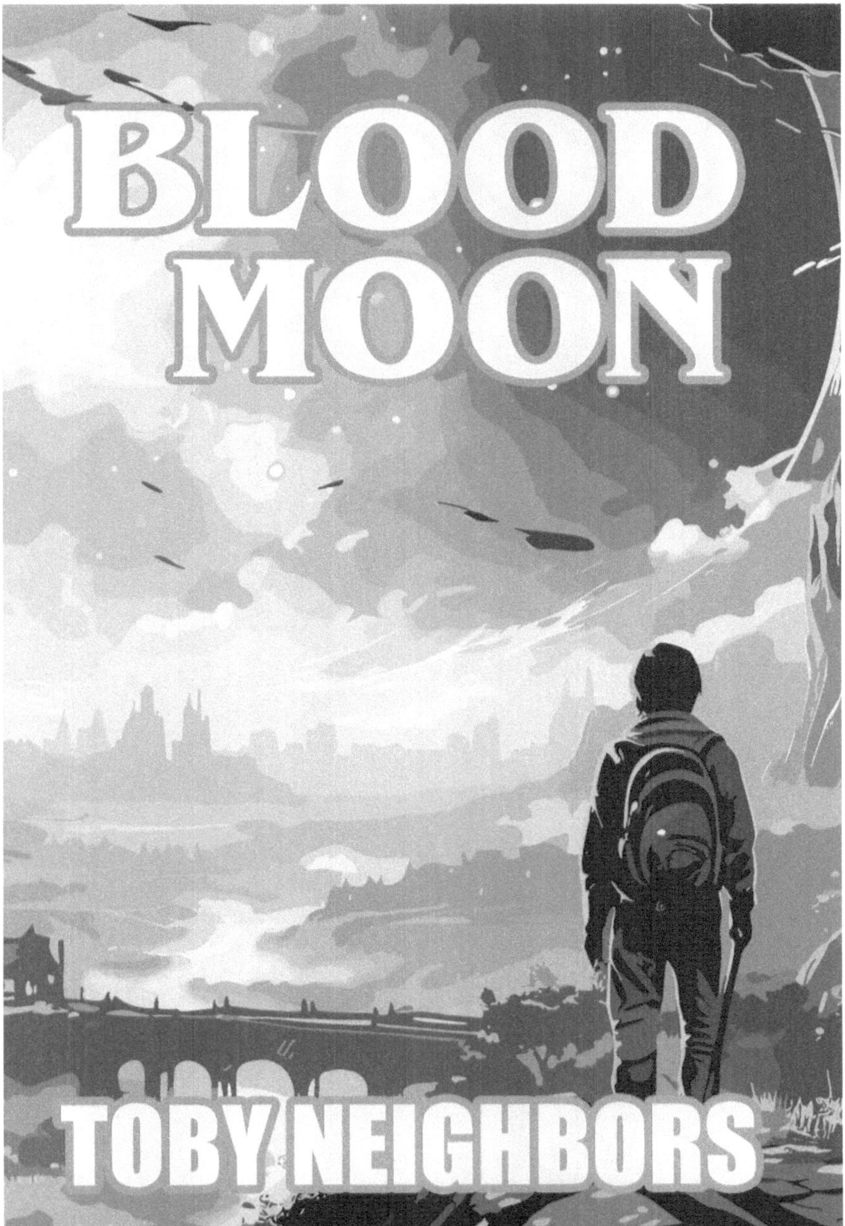
BLOOD MOON
TOBY NEIGHBORS

BLOOD MOON SAMPLE

Chapter 1

Daniel Rapp walked into the local convenience store, Jordan's Quick Stop, as he did most mornings before work. It was right on the main highway through the valley on the opposite side of the street from the Salmon River. He could still hear the rush of the waters over the round, mossy stones as he walked to the small counter where Brenda Day sold breakfast burritos.

"Morning," Daniel said as Brenda pushed a foiled-wrapped burrito toward him.

There was no need to ask what he wanted. Daniel Rapp was a man of routine. He got up at the same hour every day, and six days a week, he went into the Quick Stop on his way to work and bought the same meal from the same people. They often had the same conversations. That was the way of life in Abbie's Ford. The locals, all two hundred and eighteen of them, lived small town lives. The only industry in the valley was tourism. Anglers from all over the country made their way to Abbie's Ford, where some of the best trout fishing in the world was found. It was also a jumping-off point for hunters pushing into the Payette National Forest, where big game animals, from mountain lions to big horn sheep, could be sought and often found if a person had the stamina to trek out into the rugged terrain.

Normally, Brenda had plenty to say. Everything, from the weather to the tourists and their often odd behavior, was fair game in the Quick Stop. The Days did a brisk business selling gasoline to travelers, as well as snacks and beverages. But Brenda didn't say a word as she pushed his burrito across the counter. Daniel turned and looked around. There was no one else in the store. No vehicles were parked outside. Brenda's husband, Gary, was on his stool by the register, looking at his smartphone. One of the biggest draws to the Quick Stop was the free wi-fi, which the Days were able to get via the satellite on the roof of their store. But Daniel didn't have a smartphone and didn't need the wi-fi, just his breakfast.

He walked over to the cooler, retrieved his usual carton of chocolate milk, and went to the register. The charge for his two items was the same every day, and Daniel paid in cash. He laid seven dollars on the counter, which Gary took without a word. Daniel didn't mind the silence; he was a solitary person, but he found Gary's behavior strange.

"Everything okay, Gary?" Daniel asked.

"Sure," the proprietor said, dropping the four pennies, which were Daniels's change, into the Take-a-Penny-Leave-a-Penny jar.

"Alright then, see you around," Daniel said, before pushing open the door and heading toward the street.

The highway could be busy and was sometimes dangerous. The speed through Abbie's Ford was listed at twenty-five miles per hour. But with no police to enforce the speed limit, outsiders sometimes drove faster. Daniel looked both ways, then walked across the two lane county road. On the far side was a slight incline down to the river and a jumble of boulders stuck out into the water from the bank. Daniel walked out onto them and sat down to enjoy his breakfast. On his right was a back-flowing eddy where a big rainbow trout lived in the lee of the overhanging rock. Occasionally, it would venture out where Daniel could see it as it chased a water bug for its breakfast.

Despite the occasional highway noise, Daniel liked the river. It was why he had settled in Abbie's Ford, to begin with. There was something majestic about it. Despite whatever was happening in the world and in Daniel's life, the river continued to flow. Thousands of gallons rushed by every minute of every day. It amazed Daniel that the river never ran dry. It had been flowing through the valley since before there was a country or even people to see it. And it would continue flowing, day after day, year after year, long after Daniel was dead and gone. The river filled him with a sense of peace and helped him focus on the good things in the world. Everyone was always going on about the bad things; you couldn't pick up a newspaper or magazine without hearing about some awful tragedy. And Daniel couldn't understand why anyone would want a smart phone which kept people tethered to a constant flow of bad news. He preferred the constant flow of the river and the knowledge of how it brought life to the land around them.

Finishing his breakfast, he got to his feet and walked back across the highway. His empty foil wrapper and milk carton went into the trash can beside the fuel pumps at the Quick Stop. Then Daniel turned north and took a walking path past a few other local shops. There was Sally's General Store, the Salmon River Outfitters, Lawson's Fly Shoppe, Morgan's Deli and Ice Cream, Savanna's Beauty Supply, Tito's Pizza, and Rustler's Burgers and Beer. They were small town shops run by the people whose names were on the signs. They all catered mostly to the tourists passing through. For instance, Kyle Morgan made more selling bags of ice to fishermen than he did making sandwiches. It was a short walk to Lutum's Sportsman's Depot, where Daniel worked as the resident gunsmith. It was a quiet job, just Danny and his tools and the guns brought in for cleaning and repairs. He worked from a tiny little room in the back, rarely coming out to speak with the customers. Reginible Lutum was a seventy-five-year-old Polish immigrant who had opened the Sportsman's Depot almost forty years prior. He had done his own gunsmithing for the first thirty years, but his failing eyesight and arthritis in his fingers forced him to bring in outside help.

The Depot had a backdoor, but no one used it. The store was a square with big windows facing the highway and the river beyond. Around the other three sides of the store was a counter with a glass front and shelves inside displaying hundreds of pistols. The top of the counter was pine with a high gloss varnish, and behind the counter were racks of rifles. Most were built for hunting, although Reginible carried a few custom assault rifles that they had worked up together. The assault rifles were usually purchased more as souvenirs than shooting weapons, even though the custom rifles cost more than just about any other gun in the shop.

There were racks of camouflage clothing, hip waders, chest waders, and all sorts of accessories for the weapons sold. What the depot didn't carry was anything for fishing. Reginible and Wayne Lawson had an agreement that neither would compete for the other man's business. There were other shops, of course. A person could buy fishing gear at JC's Convenience Store or guns at the Salmon River Outfitters, which was a store at the edge of town. There wasn't much more to Abbie's Ford. There was a farm supply, a veterinary clinic, and an auto mechanic, but no churches, no doctors, not even a Post Office. All those things could be found in the towns up and down the highway. They sprang up wherever the land between the mountains widened enough, but the closest was Crossington, forty miles to the south.

Danny walked in the front door of the Sportsman's Depot, causing the little bell on the door to jingle. Old man Lutum, his friends called him Reggie, looked up wide-eyed.

"Have you seen the news, Danny?"

"No," he replied with a shrug. "Never anything good."

"Look at this!" Reginible said, spinning the computer monitor around.

It had cost him nearly a thousand dollars to have a high-speed internet connection at the store, but the state had required it of all gun dealers. Idaho still required a background check before a pistol could be sold, and they had their database online. Reginible kept one computer at the store just for that purpose, but like most people, he also surfed the internet and kept up with the news online. Lately, he had spent most of his free time reading stories about the Presidential election, but when he turned the flat screen monitor around, Danny saw something he thought he would never see again.

"It's you!" Reggie declared.

Danny shook his head. "No, it isn't."

"It's the spitting image of you, Danny!" the old man insisted.

Danny suddenly felt like he might be sick. The image on the screen was the top of a news story. In bold letters under what looked like a picture of Danny Rapp were the words *Mansfield Terror Captured At Last.*

"That's not me, Reg. That's my twin brother Nate. And I'm not surprised."

Chapter 2

Wagner bent low to see the print on the game trail. Something had passed along the path and stepped right where a spring trickled from under a rock and softened the ground. The print was pristine, and Wagner was an expert woodsman. He had seen every kind of print there was in the wild places, including some that couldn't be easily explained. More than once, he had seen the prints of human-like feet that measured over fifteen inches. Not a boot track, but a bare foot, what the locals jokingly referred to as the "big fella." Central Idaho was not a haven for Sasquatch enthusiasts. They preferred the easy country of the Pacific Northwest. Idaho was too rugged. The interior of the state was all but impassible except for a few places where a man on foot or an experienced rider could cut trail on horseback.

The single track Wagner was studying at the moment was different. He was hiking out of the forest after resupplying several caches with useful gear, everything from first aid supplies to extra ammunition. He kept everything in a water proof bag that was bright orange. He hung them from tree limbs at least twenty feet off the ground. Come mid-November, he would lead hunters into the high country. It was one of the most dangerous places in the country, with the snow and freezing temperatures making it even more hazardous. But no one would be hunting whatever had made the track on the game trail.

Reaching out with a finger he felt the soil around the track. It was still very soft, but that was from the spring. That section of ground probably never got dry, making it next to impossible to tell how old the track was, but nothing had crossed the track even though it was a busy game trail. Kneeling down, he studied the track. He stretched out his hand, spreading his fingers wide. The track, which looked mostly like a wolf print, was slightly different in the way the pads spread out and the nails dug into the soft ground. The other difference was the size. It was bigger than Wagner's hand, which made no sense at all. Wolves often had big paws, significantly larger than the average pet dog but nowhere near the size he was seeing on the trail.

"Who are you?" Wagner said. He was known for talking to

himself. It was a habit he picked up, spending most of his time alone in the wilderness. "Dire wolf, maybe? Is that possible?"

He remembered hearing about wolves in the ice age that were larger than the modern wolves, but he didn't think anything but a grizzly bear had a track as big as he was seeing. Not to mention that dire wolves were supposed to be extinct.

"It's a mystery, alright," he said.

He pulled out a little disposable camera. Wagner didn't eschew modern technology, but there was no cell phone signal in the mountains, and he just couldn't justify the expense of getting one. The little disposable cameras were still only fifteen dollars at Sally's General Store, and she only charged him five bucks to print the pictures. He started to lay a coin beside the print for scale, but the biggest he had was a quarter, and the print was enormous next to the coin. He put the quarter back in his pocket and pulled out a wrinkled dollar bill. It took the old hunter a few seconds to smooth it out, but once he had it lying straight, he checked the focus on the little camera and snapped a picture.

"Interesting," he said.

He put the dollar and the camera back into his pockets, which were stuffed with other useful bits of gear. Wagner generally wore cargo pants that tucked into his boot tops. It was a habit he picked up in the army. As he stood up, he checked the straps on his backpack. It wasn't nearly as heavy since most of the gear he had carried in was used to resupply the caches in the forest. Still, he hated a loose pack. He had a stainless steel Colt Python revolver in a thigh holster on his right leg. It was the Anaconda model with a six-inch barrel that fired .44 magnum caliber rounds. His was loaded with hydro-shock hollow point bullets that would stop just about anything that came charging at him. But the pistol was just an emergency use weapon. He had a variety of hunting rifles, but his go-to firearm was a Browning .308 with a Vortex 20x scope. It had been a gift from his wife the Christmas she had been battling breast cancer. That was half a lifetime ago, when the prognosis for this disease was dire. Wagner's wife was gone by Easter, but that Christmas was a warm memory that he still held dear thirty-five years later.

The Browning fit easily in the crook of his arm, and he continued his hike out of the woods. Four hours later, just before dark set in, he reached his Jeep. It was a little Wrangler hard top, just two doors and fifty thousand miles on her. Wagner had installed a winch on front and trailer hitch on the back. The wheels were big, knobby, off-road tires that could handle slick, muddy, or snowy trails. He tossed his backpack into the rear, slid the Browning .308 into a sleeve that was mounted against the inside of the vehicle, and settled his lanky frame behind the wheel. He had been gone for three days, and it felt good to sit in a comfortable seat again. He opened the glove box and got himself a candy bar. That was his one vice. Wagner didn't smoke or drink; the strongest drug he ever took was an Aspirin, and even though his wife was no longer alive, he didn't run around. He had only ever loved two things. His wife had passed away, leaving him only the outdoors. And he was content with that and the occasional chocolate bar.

The Jeep started easily, and Wagner began the slow descent down a narrow, twisting trail. It couldn't be called a road; no regular vehicle could make the trip. It took a rugged four-by-four with plenty of clearance and good traction. But the trip down was easier than the trip up. It still took an hour to reach the highway. Like most residents of Abbie's Ford, the cabin that Wagner called home was up the hill, as the locals called the mountains on the highway side of the river. It was a small place, just one room, but with expansive views of the valley, the Salmon River, and the Selkirk Mountains. Wagner showered, changed into some clean clothes, and traded his big revolver for a small .45 automatic that slipped into a belly holster that tucked comfortably inside the waistband of his blue jeans. Wagner didn't expect any trouble, but carrying was just a way of life in the little town where freedom and old fashioned American values still carried a lot of weight.

Wagner got back into his Jeep and headed into town. There were two things to do in town after dark. Laird's Pub was for those wanting to drink their sorrows away. And the locals had plenty they wanted to forget. Everyone lived with the pressures of life weighing heavily on their shoulders. Taxes, upkeep on their homes and businesses, and making ends meet were getting more and more difficult. Since the Covid fiasco of 2020, the world had gone mad. The locals living nearly off the grid in Abbie's Ford didn't care about masks, vaccines, or what was considered essential businesses. They continued on as if nothing had changed, except that the tourist industry, which the town depended on, vanished, and the prices of everything went through the roof. Half the town was forced to shutter their stores or take out loans to get through the hard times. And the usual strategy of just laying low until things settled back to normal simply didn't apply. Homes and property values doubled, which meant property taxes doubled. Many of the locals owned their homes and businesses, but the sudden surge in value created a hardship for most, especially as the tourist business was slow to restart once the country opened back up again. It was a nightmare the town was still struggling with ... or striving to forget.

The other option after dark was The Lighthouse Grill. Wagner had no idea why it was called the Lighthouse since they were hundreds of miles from the ocean, but it had been around longer than he had. It was a quiet cafe serving home cooked food and where most of the locals gathered to gossip after work. They served beer and wine, but nothing harder, and most of the patrons sat outside on the wide porch built to overlook the river. It was one of the few establishments on the river side of the highway, and like the rest of Abbie's Ford, Wagner was a regular.

He walked in, waved to Jessica who was working the tiny bar, and stepped out onto the back deck. He found Reggie, Kyle Morgan, and Wayne Lawson at their regular table. Wagner pulled out a chair and joined the men.

"Fellas," he said.

"You just get back?" Lawson asked.

Wagner nodded. "Up country, getting ready for the season."

"Then you ain't heard the news," Reggie asked.

"What news?" Wagner asked.

"Tell him," Kyle urged.

Reggie pulled out his phone. It was a flashy new model, the biggest smartphone on the market. Reggie didn't like to wear glasses, although he needed them. Instead, he just enlarged everything on the screen so he could read it.

"There," he said, sounding almost triumphant. "That's news."

The text on the screen filled the device. It read, *Mansfield Terror In Custody, Police Convinced They Have Their Man.* He knew about the murders. There were half a dozen of them, all runaways or prostitutes. The Mansfield Terror was big news all across the country and had been for a while, but it was on the East Coast, thousands of miles away. If that sort of nutcase had tried to kidnap or kill someone in Abbie's Ford, he would have had a real fight on his hands.

"They caught the guy," Wagner said. "I suppose that's something."

"Scroll down," Lawson said.

Wagner gave the image a flick with his index finger. The text gave way to the picture of a man that looked exactly like Wagner's closest friend. Few things in the world shocked the old hunter, but seeing the picture of a man he thought he knew very well wearing handcuffs and walking between a gang of uniformed police toward a courthouse was completely unexpected.

"This can't be," he said.

"It's not," Reggie jumped in.

"He's got a brother," Kyle said. "A twin brother."

"Really?" Wagner said. "I never heard him mention it."

"I don't think he ever has," Reggie said, clearly excited. "But when I showed him the news this morning, that's what he told me. It's his brother, and he wasn't surprised."

Before Wagner could comment on the staggering revelation, Jessica appeared with a tall, red plastic cup filled with Pepsi Cola. She set it in front of Wayne and put a hand on his shoulder.

"They telling you the news?"

"We sure are," Reggie said.

"It's not anything to be proud of," Jessica said. "You want your usual, Wayne?"

"Yes, ma'am."

"It's a shame. Everyone's talking about it. They'll be in his business before long," she went on. "Word'll get out, and there'll be news reporters poking around here before long. Mark my words on that. They'll want him to talk about it. And they'll want pictures."

"Could be good for business," Lawson said.

"Doubt that, honey," Jessica replied.

She sauntered away, and the four men watched her go. They were all older men, and Jessica was only thirty. But she was beautiful, and she knew it.

"Is he here somewhere?" Wagner asked, looking around the patio.

The Lighthouse did have lights strung up all around the outside and criss-crossing the awning that hung over the patio. There were lights along the edge of the deck, too, their light reflecting off the clear water that went rushing by night and day.

Most of the tables were occupied. Some were summer people —wealthy folks who had big homes along the highway overlooking the river. They usually only spent the summers in Abbie's

Ford and headed south in the fall before the tourists started arriving. Wagner knew that many even rented out their fancy homes during the tourist season and probably made enough for upkeep and the taxes. Many of the locals worked managing the rentals or as cleaning staff for the big homes.

There were plenty of townsfolk out that night, too, but Daniel wasn't one of them.

"Nah, he's staying home tonight," Reggie said. "Maybe for a while. He wouldn't talk about it after I showed him the news. Just locked himself up in his work area. I didn't even see him at lunchtime."

"Can't say I blame him," Kyle said. "He's a man who likes his privacy."

"He's been through a lot," Wagner said.

"But he never told you about his brother?" Lawson said.

"Never a word," Wagner said. "I don't know any more than the rest of you."

"They say his brother, Nathaniel T. Rapp, is his name," Reggie said in a conspiratorial tone, "killed at least six people. But he kidnapped more than that. Played head games with them. Drugged them even, and then let them go."

"I saw a special on it," Lawson said. "Before they caught him. Some of the victims talked about it. You could tell it scared the hell out of 'em."

"Of course it did," Kyle jumped it. "It would wreck anyone to have their life threatened in that way."

Wagner didn't argue. He knew what it was like to know that at any moment, you could die. He had served two tours in the sandbox, first in Bagdad and the second in Afghanistan. The United States forces were hated in the Middle East. Wagner had seen snipers shoot his fellow soldiers. Some were attacked while on patrol or during raids in the hostile sections of the cities. IEDs or Improvised Explosive Devices killed as many as the ISIS and

Taliban fighters. It was a stress that changed a person and not in a good way. For years after returning, the memories and nightmares had haunted Wagner. If not for his wife, he didn't think he would have made it. She was the balm he needed and helped him heal. He wished every day that he could have done the same for her.

"They'll all be back on the news," Reggie said. "And Jessica's right. Once the paparazzi find out about our boy, they'll come snooping around."

"And word will spread too," Lawson said. "It's hard to believe that someone that sick in the head could have a normal sibling."

"Twin brother," Reggie said. "Identical."

"So we form up around him," Wagner said. "We'll buffer when the vultures descend. Give the kid a chance to live a normal life."

"Yeah, the last thing we need is a bunch of people in town trying to see the freak whose brother killed all those people," Kyle said. "That can't be good for business."

"Can't guide tourists if people can't get accommodations," Wagner pointed out.

"More people coming in will drive up the rates, too," Reggie said. "It might look good at first, but if they're not here to hunt or fish..."

"Then we go out of business," Lawson said.

"So we don't let that happen," Wagner said. "He's our friend."

"Some things can't be helped," Kyle pointed out. "I don't know that there's much we can do about it. Friend or not, we don't have control of who comes and who goes."

"He might go," Lawson said. "Wouldn't be the first time bad news chased someone out of the valley."

"No, that's not an option," Wagner said.

"Agreed," Reggie said. "I could never replace him."

"Maybe if you paid a little more," Lawson remarked.

"I cannot afford to pay more and you know it," Reggie said. "A few more years, and I'll give him the store. He knows it."

"Makes sense," Kyle said. "His brother shot all the people he killed. There hasn't been anyone like that since Son of Sam. And his brother owns a gun shop."

"He doesn't own it yet," Reggie said.

"I'm just saying..." Kyle replied.

Jessica returned with a hamburger for Wagner. He thanked her and let his friends continue gossiping. It was to be expected. Few things happened in Abbie's Ford that people didn't see coming. But Daniel Rapp's brother would be all over the news, just like Ted Kaczynski or the BTK Killer out of Kansas. The press loved a gory headline. They would follow the trial, and there would be more television specials about it. Maybe movies, too, with actors that looked so much like Danny that he wouldn't get a minute's peace. Everywhere he went, people would ask him about it or, at the very least, whisper about him. It was going to be a nightmare and Wagner just hoped his friend could withstand the storm.

Chapter 3

Daniel went home after work, as he always did. *Routine is the key to not being caught*, his father used to say. In fact, he drilled it into Daniel and his brother Nathaniel. But he didn't like to think about his formative years and especially his father. That was all behind him or it had been, until Nathaniel went and got himself caught. It was on purpose, Daniel knew, because Nathanial never did anything without a purpose.

The walk up the hill was tiresome after a long day at work, but it was good to exercise his legs and get his wind up a little. He spent all day long in a workshop barely larger than a closet. He kept his door closed except when his boss, Reginible, brought him something new to work on. And there was always something new. People loved their toys, and for a great many Americans, their toys were guns. Pistols, rifles, sporting weapons, hunting weapons, show weapons, and antique weapons, there was never a shortage of toys. Most of the people who brought the weapons in were hunters. Many were sport hunters, the type with money to burn and who didn't mind paying to have their weapons modified, if only slightly. Custom was king in a world full of stock weaponry. Reginible was only too happy to do whatever the customer wanted as long as they were willing to pay. So Daniel stayed busy in his little workshop.

The truth was, he loved the job. The work was simple enough. Mechanical things always spoke to him. Every part had a function and it was satisfying to Daniel to explore that function. He would clean each part, oil those in need, make sure everything worked as it was supposed to work, and occasionally, that meant replacing something that was too far gone. But in the gunsmithing world it is preferable to fix the original parts rather than replace anything.

Daniel normally listened to the radio while he worked. He kept a small one hanging on the pegboard among his various tools. The chrome antenna was always fully extended, and still the device only picked up two stations. One was a sports talk station, the other easy listening music. Daniel liked both. But what he liked more than his tools, which he took care of in a fastidious nature, each one cleaned and always in its place, and more than the radio was the solitude. Daniel was a solitary person. Not that he didn't have friends. In fact, he walked home every day, showered, changed clothes, then walked down to the cafe for his dinner, where he usually sat with friends. His friends in Angie's Ford were just the type that Daniel liked. They didn't ask too many questions about his past, and they did most of the talking. There were nights when Daniel sat for a few hours and didn't say a single word. That was just fine with him.

But it was good to get his blood pumping and his breath

puffing just a little. It helped get the heavy tang of gun oil, which surrounded him all day, out of his head and lungs. The short walk up the hill didn't keep Daniel in tip-top shape, but it was a good little jaunt to keep him from getting too soft. His thighs burned as he walked up the winding trail. There were more trails than roads in Angie's Ford. It was another thing he loved about the little town. But he wasn't thinking about his thighs or his friends at the cafe, which he knew he wouldn't see that night. He was thinking about his brother.

Nathaniel Rapp was very much like his twin brother. They were identical, although it had been years since they saw one another. Daniel wasn't surprised to see that Nathaniel had the same haircut as Daniel. It was a twin thing, an unspoken manner that extended beyond actions. They thought the same, liked the same things, and had many of the same talents. Daniel and Nathaniel were talented in many ways, some of them Daniel tried his best never to think about. The one big difference between the twins was their interest. Daniel liked mechanical things, always had. He liked to take them apart, see how they worked, study each component, and reassemble them. When he was young, he often thought he could improve things and had been successful in doing just that. But Nathaniel was different. His interest was in living things, although his way of exploring them was much the same as Daniel's. His fascination started with dead things: a bird with a broken neck, a squirrel hit by a car, an old alley cat that died of old age. Daniel didn't like his brother's proclivities, but they were bonded on many, many levels. Still, it didn't take Nathaniel long to move on to studying living things, and so Daniel had known where the strange interest would lead.

Their home life didn't help matters. But Daniel pushed those painful memories away. He couldn't keep his father's voice out of his head, though. *Routine is the key to not getting caught.* And it wasn't just a memory; it was a command. One that Daniel couldn't break out of even after twelve years and three thousand miles of distance from the old man. Daniel still followed a set routine nearly every single day.

His home was a cabin. It had been built well over a century before Daniel showed up in Angie's Ford. It wasn't abandoned, just unmaintained. That had been just fine with Daniel. He swapped rent for maintenance and soon had the old place in good order. It was a single room, heated by a wood stove, cooled by the mountain breeze that wafted in through open windows and the occasional gap that formed between the old fir logs used to build it. In winter, Daniel mended the plaster between the logs, but every spring, new gaps formed, and Daniel let them stay. He called it poor man's air conditioning, but there were very few people who ever visited him at the cabin. It was another way Daniel had of protecting himself. *Home life is private*, his father had always said. Daniel and his brother weren't allowed to talk about their parents or their lives at home. They never had friends over and certainly no sleepovers. The family moved around a lot, so it was just Daniel and Nathaniel, the twins, brothers and best friends, until they weren't, until the bad times that had scarred Daniel's soul and drove him away from the family.

He reached the cabin door and pulled it open. He was met with silence and stillness in the tiny, one room cabin. Running water and a bathroom had been added sometime in the seventies. The add-on had been crude but effective. Daniel had improved it greatly, but the cabin was still a very simple affair: a bed, a single recliner, and a small table to eat at with mismatched wooden chairs. Everything was secondhand and well-mended. The refrigerator was as old as the bathroom add-on, but it had come back to life easily enough and still kept things cold. Daniel didn't keep a lot of groceries. Just a few frozen meals for when the odd occasion arose that he didn't feel like going to the cafe. And that was exactly how he felt on the day his brother was arrested back east.

The day his life, normally so uneventful and routine, took an unexpected hard turn.

It had been twelve years since he last saw his brother. And until that morning when Reggie showed Daniel the news on the store's computer, he hadn't thought of Nathaniel in a long time. Not that he didn't still feel the twin connection. That's what their father had called it, the twin connection, a sort of bond that Daniel shared with his brother that was unlike any other relationship he had with anyone else. Certainly not with his parents, who were abusive and controlling. And not with anyone else he ever met. No friend was ever as close; no lover ever knew Daniel as well as his brother did. And there were times when they shared emotions without ever saying a word. Even after years apart and a great distance from Nathaniel, there were times when, out of the blue, Daniel was hit by a strange emotion, usually a sense of joy that he couldn't understand, but sometimes sadness or frustration. They were the emotions his brother was experiencing, and it was just another reason why Daniel tried to avoid anything that might surprise or delight him, just the way most people tried to avoid disappointment and sadness. The last thing he wanted was to attract his brother's attention.

He walked into the dark cabin and turned on the battery-powered lamp that sat on a small side table next to the recliner and a stack of books. The old cabin had running water but no electricity. There was talk of getting some solar panels, but Daniel didn't think he needed them. The refrigerator and microwave were the only two electronic devices in the cabin, and they were kept running with a little wind turbine on the roof. It was one of the ways that Daniel kept his costs down. He didn't own a car, didn't have health insurance, there were no credit cards or student debt to repay, and other than his monthly supplies that he picked up at Sally's General Store. Reggie paid Daniel four hundred dollars cash every week. Out of that, he spent seven dollars a day on breakfast, thirteen for his lunch, and twenty for dinner, always cash. That left him with an extra hundred and twenty a week, which he saved until the first of the month when he spent around seventy-five dollars at the General store buying necessities and a few frozen meals for the rare times he didn't eat dinner at the Lighthouse. The rest went into an emergency cash reserve, which he kept hidden inside his go bag just in case he had to leave in a hurry.

He opened a box that contained spaghetti and a single piece of garlic toast. It went right into the microwave. Daniel unplugged the refrigerator and plugged the microwave into the single 110-volt outlet that was connected to the battery, which was charged by the wind turbine. The old refrigerator had no trouble staying cold while the microwave was in use as long as Daniel didn't open it up.

With his dinner cooking, he pulled off his boots and set them in the little tray next to the door. In the winter, they would be covered with snow, and in the spring, they would be muddy. The tray kept the moisture off the cabin floor. It was wide oak planking, which Daniel had refinished and sealed. When the microwave beeped, he pulled out the tray, peeled back the plastic cover, and gave the meal a stir. Then he popped it back in for another minute. When that finished, he plugged the refrigerator back in and let the steaming hot tray cool while he took a fast shower. His showers in the cabin were always fast. There was no hot water heater. Instead, Daniel filled a reservoir each morning that was, at best, lukewarm by evening. He bathed quickly and put on fresh clothes, then sat down to eat the sad little dinner he made for himself.

Most of the people living in Abbie's Ford ate wild game and fresh fish. Daniel wasn't opposed to that fare; in fact, when he was invited to dinner with friends, he enjoyed their fresh proteins, but Daniel didn't hunt or fish. He didn't kill anything, not even the spiders or house flies that often invaded his cabin. He wasn't squeamish; he just preferred not to do the dirty work himself. So he ate the microwave dinner, then poured himself a Pepsi over ice and settled into his recliner.

But that night, the books simply wouldn't hold his attention. All he could think about was Nate in a jail somewhere. The guards probably thought him strange. His crimes had made him a celebrity. And yet Daniel knew that his brother wouldn't have allowed himself to be caught if it didn't serve a purpose. That's what really bothered him. Daniel couldn't figure out what his brother was up to. He knew it would plague him all night and it did. He sat in his chair, frustrated while staring at the same page for hours. Eventually, there was a knock at his door. And that, too, bothered him. He had known she would come and would push for answers he didn't want to give her. But he couldn't disappear. That would be reactionary and he had been taught to play things cool until they could no longer be denied at any rate.

Get Blood Moon on Amazon

ALSO BY TOBY NEIGHBORS

Base Of Fire

Hard Site

Recall

Evade

Assault

Space Fever

Staying Alive

Fractal Cut

Blast Zone

Action Zone

Covert Infil

Armor Brigade

Havoc Squad

Thunderbird

Ghost Tactics

Quantum Combat

Infinite Threat

Shadow Threat

Evolving Threat

Lingering Threat

Latent Prowess

Gravity Masters

Gravity Storm

Daughter of the Night

Supernova

Artifact

Blood Moon

Renegade

Juggernaut

Retribution

With Pete Garcia

Apocalypse One Percenters

www.ingramcontent.com/pod-product-compliance
Lightning Source LLC
Chambersburg PA
CBHW031024260626
47153CB00017B/2005